"Temper, little witch. You're fighting a losing battle. You can't beat me here."

Kol leaned closer, his lips pressed to her ear. "From now on the Guardian's Keep and the streets outside it are off-limits to you."

Then realization came to her. "You saw me?"

"I saw you. I smelled you. I sensed you. I don't know what it is about you, but I can't not know when you are near."

Kelly's body shook with emotion, and not just fear. Awareness. Every inch of her skin, every hair, every pore and cell tingled when Kol was near.

How could she want someone who she was sworn to stop?

Books by Lori Devoti

Silhouette Nocturne

Unbound #18
Guardian's Keep #32

*Unbound

LORI DEVOTI

Lori Devoti grew up in southern Missouri and attended college at the University of Missouri-Columbia where she earned a bachelor of journalism. However, she made it clear to anyone who asked, she was not a writer; she worked for the dark side—advertising. Now, twenty years later, she's proud to declare herself a writer and visit her dark side by writing paranormals for the Silhouette Nocturne line.

Lori lives in Wisconsin with her husband, daughter, son, an extremely patient shepherd mix and the world's pushiest Siberian husky. To learn more about what Lori is working on now, visit her Web site at www.loridevoti.com.

GUARDIAN'S KEEP

KEEP

LORI DEVOTI

Silhouette Books

nocturne™

SILHOUETTE BOOKS

ISBN-13: 978-0-373-61779-1
ISBN-10:   0-373-61779-8

GUARDIAN'S KEEP

Printed in U.S.A.

Dear Reader,

Guardian's Keep is my second book set in a world where Norse mythology is real and a part of everyday life—at least for some.

In the first book, *Unbound,* you were introduced to hellhounds. In *Guardian's Keep* you get a peek into one of the other *forandre*'s (shape-shifters) worlds—the garm.

Garm are wolf shape-shifters. They are a tad more mainstream than hellhounds—with a much more structured world and roles they tend to fill. Garm are protectors—guardians. Protecting is everything to them. Without someone or something to guard, they have no purpose. In *Guardian's Keep* you'll see how much this means to them and what, if anything, means more. You'll also meet Kol again (bartender from *Unbound*) and Kelly (Kara's sister from *Unbound*). The two were a lot of fun to write. Both are strong and both believe they know what's right. And, of course, they both have a lot to learn.

I love my hellhounds and, rest assured, they will be back, but for now I hope you enjoy Kol and Kelly's journey.

And be sure to keep an eye out later this year for Venge's story (speaking of a hellhound with a lot to learn….).

Lori Devoti

To Meagan, Eve, Kristi, Laura, Terry, Pam, Sally, Phoebe, Kate, Barb, Bobbi, Katie, Rhonda, Bonnie, Donna, Nancy, Leilani, Monitte, Scarlet, Pat, Merri, Terrie, Missy Sue, Deborah, my sister, and all the other official hellhound lovers out there. Thanks so much for your support. I hope you can find space in your heart for a garm.

To Kathy Steffen, thanks for helping me not doubt myself quite so much—you're the best.

And special thanks to Tara Gavin, Sean Mackiewicz and Holly Root for making this journey so fun.

Prologue

The wind howled and leaves slapped against branches. The smell of damp earth and animals panicked by what was roaming the forest tonight was everywhere. Fenrir, the cause of their fear, strode on.

What was his had been taken, and he would stop at nothing to save it.

"Garm," a voice boomed.

Fenrir ground to a halt, the length of chain he held knocking against his knee at his sudden stop. He gripped the links more firmly in his fist, readied himself to use the makeshift weapon when his hidden opponent decided to show himself.

"Let him go," he called out, the chain heavy and hot in his hand, his heartbeat slowing as he let his senses travel over the surrounding woods, serching for those who had stolen what was his.

"Will you come?" the voice asked again.

"Let me see him." A demand this time. Fenrir didn't believe in playing meek, didn't know how.

"If we do, and he's safe, you'll come with us?"

Fenrir hesitated, his mind going back to Aesa, her face pale, drawn, worried. If he went with them, would he see her again? But…his fist tightened around the chain…if he didn't, if they went through with their threats? That would kill her…kill him, too.

Lifting his chin, he replied, "I'll come."

A second chain was looped around his neck, pulled tight—not cruelly, just enough to remind him that it was there, that he was no longer free.

His captor stepped in front of him—Tyr, one of the lesser gods, sent to do the bidding of those more powerful but also more cowardly.

"Aesa—" Fenrir began.

"Not part of the bargain," Tyr replied, then lowered his voice. "Too many are afraid of you, and your strength grows every day."

"How did you—?" Fenrir asked.

Tyr smiled, but regret touched his eyes. "Not all garm follow you. Some fear you almost as much as the gods."

"But he's safe? I have your word?"

Tyr stepped back, towering over Fenrir. He laughed.

"As safe as any pawn can be in these worlds." He gave the chain around Fenrir's throat a tug. "Come. There's a portal near—one of the few that can take us to your new home."

Fenrir paused, his thoughts going to Aesa waiting at home and the life he was leaving. He snapped the chain he still held against his thigh.

Tyr spun, his hand sliding up the fetter that was wrapped around Fenrir's throat until the metal dug into the garm's neck. "Safe—for now. Don't do anything to change that."

Fenrir stared at his captor, anger bubbling inside him. His rage nipped at his control, urging him to change.

"Your choice," Tyr said.

Fenrir tilted his head back and stared into the dark sky. His choice. No choice, at least not a good one. He'd go with the god, but someday he'd escape. Then he'd destroy not just the gods who feared him, but the garm who betrayed him.

He lowered his head and, letting his anger flow through his eyes, gave Tyr a short nod.

Tyr nodded back then turned and bellowed into the woods, to others who hid there, "To the portal…and Lyngvi."

Chapter 1

The bar was full tonight, the air thick with smoke—not unusual for a Friday night at the Guardian's Keep. Also not unusual, at least lately, the place was laden with tension, every customer coiled and ready for the hell that was about to break loose.

Every customer but one, that was.

Kol Hildr dropped the damp cloth he'd been using to rub down the top of the bar and stared at the tiny figure slipping through the crowd in a direct path to the back of the room, to a booth right next to the four male challengers he was going to have to battle at any second.

Did the woman actually look for danger? Or did she just have a rare talent for stumbling across it? Mumbling a low curse, he flipped the hinged portion of counter out of his way and stalked after her.

"What are you doing here?" Kol stared down at the

female now shoved into the corner booth. Two huge blue eyes snapping with annoyance stared back at him.

"You turning down customers?" Kelly Shane, a witch who had already managed once before to get herself kidnapped and traded for passage through the portal housed in his bar, pulled the ridiculous hat she wore off her head, plopped it down on the table in front of her, then smiled up at him.

"Go home." He slid his gaze to the table full of garm, wolf shape-shifters like himself, only one space over.

"I'll take a beer. Thanks for asking." Kelly pushed her hand into the pocket of her coat and pulled out a wad of bills.

Annoyance prickling the back of his neck, he leaned over, placed his hand on top of the money and shoved it back toward her. "Don't you learn?" he asked.

"Learn what?" she replied, her face full of faux innocence.

Something tightened deep inside Kol—just like it always did when Kelly was around. He tried to convince himself it was irritation at her steadfast refusal to let go of what she saw as a wrong done to her. A few months earlier he had allowed the natural order of the portal to rule; he had done his duty as the portal guardian. Portal guardians maintained balance. That was all. They did not interfere with trade or transport—as long as fees and tolls were paid. He'd tried to talk the obstinate witch out of offering herself as a toll, but she was determined to follow her friend who had been captured earlier. Thanks to her twin sister, also a witch, and a hellhound, Kelly had come out of the ordeal relatively unscathed.

Her friend hadn't been so lucky.

Kelly's hand jerked under his. His gaze shifted to her face. She frowned and tried to free her hand again.

She was an irritating bundle of prickles, but something about her brought out every protective urge Kol possessed.

Low rumbles sounded from the booth next to them. Kol muttered a curse. The natives, or in this case invaders, were getting restless. Time was running short.

Without pausing to analyze why he cared about her safety, or giving her time to argue, he scooped the little witch and her hat into his arms and strode to the door. She weighed little more than a breeze.

But her recoil was wicked.

Her thumbs pressed instantly into his trachea, a move that would have cut off the air supply of an ordinary man. Kol just blinked down at her. "You're leaving."

She blinked back, frustration warring with uncertainty in her eyes. She pulled her lip between even teeth. "I'm not."

In other circumstances, if he hadn't been in such a hurry to get her out of danger, Kol would have laughed at the statement. She hung dangling five feet off the ground cradled in his arms. She wasn't in much of a position to argue.

Then he saw it; her hand moved to her pocket. Growling deep in his throat, he shimmered, rematerializing outside the bar with Kelly still nestled against his chest.

Barely giving her time to emit a squeak of surprise, he dumped her onto the wet pavement. "Don't try your magic on me, witch," he warned her, then with a grin at her irritated harrumph, strode back into the bar.

He waited, his back to the door, his gaze flowing over the bar patrons, watching for a sign of the attack that he knew was imminent. Since the hellhound and Kelly's sister rescued Kelly, there had been one challenge after another. Coincidence, or somehow related to those past events, Kol didn't know, and at this moment didn't care.

His back pressed against the door, he closed his eyes for

a brief second. She was still out there. Disconcerting though it was, he could feel her. Up close, her heartbeat and breath had tangled with his own. But even with her on the other side of the door there was an awareness, something he had never experienced with any other being, and didn't want to experience now. He let out a loud breath. He didn't need this. A muscle ticked in the side of his face. He waited a few more seconds, until the awareness lessened.

She had moved farther away. Probably thought she was hidden.

Hidden enough so the garm he was about to confront wouldn't spot her when Kol tossed them out on their asses?

He pulled open the door a few inches, letting cool, damp air spill into the smoky space and stared out into the darkness.

He couldn't see her, but even without his senses telling him she was still lurking somewhere nearby, he'd have known she was waiting. Kelly Shane wouldn't leave so quickly, wouldn't give up that easily. He might be able to run her off, but he couldn't leave the bar unguarded—not right now. His fingers tightened around the worn wood of the door and his gaze probed the darkness one last time.

Tensing his jaw, he turned back to the bar. The door slipped closed behind him with a whisper. His irritation with the bewitching shadow who skulked out in the gloomy night still gnawed at him, but he ignored the feeling and let his dark gaze drift toward the four men seated in the back. They'd arrived not long before Kelly, reeking of arrogance and garm—wolves—but without a portal or world of their own to guard.

Challengers. They didn't even bother to hide it.

Kol sighed. This was getting monotonous.

Deciding he didn't have the patience or time to wait for their attack, he huffed out a breath, grabbed the baseball-bat-size piece of silver-coated iron he kept stashed behind the bar and strode to the back of the room, his heels making a sharp rapping noise against the wood floor.

He wasn't interested in stealth. Let them know he was coming, and he was pissed.

The biggest one, a blond giant dressed in a polo shirt and creased slacks, stood first. "You need something, bartender?" His tone was casual, but his posture was coiled and ready for attack.

The length of silver pressing against his leg, Kol didn't give the garm a chance to move on the promise. He balled his fist into the other man's shirt and jerked him close. "Question is—what do *you* need?"

The blond grinned—still arrogant. "Don't worry. I'll get what I need." He made a short motion to his companions.

Before the garm could act, Kol pulled the blond closer then quickly snapped the man's head back against the column that separated the booths. The crunch of bone hitting the iron trim of the column stopped the others just long enough for Kol to step to the side and swing the silver bar in an arc toward them. It caught the first squarely in the side of the head. He crumpled to his knees, his chin, then face, landing on the tabletop with a dull thud. His eyes still open, he stared blankly into the room.

The two remaining looked from their fallen companions to Kol, their eyes darting from his dark face to the gleaming silver bar still gripped in his hand.

"Who sent you?" Kol asked. Lately, he'd noticed a change in the challenges. They seemed more organized, orchestrated. He now suspected what started as attacks by random opportunists had changed to something much more targeted. Something directed by one individual with a goal.

He wanted that person or being's name. If he could get it, great. It would simplify his problems, but if he instead had to beat each and every challenger until there was no doubt of his dominance—he could do that, too.

He raised the bar again, letting the dim light dance down its length.

The garm still upright blinked, their eyes darting to each other, then the door.

Kol loosened his grip on the blond giant and let him slide under the table onto the sticky floor. Smacking the silver bar against his palm, Kol repeated his question.

"Who sent you?"

The two shared another glance then began to shimmer. Shaking his head at their cowardice, Kol swung the bar with both hands, hitting them both in the gut. The silver lit to bright blue, then deflected their magic, not totally, but enough that their attempt to escape ended as quickly as it began—and with both of them still stuck in the bar with Kol.

He arched one brow. Let the fun begin.

Kelly pulled the brim of her black rain hat lower on her face; rain streamed from the wide strip of material blinding her for a moment. She shook her head, cursing her idiocy at letting Kol recognize her.

She'd been staking out the bar for weeks, ever since taking on her latest case, but tonight was the first time she'd ventured inside, stupidly believing she'd go unnoticed in the crowd. But even huddled into a corner, quietly listening to the conversations going on around her, Kol had noticed her, called off the waitress and approached her himself. And damn, if a part of her wasn't excited to see him standing there, leaning over her—tall, lean and dangerous.

Memories flashed through her mind—his blue eyes blazing as he scooped her up, his grin as he deposited her on her behind in the rain. Her eyes narrowed, but something deep inside her flickered, too. Kol, just like Kelly, didn't back down from a challenge—she couldn't help but respect that.

Unhappy with the direction her thoughts had taken, she flipped up the collar of her coat against the rain and concentrated on what brought her here—what she knew about Kol.

Although her daily surveillance started with her new case, she'd been watching the place off and on since she escaped from the underwater world of Jormun, a snake shape-shifter intent on playing god. She'd escaped, but others hadn't.

Her friend Linda. Kelly squared her jaw, wrapped her arms around her middle and tried to block out the pain. Linda who trusted her, let Kelly talk her into coming here—to this bar—where she was captured and dragged through a portal, never to leave. At least not alive. And, according to Kelly's twin sister, Kara, who had seen Linda afterwards, seen her body, Linda's death hadn't been pleasant—nothing left of her but a charred, blackened corpse.

All because of Kelly…and the portal…and the man who kept it running, Kol Hildr.

Kelly stared blindly out into the night, angry tears hot against her cold cheeks.

Refocusing her gaze on the bar door, she settled in to wait and watch.

Cold crawled up her legs, her feet damp even in her supposedly waterproof hikers. She curled her toes inside her boots trying to stop the numbness, and gained a tiny bit of comfort. But almost immediately, the wind shifted, bringing with it a sheet of water that pounded against her, shoving her to the side, next to a Dumpster. Water dripped from her hat down the back of her neck like an icy finger trailing down her spine.

She adjusted her coat, halting the water's downward trek.

A miserable job on a miserable night. Hunching her shoulders, she blocked yet another wave of rain, but didn't even consider giving up her hunt.

The door to the bar edged open and Kelly stepped farther into the gloom, her body pressed against the trash Dumpster, the smell of wet wool and rotting fruit causing her to press her gloved hand against her mouth. This time instead of Kol's profile, which she'd seen earlier, right after he tossed her into the rain, a woman squeezed through the space. After glancing around the parking lot, she popped open an umbrella and scurried across the street straight toward the Dumpster and Kelly's hiding place.

Before Kelly could move to more thoroughly disguise her presence, the door to the bar opened again, this time with a loud bang, and four men tumbled out, down the steps and onto the wet pavement.

Kelly caught a quick glance of Kol's impossibly blue eyes peering into the night before the door slammed shut. *He must be on a rampage tonight.*

A muffled curse sounded from a few feet away.

The woman stood shaking, her face turned toward the immobile men scattered across the concrete.

Kelly took a step backward, planning to leave before the woman spotted her, but at her movement the woman turned, her eyes seeming to pierce the gloom.

"Is someone there?" she asked, her body rigid.

Damn. Kelly muttered a stronger curse under her breath. She'd never had such poor luck with surveillance before.

"I know you." The woman stepped forward, a frown on her face.

Kelly stepped away from the Dumpster, her arms hanging loosely at her sides, widening her stance, ready to defend herself if she had to.

"You're one of the witches…" A thought skittered behind the woman's eyes, then her frown softened.

Kelly maintained her pose, her weight balanced on the balls of her feet. She wasn't totally surprised the woman recognized her. Kelly and her sister had gained a bit of celebrity with the trip to Jormun's and back, but only in certain circles—magical ones. And the woman had come from the Guardian's Keep. Not a place normal humans hung out or even knew existed—at least not innocent ones.

"Can you help me?" The woman held out one hand, her pale skin reflecting the smattering of light from the street-lamps making its way through the rain.

Kelly made no move to take it.

The rain pattered between them, lengthening the silence.

The woman glanced to the side, then took another, bolder step forward. "I'm sorry. You don't know me, but I've been through so much. Almost given up hope." She pressed the hand she'd held out seconds earlier against her mouth, her eyes wide above it. "I heard about you. How you escaped, and hoped the garm had softened, that he'd listen to reason. My son…he's only eight." Her gaze dropped to the puddle she'd stepped in while talking. She stood there staring at it, as if she couldn't feel the cold water lapping against the thin leather of her shoes.

Kelly's eyes narrowed. She hadn't noticed the woman inside, but that didn't mean she hadn't approached Kol after Kelly left. *An innocent human after all?* She studied the woman some more, waiting for her to continue, but the woman just turned with a soft sob and hid her face with the upturned collar of her coat.

Kelly's lips formed a thin line. An eight-year-old child…surely, even Kol couldn't justify the story forming in Kelly's mind. Or could he?

"What happened to him…your son?" Kelly asked, her voice firm but her fingers curling into her palms.

The woman's eyes darted again, back to the bar—a slight movement, but telling. Another darker thought occurred to Kelly. The woman could be working for Kol. Part of a trap. Perhaps he'd sent the woman out here to ensnare Kelly somehow, to learn what she knew… *No,* Kelly didn't believe Kol would do that. Subterfuge wasn't his style.

The woman ran a hand under her eyes and then lifted her chin. "I don't know, but I heard he was brought here. Bartered or something. He's…special. Has powers. I'd been warned before that beings in other worlds would want him, but never dreamed— He's just a child." As the last escaped her lips in a shocked whisper she looked squarely at the bar, torment pulling at her features.

Something in Kelly clenched. *A child.*

Anger overpowered her earlier thoughts of caution. The Guardian's Keep was the traffic route for the sale and trade of all things magical.

And horrible as it sounded, Kelly knew trade in children happened. Her sister's new husband had suffered a similar fate, sold by his own parents to a witch who had enslaved him. It stood to reason, if someone was buying magical children, they were most likely being transported through the portal at the Guardian's Keep.

Could Kol be capable of assisting with an act so despicable?

Kelly bit the inside of her cheek until the bitter taste of her own blood coated her tongue. Kol ran the portal. He had to be involved.

How could she not help this woman? She dug into her pocket and pulled out a business card.

"Here." She shoved the card into the other woman's hand. "Come see me tomorrow. Maybe I can help."

The woman glanced at the card. "Magical Missions. I've heard of it—good things."

Kelly brushed her fingers along the brim of her hat, knocking water collected there onto the ground. "Small and new, but determined. If your son was taken by someone or something magical, I'll find him."

"But the money…" The woman tried to press the card back into Kelly's fingers.

Kelly pushed her hand away. "Don't worry about it. Anything that will bring down the Guardian's Keep I'll take care of for free—not to mention to save your little boy."

With an unsure nod, the woman shoved the card into her pocket.

One of the men across the street moaned, then sat up, his hands cradling his head.

"I'd better go," the woman murmured, her gaze darting from the men back to Kelly. She squeezed Kelly's arm with a strong grip. "But thank you." Her coat pulled tight around her and her umbrella bobbing with each step, she disappeared down the dark street.

Kelly watched her go, making sure the woman escaped safely before the men stirring in the street noticed her departure. The last thing the woman needed was a confrontation with the likes of them. Creatures Kelly hadn't even believed were real frequented this bar: trolls, dark elves, shape-shifters. Every creature from every child's nightmares seemed to find its way to the Guardian's Keep.

She tugged off one glove, then reached into her pocket and wrapped her bare hand around the carved ash dowel she kept there—like brass knuckles, except this tool not only strengthened her punch it helped store power. Not as effective as a full length staff, but a lot more discreet.

With the carved runes pressing into her palm, she relaxed. She had what she came for—proof that Kol and his portal were a danger that had to be stopped.

The men staggered to their feet. Kelly rubbed her thumb over the end of the dowel, let a little of the power drawn there flow into her hand.

Dirty red streaks ran down the face of the largest, the side of another's head completely covered with thick crusted blood. The other two remained bent, clasping their stomachs and coughing as if struggling for air.

Kelly noted their injuries with disinterest. Someone, Kol most likely, had roughed them up badly. If they hadn't just tumbled out of the Guardian's Keep, she'd be punching 9-1-1 into her phone right now, rushing to their aid, but she'd learned.

Instead she waited. Seconds ticked by as they moved about slowly at first, then faster. They were recovering quickly—supernaturally.

Kelly flexed her fingers around the wooden rod, but the men didn't even look her way. Instead, they exchanged a few low words, threw heated glances back at the bar, then as a group began to shimmer. Within a blink, they had disappeared.

Kelly released her grip on the dowel.

Forandre. Shape-shifters. Like her old captor, Jormun, and her new nemesis, Kol.

If four forandres like those couldn't defeat Kol, how in the hell would she?

Back behind the bar, Kol jostled the computer's mouse and brought the screen to life with a buzz. A couple more clicks and he was looking at the four interlopers sprawled on the wet concrete in front of the Guardian's Keep building.

The leader moved, pushing his head off the pavement long enough to let out a groan. Kol's jaw tensed.

Garm. Rogues. This was the third group in the last two weeks. Something was definitely up.

Garm were guardians by nature, not hunters, and they were loners. Something or someone had to be behind these misfits gathering together. He tapped his finger against the black plastic mouse, then quickly switched his view. The camera zoomed onto the Dumpster across the street. The image was grainy and not helped by the rain falling in a steady drizzle, but he could see Kelly standing there, her coat wrapped around her and her hat pulled low over her face.

Kol clenched his teeth. Was she behind the attacks? His hand hovered over the mouse preparing to switch the view back to the garm, when a movement in the corner of the screen stopped him. There was someone else out there—talking to Kelly.

He muttered a low curse. Who was that? The rain increased blurring his view further. He couldn't even tell if the person was male or female—human or troll.

He tried to zoom in farther, but his security system was already pressed to its limits. If the person would just turn, face the camera. He waited, leaning forward, not even re-alizing how much tension was in his body until the two forms parted, Kelly in her hard-to-miss hat staying while the second person disappeared out of view of his camera.

Hell.

Kelly stood for moment watching her contact walk away, then turned back to face the camera and the garm he'd tossed out of his bar. Kol snapped the computer back to the closer view. The garm stood now, holding their mid-sections and mumbling curses.

Kol waited again. If Kelly approached them, he'd know she was involved, but she didn't and the garm shimmered away, never glancing in her direction.

Kol punched the button on the screen, switching off his view. Tension strummed through him, urging him to stride into the wet night and yank Kelly back into the bar behind him.

The witch didn't know what she was playing with, and Kol couldn't risk any threat to the portal he guarded. If he had even the slightest hint that she was behind the attacks, he would have to eliminate her—there was no other option.

Why did the thought cause something to twist inside him?

Chapter 2

Kelly dropped her head onto her desk, agitation and frustration intruded upon her normal focus. Her anger had grown during the night, causing her to toss and turn, adrenaline pumping through her at the thought of taking on Kol. She'd known eventually she'd have to confront the dark, sexy garm. That some new crime would lead back to the Guardian's Keep, but now that it had, she couldn't seem to focus her energies, to think and plan.

Lightning, visible through the high-set windows of her basement office, sliced through the early morning sky. A spurt of power zigzagged its way to earth. She inhaled, closed her eyes, and absorbed what little leaked through the battered frames of the ancient windows—willed the tiny surge to strengthen her, to calm her racing heart.

She could do this—had to do this.

Her resolve back, she glanced at her watch; it was nearly

eight. She'd spent hours poring over the tiny bit of research she'd scraped together on portals, garm and Kol Hildr—looking for something that would make the task ahead easier. But there was nothing—no carefully drawn plans of the world's portals, no garm Achilles' heel, nothing.

She picked up the top sheet and stared down at the black lines of type. Portals led to other worlds; she knew that firsthand. The only new information she'd found was that garm, not just Kol, but other garm protected them, too—profited from them in some way, Kelly assumed. Nothing in her research said what garm gained from the job, not that the motivation mattered. What mattered was the result—innocents being kidnapped, torn away from their loved ones, and transported against their will. That was what she had to focus on—that was what she had to stop.

Another flash of lightning slashed against the cloudy sky. Screwing her eyes shut, Kelly took advantage of the storm to again strengthen her power. The energy flowed through her, adding to her resolve.

She picked up her pencil and performed a tattoo on the top of her scarred desk. Kol was a wolf shape-shifter, one of the forandre. A notoriously tough group to defeat in battle. She'd never personally tried to beat one—could she? She and her sister, Kara, as a pair of twin witches, held more power than any witch she'd yet encountered. As a pair she had no doubt they could beat anything the supernatural world had to offer, but by herself? Doubt gnawed at her.

She could call Kara, but she wouldn't help. Her sister clung to a stubborn belief that Kol wasn't evil, that his portal served a purpose—what, Kelly couldn't fathom. She turned the pencil end over end between the pads of her fingers.

No, this was a battle Kelly would have to fight without her sister. She could do it, surely.

The rain outside softened to a light patter against the window, and Kelly's mind drifted to the man she must defeat. Kol—a wolf. She could see it, his unnaturally blue eyes held a hint of something wild, untamed, something that longed to roam, run free. But instead he chose a life trapped inside that bar…why?

Lost in thought, she barely suppressed a jump as the door to the office banged open, the wind ushering in Heather, her assistant and witch-in-training. Coffee from a paper cup sloshed onto Heather's hand as she fought to pull the door closed behind her.

Kelly waited, frozen with something similar to guilt— like she'd been caught cheating on her homework, or lusting after her best friend's boyfriend.

Heather turned, rain puddling at her feet. Her eyes lit on Kelly and a quizzical look covered her face. "What are you doing here so early? Did something else happen up north?"

Kelly dropped the pencil, her eyes darting to the plastic bin where she'd dumped the Northwoods' files first thing this morning.

"No, at least not that I've heard." A flush warmed Kelly's face. In her obsession with Kol, she'd forgotten all about the problems up north—even though the case had been her justification for staking out the Guardian's Keep in the first place.

A small bed-and-breakfast concerned about loss of their winter business had hired her almost a week ago, and so far she had nothing solid to tell them, nothing to report but the comings and goings of Kol Hildr and his unique clientele.

"Mrs. Coleman called while you were gone yesterday.

I left her message on your desk." Heather motioned to a glaring pink slip tucked under a mess of papers, just one tiny corner visible.

"She wanted to know if you were coming up to check things out," Heather continued. "I guess they lost another party—a family reunion. She was pretty bummed." Heather's lips twisted in a sad little half smile. "But I still think you're right, concentrating on the Guardian's Keep that is. That place creeps me out."

Kelly fished the message out of the papers. "Still, I intended to, but—"

The door banged open again, this time with such force both Kelly and Heather jumped. For one brief heart-stopping second, Kelly thought no one was there…or no one visible. Dead leaves and an old chip bag vibrated against the wall of the sunken stairwell that served as their front stoop. The sound caused every muscle in Kelly's body to contract.

Not waiting for whatever stood outside the doorway to attack, Kelly reached toward the corner of the room for her ash staff, but before her hand had touched the worn wood, the woman from the night before stepped out of the shadows and into the room.

She hopped over the puddle left earlier during Heather's entrance, her leather pumps showing only minimal damage from the torrent outside. She smiled at Kelly and held out her hand to Heather. "Aesa Gunnar."

Kelly tilted her head. Another Norwegian, or of Norwegian heritage anyway. Seemed everyone at the Guardian's Keep had some kind of Norse connection. She frowned, then shook away the hint of suspicion that tickled at her brain. This area was settled by Norwegians and Germans, and plenty still lived here—it was hardly a sign of malevolence.

Wiping away the moment of disquiet with a smile, she tilted her head toward Heather. "Ms. Gunnar has hired us to find her son."

Her new client's face instantly folded, lines of worry making her look years older than Kelly had first assumed.

"I'm sorry…" Kelly let the words fade as the woman waved her to silence and slid into a seat.

Kelly followed her lead, reseating herself behind the desk. Feeling awkward and not sure what else to do, she shoved a box of tissues toward her client.

"Call me Aesa." Her newest client accepted the box with a short nod, and dabbed at her eyes. "And don't apologize. It's silly of me to cry. It's just…" She waved the tissue in front of her, then letting out a loud sigh dropped her hand to her lap.

"Coffee?" Kelly asked, then looked at Heather. "Maybe some coffee?" Witnessing such raw emotion made something clench in Kelly's stomach, made her eyes dart toward the door, wishing for a reason to run from the room and hide. But she couldn't. She had a job to do and she needed information from this woman to do it.

Water pinged into a metal bucket, dripping in a steady flow from a pipe overhead, emphasizing each second Heather was gone. Tissue fisted in her hand, Aesa turned eyes dark with sorrow toward Kelly. "Have you ever lost someone?" she asked.

Thoughts of Linda rose up in Kelly. The older, but insecure witch glowing with each new power she learned, believing Kelly when she said they had nothing to fear.

Pushing herself to a stand, Kelly muttered an apology and strode into the other room.

Heather stood right outside the door, two cups of coffee in her hands.

"We were out of filters. I had to use a paper towel."

Not sure why that took triple the time, Kelly grabbed the lukewarm cups from Heather's hands and nodded. After allowing herself a second to take a deep breath and block painful memories from her mind, she strode back into her office.

Aesa was bent over Kelly's desk, her hand hovering over the stack of papers Kelly had left there. Unease ran down Kelly's spine.

Spotting Kelly, Aesa held up the empty tissue box. "Do you…?" Her weak smile making Kelly shift from foot to foot. The woman was here for her help. Why did Kelly have to be so suspicious?

"Sure, sorry." Kelly set the cups on the desk and pulled a fresh box of tissues from a drawer. Back behind her desk, she waited for Aesa to blot her damp eyes and pick up her coffee.

"I'm so happy you're going to help me. Terje is all I have. His father…" Aesa's eyes grew hard for a second, then as if remembering where she was, she glanced back at Kelly. "I raise him alone."

Assuming the father had deserted them, Kelly hurried to guide the conversation in a new direction.

"Can you tell me what happened?" she asked, trying to keep her voice soft, supportive.

Aesa took a tiny sip of coffee, the cup shaking in her hand. "A week ago. Terje was playing in the backyard." She glanced up. "He likes the woods, builds forts, keeps a book of animal tracks he finds, that kind of thing. I thought it was safe." Her voice cracked.

Kelly glanced at the doorway willing Heather to appear with coffee or more phone messages, anything to save her from another onslaught of undisguised emotion.

Her body shook for a second, but Aesa seemed to

recover, only brushing one tear off her lower lashes. "Anyway, he went out to play right after school, around four. Around five I went to check on him and…" She looked at Kelly, her eyes glimmering.

Kelly felt her own eyes begin to tear in response. She blinked and looked down at her desk.

Aesa continued, "He was gone. I looked everywhere, checked at the neighbors. No one had seen him."

"Did you call the police?" Kelly asked.

Aesa shook her head. "They can't do anything."

Kelly pursed her lips. A little boy disappearing was certainly disturbing, but not necessarily supernatural. "Why do you say that?"

Aesa gave Kelly a long glance, then reached into a leather purse she had slung over one shoulder. Cold discomfort crawled over Kelly's skin, her hand twitched, thoughts of the ash dowel tucked in her coat pocket only inches away offering her some reassurance.

"What I didn't tell you," Aesa continued, "is who my son is, or who his father is." She waited, her hand still inside her purse.

Without changing her expression, or moving her eyes, Kelly pushed herself away from her desk slightly and slipped her hand into the pocket of her jacket, which was slung over the back of her chair. With the ash dowel gripped in her hand, she asked, "Who *is* his father?"

Her face expectant, Aesa replied, "Fenrir."

Kelly's mouth formed a soft O. *Fenrir*. Almost half the information on her desk involved the mighty garm in one way or another. Son of Loki and brother of Jormun—the forandre who had held Kelly and her sister captive—he was seen as one of the biggest threats to the gods. So much so, they had imprisoned him on an island in Lake Amsvartnir.

"And you think Fenrir took him?" Kelly asked, circling the top of the dowel with her thumb.

Surprise lifted Aesa's eyebrows. "No. His enemies or—" she seemed to consider the question for a moment "—or someone for him. Fenrir is trapped. He hasn't escaped. I'd *know* if he escaped."

The intensity of her answer pulled at Kelly. *Aesa must live in fear that Fenrir would escape and come for his son. But someone else had gotten to the boy first. Who?*

"Which do you think it is? Who would gain the most by having Terje?" Kelly asked.

Aesa studied Kelly, then let her gaze drift to the slew of papers on Kelly's desk. "It doesn't matter. Either way, I know where they took him." She swallowed, her Adam's apple moving up and down. "To Lyngvi."

Lyngvi, an island incapable of hosting any life save its one high-profile prisoner and his keepers. Home of Fenrir.

Kelly tightened her fist around the piece of wood still warming in her hand, the tiny bit of security helping her to shove down the disquiet of Aesa's declaration. "But why are you so sure?"

Aesa slid forward on her seat. "If it's Fenrir behind Terje's abduction, he'd want his son near him, right?" Her eyes glittered with the intensity of her emotions.

Kelly tilted her head in agreement.

"And his enemies? To them Terje is nothing more than another tool to taunt his father. Again, they'd want Fenrir to see him, so they could hold him just out of reach, torture them both…" She paused, swallowing hard. Then with a slight move of her head, as if shaking off ugly thoughts, she continued, "Either way, I have to get him back, and soon." Her hands gripped the arms of her chair until her knuckles glowed white.

Kelly pushed herself back against the cushion of her seat, away from the intense emotion pouring out of her client, but she agreed with the woman.

Lyngvi.

She didn't know much about the isle; she'd only heard a few whispers here and there. Everything she had heard screamed danger: rocky, foreboding and unforgiving—not at all the place for an innocent eight-year-old child.

A shiver crept up her spine.

Tamping it down, she forced herself to keep her gaze steady, strong. "So, you want me to rescue him?"

Surprise darted across Aesa's face. "No, I couldn't ask you to do that. Just find out how to operate the portal, then get the guardian away from it long enough so I can go through and find my son." Her fingers relaxed slightly around the wooden arms of her chair. "I'd never expect you to go through the portal yourself. I've got family willing to go with me, and I know Fenrir. If he's behind Terje's kidnapping, I can deal with him."

Kelly's gaze flicked over the other woman. She sounded awfully sure, but from what Kelly had heard, the gods themselves struggled with controlling the fierce garm. How did this woman, not all that much bigger than Kelly's puny five-foot height, expect to accomplish the act?

As if reading Kelly's thoughts, Aesa leaned forward enough to place her hand on Kelly's arm. "Don't worry about me. Dangerous as Fenrir is, he would never hurt me. It's my one sure card."

A slight tingle of power, like a static charge, zinged into Kelly's arm where Aesa's hand touched her. She stopped herself from flinching, but barely.

Keeping her gaze cloaked with sympathy she studied

the other woman more carefully. Aesa had never said she was human, but from how the other woman acted, Kelly had made that assumption.

Always a mistake. Of course, it made sense. She'd just admitted her son's father was Fenrir. Your average suburban mom didn't have many opportunities to hook up with the fiercest garm of all time. So there was more to Aesa than she was telling Kelly, but did it matter? Maybe Aesa assumed Kelly knew what she was. Kelly could ask, but it seemed rude somehow, like asking someone's income. And it might shake Aesa's confidence in Kelly if she thought Kelly such a greenhorn she couldn't tell what Aesa was.

Kelly rubbed her thumb over one of the runes carved into her ash dowel. Did it matter?

Aesa pulled out the hand that had still been nestled in her purse, revealing a four-by-six-inch picture of a young boy, his arms wrapped around a stuffed rabbit. The distraught mother stared at the photo for a moment, then with her hand shaking, as if parting with the memento was almost more than she could bear, she dropped it onto Kelly's paper-strewn desktop.

"Here. I thought you might want a photo."

Kelly stared down at the image. The boy's eyes were bright with happiness as he squeezed the blue bunny with such gusto it appeared he might rend the toy in two. She laid the pad of her index finger lightly on the white border of the photo.

No. It didn't matter. No matter the sins of the father or the origin of the mother, this little boy did not deserve the fate of Lyngvi.

Kelly had no choice but to rescue him—no matter who stood in her way.

* * *

A forandre—fox, Kol guessed based on the other male's earthy scent—wandered up to the bar, tossed down a cloth bag with a clink of the coins inside and barked out, "Drink."

Kol cast him a dark look.

The other forandre twitched his nose, plucked the bag off the bar top and scurried back to his table.

Kol's glance returned to his computer screen and the blinking alert he'd found there when he logged in. The message was from the Garm Council, a small group who oversaw the guardians of the most important portals, landmarks and beings. For centuries there had been no communication at all between the various guardians, but like the world around them, even magical beings had to change. Turning some element of control over to the Council had been one such change.

This alert, like most Council communications, was arrogant, uninformed and worth less than the tiny bit of bandwidth it took to relay it.

Portals around the human world are being attacked. All guardians should be on alert.

That was it. No information as to which portals—for all Kol could tell it might only be his—when and where the attacks started or what, if anything, the Council was doing to stop the attacks.

He flipped off the screen with a grunt.

As always, he was on his own.

A Svartalfar, dark elf, signaled him from the end of the bar, and still glowering over the uselessness of the Council, Kol reached for the vodka to top off the elf's glass.

As he was pouring, the door to the bar popped open and Kelly Shane dressed in a floor-length black coat and her wide-brimmed hat strode into the room. She stopped, the door still open behind her, her feet shoulder-width apart and her gaze brimming with determination.

With her nose red from the cold, her too-big-for-her-face eyes snapping and her diminutive height, she looked no more intimidating than a pissed-off puppy.

Kol hid a grin and growled, "Shut the door."

Narrowing her eyes, she complied, shoving it closed with the heel of her boot.

Purposely turning his back on her, Kol moved down the bar, snagging an empty beer mug and an overflowing ashtray as he went.

"I'm here to talk to you, garm." Kelly stared at him from under her hat, her eyes wide and blue as a mountain sky.

"Really, witch?" He raised one brow, placed both hands on the bar in front of her, and leaned in—close enough to smell the musk of her cologne and the undeniable scent of female. His nostrils flared, but he kept his voice firm, unmoved. "This is a bar. You want to talk, you better order first." He started to spin away, but stopped. "Oh, and lose the hat. Customers here like to see who they're drinking with. Isn't that right, Bari?" The dwarf perched on the stool next to Kelly grinned, revealing white teeth against his dark skin.

Her gaze shooting to Bari and the heavy axe hanging from his leather belt, Kelly edged sideways.

Kol was hiding a second grin, when his computer beeped signaling another message. The smile fading from his face, he remembered the attacks and his suspicions about the witch.

He strode back to where she stood, her hat now lying in a puddle on the top of his bar. "Why are you here, witch?"

Purposely ignoring both him and Bari, who was watching her every move with more than a little interest, she flicked water off her coat, pulled the tail of it out of her way and sat down. "I'll have that beer I ordered last night." She glanced at the other patrons, then added, "Bottled."

Kol growled again. This time in earnest, but she simply placed her delicate little witch hands on his bar and tapped her fingernails against the wood. "Light, if you have it," she said.

He stood there, his muscles tensing, his brain warring with his instincts. Why did the little piece of fluff get under his skin? Why did he let her?

Because something about her pulled at the most basic parts of him. The wolf in him snarled when she was near, snapping to be set free—but for what? To claim or kill? He couldn't decide.

Mumbling a curse, he strode to the beer cooler and yanked out a bottle.

Not bothering to twist off the cap for her, he plunked the beer onto the counter.

"Thanks." She arched one brow. Her gaze was cool, but he could feel her reaction to him. Her heart sped, the blood moving more swiftly through her veins, adrenaline pumping despite her calm exterior. She might act unaffected, but little witch Kelly was every bit as aware of him as he was of her.

The realization made him feel better, much better.

He smiled—a slow deadly smile.

Why was he smiling? Dropping her gaze for a moment, Kelly draped her leather coat over the top of the beer bottle and twisted off the lid. The piecrust-shaped disc fisted in one hand, she lifted the beer and took an unconcerned sip. *He'd served her, that was an improvement, but it just added to her suspicions. Had he known Aesa was waiting to talk to him last night? Had he tossed Kelly out to keep her from overhearing?*

"You've been busy." She made it a statement. She didn't want to show any weakness now around Kol—not that she had ever wanted to.

His eyes sparked for a second, then he raised dark brows. "Why would you say that?"

Something simmered under the question, something dangerous just waiting for one wrong move from her to bubble to the surface. Sensing a trap, she twisted slightly in her seat, taking a second to study the patrons and refine her plan.

If she had a plan. She'd thought she did before she strode into the bar. She was going to confront Kol, give him a chance to do the right thing—help her find and free the boy. But now staring into his sizzling gaze, she saw the foolishness of such thoughts.

"So, you haven't been busy?" She tilted her bottle, let the cool liquid roll down her throat.

He pulled back slightly, as if weighing something. "You tell me."

She placed the bottle onto the bar between them with a clunk and curled her fingers into her hands. "How do you justify it?"

"Being busy?" He picked up the drink of the man next to her and wiped under it with a damp cloth. "You have some preference for slothfulness?"

The edges of the bottle lid dug into her palm. She dropped the tiny piece of crimped metal onto the bar, let it roll across the wood and patter to stillness next to Kol's hand. Then she leaned forward, her forearms resting on the countertop. "You know what I mean."

He dropped the cloth and leaned forward, too. Their noses an inch from touching, his gaze bore into hers. "Maybe I know more than you think."

Kelly flinched inwardly, her heart skipping faster with each second. She resisted the urge to lick her lips, her eyes dropping to his instead—firm, masculine, tempting. With a start, she jerked her gaze back to his eyes. He watched her with those ice-blue eyes, cool one second, boiling the next. A shiver ran over her. Her jaw clenched, she fought off her disturbing reaction to him and concentrated instead on his words.

Did he know she'd been watching him? She'd been so careful. Deciding to go on with her bluff, she tilted her chin. "Maybe *I'm* the one who knows more than *you* think."

"Maybe you do." He leaned back, his gaze apprising, then glanced down toward his computer. "Why don't you tell me *exactly* what you know?"

Kelly frowned. This wasn't supposed to be about her— it was supposed to be about Kol and saving a little boy.

He crossed his arms over his broad chest and stared at her. "I'm waiting. You came to talk— Talk."

Kelly made tiny little circles over the top of her beer bottle with her thumb. She did come to talk, but suddenly she wasn't eager to confront Kol with what she'd learned.

As she considered this twist of emotion, the air around Kol began to shift and before she could move, he shimmered, appearing almost instantly behind her.

She stiffened, her hand slipping into her pocket searching for the ash dowel.

His chest pressed against her back, he whispered in

her ear, "Tell me what you've been up to. Maybe it's not too late."

Around her, bar stools squealed as patrons shoved them out of their way and scurried for the door or just evaporated into mist and disappeared. As the last being wafted to nothingness a few feet away, Kol added, "Just you and me. Might as well talk."

His body was warm against hers, his breath moving her hair ever so slightly. Kelly's legs shook with the effort to resist the attraction boiling inside her. Despite the emotion, or perhaps because of it, Kelly wrapped her fingers around the wood, and quietly willed power to flow from the rod into her body.

Kol's lips brushed against her ear as he whispered again, "Talk."

Kelly sighed out a breath, let her body soften against his. He jerked, a tiny movement of surprise, but quickly recovered. Taking advantage of his few seconds of confusion, she held up her free hand and let power shoot from her palm.

"Damn." He jumped back, squatting below the line of energy as he did so.

As he moved, Kelly lost track of where he stood. With her foot braced against the bar for leverage, she pushed off, spinning her body on the bar stool.

There was a blur of movement to her left and with a quick deft move, Kol slipped his hand into her pocket and pried the dowel from her grip.

Dangling the rod in front of her, he raised one brow. "Again with the magic. That wasn't nice, was it?"

"Like sneaking up on me was." She forced the expression in her eyes to stay cool, not to reveal the fascination her body felt for his. She quickly let her gaze dance once around the room. Good or bad—they were alone. She grabbed for her tool.

He jerked the dowel back with animal grace, then tapped it lightly against his chin. "You've been up to something, little witch. We both know it. Then tonight you come banging in here like you're ready to fight in the open. Why the sudden change of heart?"

Kelly kept her senses focused on the ash dowel as he dangled, then twirled it, through his long tan fingers.

"You can't keep victimizing people. They're getting fed up," she replied.

He paused, his hand wrapping around the suddenly still piece of wood. "Really?" His tone was amused—a fact that fed Kelly's anger.

"Really. Like adult witches weren't bad enough—women with families who loved them. But a child? How can you justify that?"

Disgust sent her to her feet. She glared up at him for a second, then pushed past him headed to the door. This conversation was a lost cause. She'd known it all along, but if for no other reason than her sister seemed to trust Kol, she'd had to try.

Before she reached the exit, he was behind her. He grabbed her by the arm and spun her until she was trapped between his hard length and the battered door. His eyes blazing, he stared down at her.

"Child. You said child. There are so many. Care to tell me which one you've chosen to champion?"

God. It was worse than she'd thought. So many kids he needed her to name the boy? Maybe Aesa was wrong. Maybe Terje's abduction had nothing to do with his famous father—maybe he was just one more commodity to be traded through Kol's portal. Balling up her fist, she pulled back and landed a punch directly in Kol's gut. He took a step back, giving her enough room to lean back and put more power into the kick she had aimed at his groin.

Murmuring a curse, he sidestepped and slammed her back against the door.

"Temper, little witch. You're fighting a losing battle. You can't beat me here. Not anywhere." He leaned in closer, his lips pressed to her ear. "Best give up whatever cause you think you've uncovered and get back to investigating stolen brooms or whatever you're up to in that office of yours. From now on the Guardian's Keep and the streets outside it are off-limits to you."

He pushed away from the door, leaving her standing there, her heart beating loudly in her chest, her breath coming in ragged puffs, her traitorous body wishing he'd come back.

Then it hit her—he had seen her, not just last night, but previous nights when she'd huddled out in the cold watching the bar. "You saw me?" she asked.

He laughed, a low disbelieving sound, turned as if to leave, then stopped and closed the distance between them again. She stood still this time, pretending he didn't intimidate her, that her heart didn't race every time he drew near.

"I saw you, I smelled you, I sensed you. I don't know what it is about you, but I can't *not* know when you are near. My advice, little witch? Get away, and stay away— it's the only way either of us will ever be safe from the other."

Then shoving the wooden dowel back into her pocket, he spun and stalked through the doorway behind the bar.

Kelly stood there unable to move. Her body shook with emotion, and not just fear, awareness. Every inch of her skin, every hair, pore and cell tingled with awareness when Kol was near. It wasn't fair—couldn't be right.

How could she want someone who was everything she had sworn to stop?

Raising a trembling hand, she brushed her hair from her face and stared into her own image reflected back at her from an advertising mirror hanging on the opposite wall. Lips parted, eyes wide, she looked like a woman fresh from seduction.

Cursing her own weakness, she yanked open the door and strode into the wet night.

Chapter 3

Kol sensed the frustrating witch's exit. He leaned the back of his head against the hall wall and stared blankly at the water-stained ceiling. Why couldn't she just take his advice and stay away? What had she hoped to gain by coming here tonight? And what was all this talk about a child? The woman spoke in riddles.

He ran his fingers through his hair, pulling it away from his face. The woman *was* a riddle, and unfortunately, one that intrigued him to no end. Whether she was behind the attacks or not, she was trouble—with a capital pain in his ass.

He smacked his head against the wall just to experience the ache, to remind himself that now was not the time to be getting sidetracked by a testy little piece of temper.

The crash of a table overturning and glasses smashing to the floor jerked him out of his reverie and back to reality.

He spun on the balls of his feet and peered out into the bar.

The four garm from the night before strode toward him with what looked like silver baseball bats gripped in their hands.

Who said you couldn't teach old dogs—or wolves in this case—new tricks?

Heaving out a sigh, Kol gripped the sides of the doorway he stood behind, then waited as the other garm stormed toward him. When they were only a few feet away, he pulled his weight up and using the doorway for leverage, kicked out with both feet.

The two leaders fell backward, knocking the other two to the ground beneath them.

At best it was a two-second slowdown. Not waiting to see how quickly they would regain their feet, Kol leaped over the bar and landed in a crouch in front of his computer. Hidden from view he quickly reprogrammed the portal.

These garm wanted a trip—he was ready to oblige.

Cursing and the crunching of broken glass under heavy boots signaled the four garm had made it back to a vertical position. Kol waited, hoping they wouldn't sense him crouching just a few feet away, and would instead decide to investigate the apparently unguarded portal.

"Where'd he go?" one growled.

"He shimmer?" another asked.

"Let's find out," the voice of the big blond Kol had introduced to the iron-trimmed column the night before replied. The whir of metal slicing through the air followed, then with a teeth-jarring crash, glass splintered to the ground.

Hell-bound curs. Kol resisted the urge to peer over the top of the bar, but let his hand slide along the ledge near his knee until the silver-covered iron bar he kept stored there warmed in his palm.

Another round of crashes, a few rough laughs, and the garm's destruction slowed.

"Thought she said he'd fight to hold this place?" one asked.

At the mention of a female, Kol's breathing slowed and his eyes narrowed.

"She's got him all built up into the big bad wolf, doesn't she?" another added with a grating chuckle.

"More like a piss-in-his-pants pup," the leader added. Anger twisted and twirled around Kol, threatening to engulf him. But letting rage take over wouldn't help him learn anything more about who sent these interlopers.

She—who was *she?*

"So, what now? He's not here." Another crash, like the speaker had tossed a table over with his boot or hand. "Should we call her? She can't be far. Every time we need her, she's circling the place."

One of the men growled. "She made a lot of promises, and not one's been met. I'm tired of waiting."

The others grumbled their agreement.

"Maybe we should claim this portal—make her come to us to get her lover free."

Lover. The word hit Kol in the chest. Could Kelly have left a lover trapped on the other side of the portal? Some witch she met in Jormun's world?

Before he could contemplate the possibility more, the other garm moved closer. Now just a few feet away, on the other side of the wooden bar, they continued their discussion.

"I say we do it," one declared.

"Yeah."

Kol waited, the bar heavy in his hand. Who was "she"? If he charged the garm, could he get them to talk? Could he even reach them in time to keep them from shimmering away—if not, whoever "she" was might realize how much he'd heard.

They'd destroyed his bar, insulted him, and they knew who was behind the attacks on the portal. The temptation to throw himself across the wooden countertop, his silver bar swinging in retribution for every broken glass and splintered table, was almost overwhelming. But it also wasn't logical.

His best bet was to weaken his enemies by lowering their numbers. Best to stick with his first plan.

Wait—let their own arrogance and idiocy do them in. Shouldn't take long.

The group's murmurs grew louder, until finally the leader barked out a curt order, and they all fell silent.

"So, anyone worked a portal before? Know anything about it?"

Low rumblings said no.

"Saw someone go through it, though," one finally tossed out.

"Really? Where?" another asked.

"Right there."

Kol could feel the group's energy shift, their greed for power pulling them toward the open doorway that when active was the portal.

"Just looks like a door to me," the leader said.

"Go through it," another challenged.

Yeah, go through it, Kol seconded silently.

They shuffled forward, none quite touching the doorway, but none wanting to be left behind.

A cramp shot through Kol's thigh—his body's complaint for staying in the uncomfortable crouch for so long.

"You think we operate it somehow here?" one asked.

Just get on with it.

A few more shuffled steps back and forth, and Kol could handle the wait no longer. With a roar, he leaped to his feet, the bar swinging as he moved.

The garm moved almost as quickly as Kol, spinning toward him, surprise written across their faces. As a unit they stepped backward, preparing to fight, but Kol's bar hit them first—knocking the leader across the chest and pushing him into the garm behind him. He teetered, his hands gripping Kol's weapon, then fell, his weight hitting his companions. One by one they fell backward, like dominos, and tumbled through the open doorway.

Kol landed on the concrete floor in front of the doorway, just as the blond leader disappeared through the gray ripples of the portal, Kol's bar still gripped in his hands.

Kol cursed under his breath.

The silver-covered iron wasn't cheap to come by—especially if formed by dwarves. Kol would have to promise Bari at least twenty toll-free passes to earn another one.

And the garm escaped without Kol learning anything more of the "she" they had referenced. His luck couldn't get much worse.

As he stooped to upright an overturned table, the door to the bar flew open. Four more garm stood in the doorway—three males and one female, and all four wore the singing wolf neck badge of the Garm Council.

Kol cursed again, this time out loud. Lucky him—this night just kept getting better and better.

The next morning, as the wind hammered against the window above her, Kelly sat at her desk staring into the depths of her half-drunk cup of now-cold coffee, her mood quickly growing darker than even the day-old brew.

Her latest visit with the owner of the Guardian's Keep made her sick to the pit of her stomach, and not just his reaction to her questions—his nonchalant lack of concern over a missing child—but her own reaction to him as a man.

She was attracted to him. The thought sickened her, but she couldn't deny it. Her heart beat faster when he was near. Her palms grew sweaty, and her body turned toward him almost of its own accord. Disturbing as it was, her body, if not her brain, wanted him. The realization clawed at her, making her doubt everything she'd ever thought about herself. How could she be attracted to someone so, at best, amoral?

She picked up a freshly sharpened pencil and flung it at the cork board beside her door. It bounced off an image of the Guardian's Keep front door, just one of the set of surveillance pictures she'd been tacking up for the last week.

She'd watched. That got her nowhere.

She picked up a second pencil and aimed for another photo—this one of the parking lot where a group of patrons congregated. Another glancing blow, but this time leaving a black line of lead across one man's face.

She'd talked. Waste of time.

She weighed the third pencil in her hand, taking her time with the shot.

There really weren't many options left to her.

Narrowing her eyes, she concentrated on her target, a close-up of Kol, his eyes bright against his dark complexion, his face tilted to the side as if he was listening to something. Squeezing the pencil until its octagon shape bore into her skin, she took a deep breath, and made her decision.

Time to attack.

With the thought, she let the pencil fly, nailing her target right between his gorgeous clear blue eyes.

Kol flipped on the warming plate under the bar's coffee-pot and slid five mugs onto the bar, his gaze on the front door.

The wind howled outside, last night's rain threatening to harden to sleet, the savage weather mirroring his mood.

The Council would be returning soon. They had spent an hour last night grilling Kol as to why the bar was destroyed, but empty, and where the garm they'd tracked there had gone.

Kol had remained silent, staring at them one by one with cool indifference. The garm were gone—transported to a sparsely inhabited part of the land of the giants. Without the aid of a portal guardian, like Kol, it would take them years if not eternity to find their way back. Why discuss what was done?

Finally, the Council had given up, the most senior member saying they had bigger worries, and had to trust that Kol had used a sliver of good judgment. Kol'd let the old garm's condescension roll off him. He knew their tricks—taunt him into losing his temper and revealing what few secrets he held.

After a few more carefully aimed shots, they'd departed for the night—the old garm, Magnus, issuing an order to reconvene at seven this morning.

It was now six-fifty-nine.

Kol tipped the steaming pot of coffee over the first cup, the rich aroma of the dark roast filling the bar at the same time the room shimmered with the Council's reappearance.

"No door today?" Kol asked, pushing a cup toward Birgit, the female member and the only one deigning to look his way.

"Magnus saw what that bit of politeness did for us last night," she replied with dry disinterest, her gaze drifting to the Council's leader.

"Not that we're spying. A portal guardian of Kol's level knows better than to hide facts from the Council. Correct,

Kol?" Magnus stood erect, his gray gaze traveling over the bar. "When do you open?"

Kol shrugged. "Whenever. But I can close for the day."

"Best. I don't want word of our arrival leaking out until we've formed a plan." With that Magnus pulled out a chair at the table farthest from the door and sat down. The other Council members followed his example, leaving Kol to carry their coffees to them on a tray.

He considered leaving the drinks—the bar was closed, his bartending role shut down with it. But it was a small matter, let the Council keep their delusions of authority, for now.

Once everyone was seated with their coffee in front of them, Magnus dove right to the point.

"We believe your portal is in danger of being lost."

Kol tapped his index finger against the lip of the thick ironstone mug. "Is that a fact?" His gaze zeroed onto the older garm. The forandre had been great at one time, a legend, but easy living had softened him, taken away his edge. "And you base this on what?"

"Don't be a fool," Birgit broke in. "We've been monitoring you for months—ever since that witch slipped into Jormun's world with her hound."

Kol's eyes narrowed, his hands pressing against the top of the table as he turned to address her. "That witch—"

"Enough." Magnus held up one hand. "What happened with the witch isn't our concern, not now." He shot a quelling gaze at Birgit. "It's another witch that brings us here."

"Another witch?" Kol leaned back, wiping all expression from his face.

"Like you don't—"

"Birgit," Magnus warned, then turned to Kol. "This witch has been watching you for months. We're sure you've seen her." He reached into a leather folder resting near his elbow and pulled out a photo.

Kol glanced at the image, even though he knew what…who he'd see there.

Kelly in that ridiculous hat. Could she have been any more obvious?

Birgit placed her elbows on the table and leaned closer. "Know her?"

Her gaze said she knew the answer, probably knew or thought she knew more about Kol's relationship with Kelly than Kol knew himself.

"I've seen her," he replied.

Birgit huffed out a breath of disbelief. "Is that enough for you?" she asked Magnus. "I told you. She's got him… charmed. He can't be expected to hold the portal in a condition like this."

Despite his resolve to remain cool, Kol's nostrils flared. "I'm holding this portal just fine."

"Are you? How many attacks have you had in the past month? And what happened to the garm we sensed here last night? They got too close, didn't they? Caught you off guard, maybe because you were sidetracked…" She tapped a blunt nail against the brim of Kelly's hat. "You couldn't fight them off so you sent them somewhere, somewhere through the portal in direct violation of portal-guardian regulations. Unauthorized use. It's grounds for losing your portal, you know."

Kol pulled his hands off the table, pressed them into his thighs, fighting the temptation to wrap them around the female's throat and squeeze until her words of threat gurgled to a stop.

Birgit, her eyes blazing, shifted in her seat toward him, ready to face his attack.

"Birgit," Magnus bit out the name. "Stop acting like a pup new to the hunt. And, Kol, you have this post in great part because of your judgment and control—don't give me reason to doubt that now."

Kol relaxed his fingers and picked up the cream. He held it out to Birgit.

Her lips thinning, she ignored him.

"Tell him," she said to Magnus.

Kol set the metal pitcher down, his fingers moving to the thin strip of stainless steel that formed the handle. "Tell him what?"

The men shifted in their seats, their gazes meeting briefly then darting back to their coffee, their hands, anywhere but Kol. Birgit leaned back, twisting her body to rest her elbow on the back of her chair. "Should *I* tell him?"

Magnus shot her an annoyed look, then wrapped both hands around his cup. Staring at Kol, he said, "The Council has decided the risk of losing this portal is too great. We can't justify leaving its protection to only one garm—not until whatever has been stirred up is captured and dealt with." His gaze flicked to the photo of Kelly.

Kol's fingers tightened around the pitcher's metal handle. "Interesting thought," he replied.

"It isn't a thought, Kol. It's a plan," Birgit interrupted.

Kol didn't bother looking at her. She was nothing more than a burr in his coat—Magnus was who he had to deal with.

"The portal is secure. If things get too dicey I can shut it down."

Birgit made a noise in the back of her throat.

"And risk angering the entities in the other worlds?" Magnus asked, then shook his head. "You don't have to like this, Kol, but you have to do it."

Did he? Kol held the older garm's gaze, measuring his

choices. Now he understood the purpose of the other two males with Magnus. They were nothing more than goons to enforce the Council's edict, but Birgit…. What was her role?

Suspicion tickled at the back of his mind. His gaze slid to the female. She smiled back at him.

"You cannot think—" he began, his eyes snapping back to Magnus.

"I'm as experienced as you, Guardian," Birgit broke in. "And not as easily distracted."

The little metal handle crimped under the pressure of his fingers. Kol closed his eyes briefly, reopened them when he was back under control. "She has never guarded a portal," he said to Magnus.

"But she's operated them, and she was instrumental in the modernizing we started two decades ago."

"And the upgrades," Birgit added.

Kol stared at a spot above Magnus's head. A computer geek. He was being attacked by groups of rogue garm and the Council thought to stop them by saddling him with a techy. "She can't fight," he finally added.

"With good security, you don't have to fight." Birgit slid her empty mug across the table, letting it smack into Kol's.

Black coffee lurched from Kol's mug onto the table, settling into a dark, ugly puddle.

"Besides, I can fight. I just haven't had to." Birgit rapped her fingers against the table top, and for the first time Kol sensed unease from her.

"Think of it as training," Magnus said. At Kol's menacing look, he continued, "For her. Birgit wants her own portal, but has no real-world experience. You need backup." He held up his hand as Kol moved to correct him. "We say, you need backup. Bottom line, this is our decision. You can live with it—or not."

The two thugs stood and stepped away from the table, ready to fight.

Still seated, Kol studied the group. He could battle the Council and he might even win, but what would it gain him? Continued ownership of the portal? For now—but he'd also be a marked man. Marked as a rogue, open to attack from everyone, whether they opposed or supported the Council.

Kol was independent, but he wasn't rogue. He respected the rules that kept chaos from reigning. He'd even spoken up more than once in support of the Council—not because he agreed with their decisions, but because he believed in the necessity of a regulating body.

If he walked away now, both he and the Council would suffer. He'd be making a stand for chaos. And that was something Kol could never do—no matter the cost to him personally.

His gaze clicked back to Magnus.

The older garm's eyes met Kol's and with a short incline of his head, Magnus signaled he accepted Kol's assent.

"There're rooms upstairs. Take your pick." Kol's chair scraped across the floor with a shriek.

"So, I'm in?" Birgit glanced from Kol to Magnus.

Magnus stood, too, slipping his leather portfolio under one arm. "We'll leave it to you two as to how you work out the details. All we care about is that the portal is safe, and whoever's behind the attacks—" his gaze dropped back to the photo of Kelly "—is contained."

Contained. The word echoed through Kol's mind as he tipped his nose to the wind and waited for a scent of Kelly. In his wolf form, he'd know if she was anywhere within ten miles of the bar.

The breeze brought back the smells of a human city—rotting garbage, auto exhaust and hamburgers grilling at a nearby greasy spoon. But no Kelly.

He should be glad. She wasn't here. She wasn't watching the bar. Maybe this meant she wasn't involved in the attacks, or maybe it just meant she'd taken a night off.

It also meant he had a decision to make. Before he'd left, Magnus had made it clear someone was going after Kelly. It could be Kol or it could be another garm—probably Birgit—but before twenty-four hours were up, someone had to question her and prove she either was or wasn't involved in the attacks.

Now, for Kol to do that, he'd have to leave his portal for one of the few times in over a century. He never liked to leave his post. Why was he even considering the option? Why not leave the task of questioning Kelly to Birgit? She was eager enough for the job.

Kol stretched his front legs out ahead of his body, then leaned back on his haunches and catapulted himself onto the top of the Dumpster Kelly had hidden behind a few days earlier. A faint scent of her still hovered in the air.

He inhaled, felt the reaction vibrate through his body, down the length of his spine to the tip of his tail.

Damn whatever hold she had on him—maybe Birgit was right, maybe she had cast some kind of charm on him.

All the more reason to let Birgit carry out the unenviable job of questioning her.

Except…he stared at the bar where Birgit sat waiting for his decision.

Except Birgit was too eager for the job, too anxious to prove her worth to the Council. Any interrogation session she conducted, Kelly might not survive.

Chapter 4

Kelly dropped the manila folder onto the top of her kitchen table and stretched forward, resting her head on her arms. Closing her eyes, she tried to relax, to let the darkness settle over her, slow the pinging thoughts in her brain.

The day before, filled with anxiety and a bit of desperation, she'd boldly told herself she was going to attack Kol—force her way through the portal to rescue the kidnapped boy, then shut the whole operation down—single-handedly.

Sound the trumpets. Maybe she'd even leave a silver bullet behind when she was done.

She groaned. God save her from her own arrogance.

Her eyes flew open. Time to face facts. She needed help. She needed her sister.

She pushed herself up and walked to the phone,

glancing at the clock on her stove as she did. 5:00 a.m. Not that time mattered, she couldn't call her sister directly anyway. Kara and her new husband, Risk, were staying at his cabin—somewhere. Somewhere not quite in the human world, Kelly gathered. She hadn't been invited to visit yet.

She frowned. Call your brother-in-law a slathering beast a few times and get banned from the home front. Who knew hellhounds were so sensitive?

Anyway, Kara and Kelly did have a way to communicate; very mundane, and not exactly speedy—voice mail. Kelly could leave a message and when Kara came up for air in her little love nest, maybe she'd check for messages and maybe she'd call Kelly back.

Muttering to herself, she picked up the phone. Mid-dial a knock sounded at the kitchen door.

Odd. No one but Kara came to the back door. The thought spurring her forward, Kelly rushed to answer.

She flung the door open and peered out into the murky morning fog. No one. Her brows lowered, she leaned out a bit farther and glanced toward the drive that dead-ended into her detached garage. No vehicles. Had she imagined the knock?

Something rattled against the metal trash can she kept stored near the drive. She placed a bare foot on the damp concrete stoop, ready to go investigate, but a breeze caught her short robe, blowing it open and reminding her she wasn't dressed for battle.

Still, she didn't like the idea of someone lurking outside her house. She hesitated. The trash can rattled again, this time tumbling onto its side.

Kelly jumped, then laughed as a neighborhood cat sauntered around the spill of garbage.

Still smiling, she placed her hand back on the knob

and started to turn. The hairs along her arms raised. She could feel someone…someone behind her…inside her house.

Without pausing to think, she gathered power in her free hand, and spun, letting the baseball-size sphere of energy shoot across her kitchen.

Directly at Kol Hildr.

Busy admiring the length of bare leg showing from beneath the short robe Kelly wore, Kol almost missed the witch's sudden attack. As the sphere shot toward him, he dropped, letting the ball of energy smash into the wall behind him. The smell of smoldering plaster filled the room.

"What are you doing here?" Kelly strode toward him, another ball of energy sizzling in her hand.

Cocking one eyebrow, he stood and held out one hand to stop her advance. "I knocked."

A frustrated puff of air escaped her lips and her eyes narrowed. "It's polite to wait for an answer before you come in."

"Really?" He shrugged one shoulder. "I didn't know." He glanced around the room, purposely ignoring the powerball she still held and the blackened hole in the wall behind him. "This is your house? It seems a bit…cheery for you."

He could feel her tension, then indecision. The powerball let out a low snapping sound, like a fire before it builds to a roar. Kol's muscles tightened, his body ready to spring.

"Kara decorated," Kelly ground out the words, like they pained her. Then she jerked her fingers closed around the sphere, extinguishing its magic. "I'm not much on domestic issues."

Kol half turned; glancing at her over his shoulder, he cocked one brow. "Really? How surprising."

She tapped her fingertips against her bare leg. "What are you doing here?"

"Visiting?" He folded his arms over his chest. "You've certainly been dropping by the bar often enough. Although, you don't often actually come in. Why is that?" He stepped forward, until the bottom of her robe brushed against his jeans.

She stared up at him, her gaze determined. He made her nervous, he could feel it, but she was damn good at hiding it.

He smiled.

Her teeth snapped together, as if she was stopping herself from replying.

"Tell me, Kelly. Tell me why you've been watching my bar…me." He leaned forward, letting her scent waft over him—she smelled like the woods: sharp, sweet, irresistible.

"I'm not watching you." The words came out too quickly. *She was lying*.

He smiled again. His hand drifted upward, capturing her chin and tilting her face toward his. "I'd like to think it was because of…" He lowered his mouth. Her lips parted, whether in greeting or objection, he didn't wait to discover. He pushed all thoughts of what brought him to her house to the back of his mind and sank into the sensation of kissing her…his arms slipped around her slight form, pulling her against him…holding her.

Kelly moved closer, her breasts pressing against his chest. His hands wandered down the length of her back. He cupped her buttocks, and pressed her sex against his fast hardening length.

Kelly snuggled closer to the strong chest in front of her. Her fingers barely skimmed the smooth cotton of Kol's shirt, as if touching him too solidly would make this dream real—too real. As in, her rational mind would force her to snap out of the fantasy her body longed for.

Cool air brushed against her almost bare bottom, her robe riding up as Kol pulled her closer. Her sex pushed harder against his steely erection. She would be bruised tomorrow, and she didn't care.

Moaning, she opened her mouth to greet his tongue. He tasted of wintergreen: cool and enticing. He stepped forward, pushing her ahead of him. She clung to him, shutting down any part of her that might object. Her butt knocked into the edge of the table, and she let herself relax on top of it. Her hands wrapped around Kol's neck as she pulled him down with her. Files fanned out beneath her, tumbling to the floor, one soft plunk followed by another.

The rough stubble on Kol's chin rasped against her face as he angled his mouth toward her neck. A gasp of pure sensory pleasure escaped her lips.

"What's this?" Kol's hand pressed against an open file; his lips lifted from her neck.

Still caught up in the moment of passion, Kelly blinked, her mind blank of anything besides what was happening right now on her kitchen table.

Kol stood, cool air replacing the warmth of his body pressed to hers. Kelly barely stopped herself from clinging to him, keeping him clasped against her.

"What are you up to?" The words were low, as if he spoke only to himself, but they broke through the fog that had engulfed Kelly as surely as a chisel could break through glass.

She turned her head, her gaze landing on Kol's wide-spread fingers placed firmly on top of the picture of him with the pencil hole decorating the space between his eyes.

She twisted, slipping under his arms then standing. Her fingers dug into her upper arms. Her nostrils flaring as she struggled her way out of the lust-filled haze, she watched him through cautious eyes.

He picked up another batch of photos, then the notes she had made on garm.

"You seem to be spending a lot of energy researching garm—should I be flattered?" He held up the photo of himself, and flicked a fingernail over the pencil prick between his eyes. "I guess not."

Suddenly feeling silly and confused, Kelly grabbed for the picture.

He jerked it back, out of her reach. "Are you going to tell me what you're up to now?"

Kelly frowned. She'd already told him what she was doing, what she wanted from him—Terje.

He glanced at her, a frown of his own darkening his face. "This isn't a game you know. There are others involved now. They know you've been watching the bar, know…or think they know what you've been up to."

"You called in reinforcements?" She laughed. "I'm the one who should be flattered. I didn't realize I was so intimidating."

He stepped forward and grabbed her by the upper arms. Kelly met his gaze, her eyes snapping with anger.

Kol continued, "I just told you. This isn't a game. You need to tell me what's going on—why you've been watching the bar. Who else is involved? It's the only way I can protect you."

Kelly rounded her eyes. "Protect me? I don't remember asking you to protect me. Maybe you need to worry about protecting yourself."

He dropped his hands and shook his head, like a disappointed parent. "So, it's true. You are behind the attacks. How'd you get the rogues to help you? What did you promise them? Do for them?" The questions were low, his voice controlled, but Kelly could sense his fury, like a volcano giving off a low rumbling before exploding.

Kelly took a step backward. She regretted it instantly. She didn't have to explain things to him, especially when he was spouting nonsense. "What attacks?" she asked, her hand dropping to her side, ready to pull more energy from the room, to do what he accused her of—attack, if necessary.

Kol could barely look at the woman in front of him. Rage clouded his mind, knocking out all rational thought.

Rogue garm wouldn't follow just anyone. They had to have a reason, a promise of something. And he had no doubt what *he* would want from Kelly in exchange for his service—how could the other garm not ask the same?

"Terje. I want Terje." She spat out the words, like it pained her to release them.

Terje—was that his name, the lover the rogues had mentioned before Kol shoved them through the portal? Feeling his control slipping, the wolf in him threatening to come out, he spun, turning his back on her.

"Is he that important? Do you really understand how much danger you've brought upon yourself?"

She didn't answer. He glanced over his shoulder. She stood there, confusion on her face and another squirming ball of energy glowing in her hand.

Without hesitating, he shimmered, reappearing directly behind her. He grabbed her hands by the wrists, then shook, sending the sphere of energy dropping to the floor where it sizzled and popped like an angry rattler ready to strike. His mouth pressed to her ear, he murmured, "Don't mistake my attraction for weakness. I said I would protect you, but I can't let you endanger my portal."

Her body stiffened. He could feel her reaching for power, siphoning it from the room around them. With a growl, he dropped her wrists and spun her around in his arms, bent down until his nose was inches from hers. "Don't make me do something I don't want to do."

"I think you should leave." Her gaze was steady, her blue eyes giving away nothing to indicate her emotion.

He stared back at her, his own frustration threatening to push him over the edge. He wanted to shake her until she gave up whatever crazy mission she was on, until she saw him not as an adversary but a—

He yanked his hands from her body and held them up in front of him. "I'm done." Then he shimmered away, back to his bar and the portal.

"Why didn't you throw the powerball?" Heather asked, her brows lowering.

"I did. It just didn't hit him." Kelly pulled the coffeepot out from under the still dripping stream.

"Not the first time. The second time. You already said you didn't realize it was Kol when you threw the first one." A line of worry formed between Heather's eyes. "Would you have thrown it if you'd known it was him?"

Coffee slopped onto Kelly's hand. Murmuring a curse, she blotted at it with a paper towel. "Of course, I would have."

Heather cocked a disbelieving brow.

"And I didn't *not* throw the second one, I just...hesitated."

"Hesitation can get you killed." Heather punctuated her statement by ripping another towel off the roll with a savage jerk of her wrist.

Kelly ignored both her assistant's statement and

obvious disapproval. "And it's not like it matters. I couldn't have hurt him anyway—he's forandre. He'd just have shimmered or something."

"Maybe." Heather dropped the roll of towels and stalked to her desk.

"Forandre are known for being dangerous—and tough. Only another forandre, or a god or something, could beat Kol."

"But you didn't even try." Heather flipped on her PC. "I've wondered all along why you haven't been more direct. Now I think I know."

Kelly let out a humph. "You don't know anything."

"Touchy, aren't you? I'm not saying anything bad, just that maybe you trust Kol more than you think you do. More than you should. I've seen you in action. If you had really felt threatened, you'd have thrown that ball."

Not bothering to reply, Kelly picked up the coffee-soaked paper towels, tossed them into the trash then strode out of the room. Back in her office with the door snapped closed behind her, she collapsed behind her desk.

Heather was right. She could have thrown that power-ball, and followed right behind it with another and another. Alone and unprepared, she might not be strong enough to defeat Kol, but she could have bought enough time to have escaped the house.

So, why didn't she?

The thought made something in the front of her brain start to pound.

She just didn't that's all. It was early. She was caught off guard, confused by his kisses.

His kisses…her reaction…Kelly pressed her fingertips to her forehead. The pounding was getting worse. What had she been thinking?

She hadn't—simple as that. He caught her off guard and used the one weapon she never would have thought she'd have to fight against—her own body and its irrational desires.

Well, now she knew and next time she'd be more prepared.

Her hand dropped to her phone. Enough time wasted worrying about how she had messed up. Time to concentrate on what she could do to make sure it didn't happen again. Time to call Kara.

Hopefully, she'd be able to convince her sister to leave her love nest and come back—at least long enough to help Kelly defeat Kol.

"Bar's supposed to open in five minutes." Birgit tapped the face of her wristwatch.

"And I'm here." Kol strode to the front and yanked the door to the Guardian's Keep open. Six of the desperates who frequented the place filed inside.

Birgit waited for him to take his place behind the bar then leaned forward. "Was there a problem? Did you learn anything? Stop her?"

Ignoring her, Kol checked the papers two dwarves handed him in exchange for passage through the portal. "This is forged." He tossed the papers back at the stouter dwarf. "Try that again, and you'll never see Nidavellir."

The two left muttering to themselves.

"You didn't learn anything. Did you?" Birgit shook her head, dropping the spoon she'd been using with a clank. "So, what were you doing?" She sniffed. "You smell of her." Pushing her cup forward, she stood.

"Where are you going?" Kol turned from the dark elf he was serving to glare at the female garm.

"To finish what you're too besotted to do yourself." She began to shimmer.

Kol leaned across the bar and grabbed her by the wrist. "No, you're not. You'll leave Kelly alone."

Birgit smiled. "So, it's *Kelly*. I knew I was right—that Magnus was giving you too much credit." She stared at Kol for a second then shook her wrist free. "Fine, the more you screw up, the better my chances of getting your portal. But—" she pressed her fingers onto the bar until the tips turned white, then baring her teeth, continued "—you endanger the security of the portals and I'll take you down."

Kol lifted one brow.

With a smile, Birgit pushed away from the bar. "By the way, I ran a vulnerability scan on your system this morning. Your passwords wouldn't slow down a dwarf drunk on four kegs of ale. I changed them."

Kol's hands balled into fists. "Don't mess with my computer."

Her gaze drifted down to his fists, then back up. "Don't worry. I'll tell you the new ones—this time. You just remember what I said." Then, giving her coffee cup one last shove, she slipped through the doorway that led upstairs.

Chapter 5

"Any calls?" Kelly peeped at Heather out of the corner of her eye as she strode past her assistant's desk on the way to her office.

She tossed her gym bag onto her desk a little harder than necessary. Her MP3 player inside clinked against the hard wooden surface. She muttered a curse, and jerked the bag open to check on the electronic device.

Assured the player was still functioning, she shoved it back inside the bag and collapsed in her chair.

After her conversation with Heather earlier, she'd found it impossible to concentrate on anything. Her thoughts kept wandering back to Kol—him pressing her back against the table, her pulling him down on top. She'd hoped a few rounds with a punching bag would clear her head, knock the asinine thoughts out. But, to her chagrin, even an extra hour with the speed bag hadn't helped.

Heather followed her into her office, one pink slip of paper in her hand. "Just Mrs. Coleman. She said she was going to e-mail some pictures."

"Of the wolves?" Kelly asked.

"I guess." Heather laid the slip on Kelly's desktop. "Aren't garm wolves?"

Picking up the paper, Kelly nodded. "That's why I was watching the Guardian's Keep." Shaking her head, she tapped a finger against the message. "But that was before I researched garm as much as I have. Apparently, they don't hang out in packs all that much, and I really can't see Kol bonding with others, even his own kind."

"Well, they aren't werewolves." Heather pursed her lips.

Kelly snorted. "Of course not, but that doesn't mean they're garm, either. The Northwoods case may wind up being nothing more than a stray pack of perfectly mundane wolves moving south from Canada."

"Mrs. Coleman sure doesn't think so." Heather picked up Kelly's empty coffee cup from earlier and turned to leave. She paused mid-spin. "You aren't giving up on—"

Kelly shot her a sharp glance, cutting her off.

Heather sighed. "Maybe the pictures will tell you something."

"Maybe." Kelly tilted back her head, her eyes closing briefly.

"Oh, and the new client—Aesa. She stopped by, too. Right after you left. She seems so nice. That's just terrible about her son."

Letting out a breath, Kelly opened her eyes. "What did she want?"

"Didn't say, but she did say she'd stop back by." Heather paused again, her gaze wandering toward the clock on

Kelly's wall. "Would it be okay if I left early? I've got to run by the bank and—" she made a flicking motion with her wrist "—stuff."

Not giving the request too much thought, Kelly replied, "Sure." As Heather wandered out of the room, Kelly stared at her assistant's back wishing she still saw things as clearly as Heather seemed to. With a sigh, Kelly shifted her gaze, letting it fall on her phone.

When would Kara call? She needed her sister.

As soon as the thought formed, Kelly realized how true it was—but she needed Kara for something more now— not just to help her take on Kol.

She needed her sister's help explaining why something in Kelly seemed resistant to even try battling the disconcerting garm.

Kol stood outside Kelly's office, the wind blowing the ruff of hair around his neck to standing. In wolf form, he'd trailed her from her office to the gym and back to her office. Her assistant had left a few moments earlier. The entire time he'd watched Kelly, she had met with no one. Talked with no one, except, he assumed, her assistant—not even the other gym patrons.

He had watched her through the smeared windows of the old boxing club, kicking and punching with all her strength into the black bag. Her body had quickly developed a slight sheen, the muscles of her buttocks taut and clearly visible in tight-fitting shorts, her hands jabbing with a rhythm that was almost hypnotic. Even in his wolf form, he'd felt a physical reaction—wanted to get closer, past the glass that separated them so he could fill his lungs with her scent.

She was dangerous.

But was she behind the attacks on his portal? And who was Terje? Questions he needed answered. Talking to her didn't work. Following her was time-consuming, time away from his portal. Time with Birgit left to her own devices.

No, he needed to watch Kelly, but he needed to do it on his own turf. His ears twitched forward at the thought. His turf. That was the answer to all his problems. If he could get Kelly to stay at the bar with him, he'd be able to watch her, make sure she wasn't causing the attacks, *and* make sure she was safe. All and all the best solution to everything.

Now he just had to get Kelly to agree. How hard could that be?

Barking out a laugh, he shimmered back to the bar to change.

Heather left her car hidden inside a deserted lean-to and crept toward the entrance of the cavern. The thick fog that seemed to have swallowed the Northern region for the past few weeks was on her side tonight, disguising her visit from anyone glancing out the window of the nearby bed-and-breakfast. Her shoes made a squelching sound in the soft mud. She shot the beam of her flashlight onto the path. Gigantic paw prints marred the earth in front of her. She frowned.

Ahead, light leaked between two boulders. She flipped off her flashlight, and moved forward, sidestepping to avoid knocking any stray rocks off the path and alerting what waited inside.

A curtain of power, designed to confuse anyone who wandered onto the hideout, had been left open. Heather frowned again, this time adding a low curse under her breath. Discarded beer cans and chip bags littered the floor.

Letting out an irritated breath, she stepped into the brightly lit cavern, and purposely kicked one of the cans, sending it skittering across the cavern floor.

Not one of the hundred or so garm gathered there looked up. She yanked off her coat, draped it over her arm, then took a bracing breath and strode forward.

"I've found the guardian's weakness," she announced.

Leifi, one of the more dependable of the rogues, looked up from the cards fanned in his hand. "Really? And did you discover what happened to the last group of stooges she sent?"

After brushing chip crumbs off a folding chair, Heather risked a sideways glance at a line of garm slouched against the cavern wall behind her and sat. "Like you care."

He glanced at the others in the room, then shrugged. "Of course, I don't care—not about them. But I do care about me." He tapped his chest with one finger. "She's been feeding us bits for months, constantly claiming she's found the solution to stealing the portal. I'm beginning to doubt we'll ever get what she's promised us—or you, either."

"So it's *my* success you care about?" Heather slipped fingers into her pants' pockets, hiding the slight trembling caused by the suggestion everything she'd done so far would be for nothing. She was so close to getting the power she wanted. After all this…she glanced around the dim cave, taking in the aroma of unwashed garm then fidgeted on her seat a bit as one of the rogues noticed her perusal and grinned. She gave her shoulders a little shake, knocking off the unease that always encompassed her when alone with the rogues. Staring down at the table, she refocused her thoughts.

She'd done too much, committed…she couldn't fail now.

"The Council is here," he replied.

"What?" Her head snapped up.

"Karl and I went to the bar last night. The guardian has a keeper—a female. She was wearing the singing wolf emblem."

Heather licked her lips. She'd heard a lot of talk about the Council. They seemed to be some kind of obsession for the garm, but she didn't really see why their appearance was an issue.

"So, they're not even trying to hide their involvement." Aesa stepped out of the shadows, a low hiss escaping from between her teeth.

Heather straightened.

Leifi barely gave Fenrir's lover a glance. "Why should they? All they care about is restoring their all-important order. We're nothing to them." He dropped the cards on the table and stood.

Tension thickened the air, the other garm deserting their cards and conversations to watch Leifi and Aesa. Heather shot a nervous glace toward the cavern entrance. The garm were a strange and powerful lot, constantly fighting amongst themselves for domination. She had no desire to get caught in the middle of yet another scramble for power.

Aesa strode forward, a determined look on her face. Even a novice witch like Heather could feel the energy of Aesa's anger swelling, pushing against the rock walls that surrounded them.

Aesa glanced around the room. Heather followed her gaze. The look of disgust and dismay on Leifi's face was mirrored by every other garm in the room.

Placing a hand on Leifi's back, she spoke to the room. "They'll mourn their mistake. Once Fenrir is free, we'll find roles for everyone—portals and beings for every garm to guard. No garm will be deemed unworthy of responsibility and respect."

Heather pulled back against her chair, almost afraid to breathe, the emotion rolling through the cavern had grown so threatening.

Leifi didn't move, his muscles still tense with anger, he asked, "No garm?"

Aesa paused as if weighing her words. "None here."

He turned to look at her. "None at all—except maybe the Garm Council themselves."

Heather pulled her hands from her pockets, wished she'd chosen a seat closer to the cave's opening.

Aesa stared at him, her face free of emotion, nothing to give away what thoughts lay behind her eyes. Then, with a short incline of her head, she signaled her agreement.

Heaving out a sigh, Heather placed her fingertips on the edge of the table. "He says the Council is already involved."

Aesa raised her chin and switched her gaze from Leifi to Heather and back again. Addressing the rogue, she said, "We need to move fast then—before they relieve the current guardian of his portal." She flicked her gaze back to Heather. "Did I hear you say you've discovered his weakness?"

Heather licked her lips. "It's been right under our noses all along. I just never guessed…"

Aesa frowned. "Tell us."

"Kelly. The guardian is hot for her."

Warm welcoming light glowed from the other side of the windows when Kelly arrived at her office the next morning. She tromped down the stairs, determined to make this a better day, to shove aside her doubts and move forward—to do whatever she had to, to find Terje. As her foot moved toward the bottom step, she heard ringing coming from inside. She skipped the last step and rushed through the door.

"Heather, was that the phone?" Not waiting for a response, she dove for the handset. A dial tone greeted her.

Frustrated, she clunked the handset back down. Shaking her head, she called out for Heather again. A strong hand on her shoulder halted the words in her throat.

What did it say that this time even before turning around she knew who she would see? Was her body that attuned to his touch?

She sidestepped, putting room and a powerball between her and Kol. *She would do what she had to do.* "What are you doing here?"

Kol's hand fell to his side. His blue gaze skimmed her body as though he could see through her heavy trench coat—as though he was remembering her as he'd last seen her, dressed in only her short terry robe. Kelly swallowed and tried to push thoughts of their last encounter out of her mind, off of her face.

Neither spoke, then slowly Kol's hand began to rise, his gaze now focused on her face. Kelly stood there frozen until a loud noise knocked her out of the spell.

She turned to see the front door banging against the wall and Heather hurrying into the office, a carton of milk in her hand. "This was all they had. I hope it's…" She stopped, her face flushing as she caught sight of Kelly.

"You have a visitor. I offered him coffee, but he asked for cream and you drink yours—"

Kelly held up a trembling hand. "That's fine." She flicked her gaze over her harried assistant. Yesterday Heather had seemed dead set on Kelly challenging Kol; today her assistant was running around waiting on the garm. What had changed?

She glanced back at Kol. His expression revealed nothing. Lips pursed, she said, "Maybe you'd better come in here." Slipping past him, she walked into her office. Her heart hammered against her ribs.

She slid behind her desk, her coat still wrapped around her. The combination of the coat hiding her body, and the solid piece of furniture now between them, made her feel a little more in control. Her voice firm, she repeated her earlier question, "What are you doing here?"

"Don't you want to take off your coat?" Kol cocked his head.

"I'm fine. Answer my question."

Instead, he wandered around the room, picking up odd objects—the medal she won last year during a kickboxing tourney, then the picture of Kara and her new husband on their wedding day.

"It was a nice wedding," he commented, setting the photo back down.

Kelly tapped her fingers on her desk blotter. Kol had attended the wedding. Something that at the time both infuriated and amazed Kelly. Kara insisted the garm was instrumental in her having the chance at a life with her husband, but it was beyond Kelly to understand such logic.

"Overall," she replied. "So, why are you—"

"Here?" he completed, coming to a stop in front of her desk. "I have a proposition for you."

"Really?" Kelly couldn't keep the surprise from her face.

He smiled, a slow angling of his lips that made Kelly's insides tighten in a delicious, dangerous way.

"Not that kind of proposition, although…" He let the words die off, then continued, "A business proposition."

"Really?" Kelly repeated.

"Really."

The computer beside her beeped.

He glanced toward the machine. "You've got mail. Do you need to check that?"

"No, I…" Kelly's gaze slid to the monitor. Kara wouldn't e-mail, but the interruption offered her a chance to call her meeting with Kol short. "Maybe I should. I'm expecting some important files from a client. If you want, you could make an appointment with my assistant. I'm sure I'll have time free…sometime."

"No worries. I can wait. Go ahead and check." Nodding to the computer, he sat on the edge of her desk.

Kelly shot him a killing look, but it seemed to roll off him like water off a wolf's coat. Not sure what else to do, and needing a moment to gather her thoughts, she spun in her chair and clicked open the highlighted message. A picture of four giant wolves backlit by the afternoon sun filled the screen.

Behind her, Kol's body went rigid. "Friends of yours?" he asked, his voice low and severe.

Kelly glanced at him over her shoulder, her mind grasping for a response. The intensity in his eyes did nothing to soothe her stammering brain. She opened her mouth praying some answer would come, but before a word could pass her lips, Heather ran into the room.

"Kelly, I think—" A table crashed through the open door behind the apprentice witch.

Kelly stood, her wheeled chair shooting across the room and slamming into the wall behind her. Someone was attacking her office, her assistant—her. She strode as quickly as she could toward the open doorway, gathering power as she moved. She was within a foot of crossing the threshold when an arm wrapped around her waist and pulled her backward, jerking her off her feet.

"What the hell?" she bit out.

Power surged to her hands ready to spill over and sear whoever had stopped her forward motion, but just as quickly as the energy gathered, she realized it was Kol gripping her from behind, pulling her body against his. "Damn," she muttered, as the energy shrank back almost of its own volition.

Her body shaking with the effort of containing the power she'd drawn from around them, she twisted and glared up at him. "Let me go."

He didn't even glance at her. Just shoved her behind the desk and crossed the room—shimmering as a chair blasted through the doorway in front of him.

Kol materialized in the center of Kelly's reception area. Four garm, in human form, stood near the door, each with some piece of furniture in his hands. A short, broad-across-the-chest male held Kelly's assistant's chair. At Kol's appearance, he lifted it overhead and tossed it at the guardian.

Kol rolled across the floor, ignoring broken pieces of plastic and pottery that gouged into his arms and sides as he went. The chair missed him by a good foot, but a computer printer soon followed.

What were the rogues doing here—attacking Kelly? Had she done something to anger her coconspirators?

Crouched behind Heather's desk, Kol watched for an opening. A taller male, with a snarling wolf tattoo on his forearm, darted his eyes at the other three, giving them some type of silent signal. *A leader, among rogues.* Kol was intrigued. Then without further warning, the three followers shimmered. Remembering Kelly unprotected in her office, Kol's breath stopped in his chest, but before he could move to save her, she appeared, her eyes blazing and powerballs dancing in her open palms.

The first one she threw directly at his head.

Kol rolled again, this time a backward flip—his feet aiming for the corner of the room where a six-foot-long wooden staff stuck out of a silver umbrella stand. Instead, he collided with the short garm, who had just materialized behind him. The other male stared down at him, his lips pulling back into a snarl, a cloud of power engulfing him as he began his change into a wolf.

Kol began his own change, but he knew it was too late. The other garm would beat him, not by much, but enough to rip out Kol's throat before he had a chance to complete his transition to wolf.

"Damn it," Kelly yelled, tossing the second ball. This time her missile hit, colliding with the short garm's stomach, stopping his change and sending him plummeting to his knees. Kol barely had time to roll again before the other garm fell face forward onto the floor.

Now fully in wolf form, Kol twisted, dancing out of the way as Kelly shot two more powerballs toward the fallen garm's companions. As the two dove out of the way, Kol paused to shoot a grin at the grim-faced witch. Maybe she could take better care of herself than he'd thought.

The grin slipped from his lips.

The garm Kol had pegged as the leader stood behind her, a silver blade a hair's width from piercing her throat.

Chapter 6

Power thrummed through Kelly. The energy level in the room was so high she had to fight to keep from absorbing more than she could control. Kol, as a wolf, glanced back at her with something akin to pride shining in his eyes, his mouth breaking into a grin. Kelly started to grin back, but then his expression changed from joy to pure animal hatred.

Instinctively, she pulled back and felt the sharp tip of a knife slice into her neck.

"He is caught, isn't he?" A harsh voice murmured in her ear. "Who knew the least experienced of us would stumble on the truest trap of all?"

Kelly didn't understand a word of the man's ramblings, but was happy for his apparent split in attention. Flexing her hands, she willed a stream of energy to her fingertips.

Other fingers dug into her arm.

"Don't try it," the voice ordered. "We're not here to hurt you anyway. Just keep still, play the frightened little lamb, and you'll be fine."

Kelly almost snorted at the insanity of such a suggestion. Barely breathing, she released the constraints she'd put on herself and began sucking power from the room.

On the other side of the desk, Kol snapped and growled, his hackles raising, his hair expanding. He looked three times his previous size.

The man behind her spoke, his words floating past her, obviously not meant for her ears. "You know what we want. Give it to us, and we'll hand her over."

Kelly blinked, confused by the one-sided conversation. Then she noticed Kol angle his body closer, his teeth bared, his eyes flashing. *Kol.* She'd forgotten the forandre could speak telepathically when in their non-human form. Unfortunately, Kol had apparently chosen not to share his current conversation with her. She was left trying to interpret what was happening based only on the words of her captor.

"She'd still be dead, Guardian."

Kol growled.

The power continued to build inside Kelly. She could feel it, like a taut guitar string running through her center. A humming filled her ears. She wasn't sure how much longer she could hold the magic or what would happen when she let go. Uncertainty sent her gaze back to Kol.

One of the garm Kol had downed earlier began to stir. Kol jumped at him, his teeth hovering over the other man's neck. Kelly's eyes rounded. It was one thing to toss a powerball at someone, injure, even kill them that way. But to rip their throat out? Despite the power crackling through her, she shivered.

"Kill him. I don't care." The knife at her neck bobbed as the man behind her shrugged.

She could see the indecision in Kol's eyes. Something in him *wanted* to kill the other man, but the threat to her held him back. His chin dropped lower, his mouth gaped, and his lip curled upward, then just as suddenly, and without apparent reason, his gaze lifted and he cocked his head to the side.

Surprised by the sudden switch, Kelly jerked sideways. The end of the knife stabbed into her neck. She cried out, drawing Kol's piercing blue gaze back to where she stood.

"We're leaving," his voice declared in her head.

Blood running down her throat, Kelly stared back at him in disbelief. Did he think she chose to stand here and have a knife shoved into her neck?

"In five seconds, do whatever you have to, to put distance between you and the rogue."

Kelly blinked at him.

"Oh, and lean to the left."

"Five, four, three," Kol muttered in her head, his eyes focused on the man behind her the entire time. "Two—"

Kelly twisted her palm up, letting a stream of energy shoot where she guessed by the pressure of the knife the garm holding her stood, then leaned hard to the left.

The man behind her cursed, and the knife clattered to the floor, but his other hand still gripped her arm. Kelly swung her free arm around, placing her hand on the fingers that held her, and let pure raw power race free.

Another curse, and she was falling. As she started to twist, to protect herself from the impact, Kol sailed toward her, feet out in front of his body. She steeled herself, but instead of the expected impact, her body tingled, like a thousand pinpricks. Then just as quickly, she hit the ground with a loud thump.

She barely had time to take a breath before Kol's teeth sunk into the collar of her coat and he began dragging her backward, behind an overturned table. A beer bottle smashed into the wall at her back.

She blinked, her mind suddenly clicking back into action. The bar. She was in the Guardian's Keep now—and in the middle of what sounded to be an even bigger fight than the one she had just left.

Bottles slammed into the wall behind Kol, beer exploding out of them and drenching his fur. He blinked the liquid out of his eyes and concentrated on dragging Kelly to safety. He'd have preferred her somewhere else entirely, but when his senses told him the portal was in danger, he'd had no options. He had to get back to his bar, and he couldn't leave Kelly behind.

Kelly stirred. Her heels dug into the floor, slowing his progress. With an impatient tug, he jerked her behind an overturned table. She pushed herself onto her elbows, her gaze darting around the room.

"Stay here," he ordered, projecting his voice into her head.

She blinked at him, then made a move to flip over— onto her knees. He bumped against her with his hip, sending her back onto her seat. He shot her a warning gaze, then after a quick swipe of his muzzle against her hair, launched his body over the tabletop and into the fray.

There were rogues everywhere. Birgit, in wolf form, stood in front of the bar guarding the space behind and the computer that operated the portal. Magnus and three of his thugs fought as humans, parrying blows with anything they could grab.

Another beer bottle crashed against the wall, quickly followed by a chair. His eyes narrowed, Kol scanned the room, looking for a leader. There had been one at Kelly's. Was there one here, too?

A shimmer of light near the portal doorway caught his eye. Not waiting to see who was materializing, he leaped. The garm with the snarling wolf tattoo that Kol had just left at Kelly's office solidified seconds before Kol landed on him, his mouth open and directed at the other garm's neck.

The rogue's eyes flashed and he raised his arm. Kol's teeth sunk into skin and through muscle. An image of the rogue standing behind Kelly, the knife pricking her, blood running down her neck flashed through Kol's mind. A low growl formed deep in his throat, and he sunk his teeth deeper, jerking his body side to side determined to break the arm that had threatened to harm the twin witch he was quickly thinking of as his.

The rogue snarled in response, his lips pulling upward, revealing white, even, human teeth and his wolf nature at the same time.

"Give it up, Guardian. Your time is past. If you're lucky, we'll let you join us." The rogue raised his hand, signaling to one of the garm pressing Magnus back against the wall. Silver flashed through the air as the second garm tossed a silver-coated bat to the rogue Kol was determined to take down. The bat clasped in his hand, the rogue looked down at Kol, something close to regret in his eyes. "Last chance."

Kol's only response was a shift in his weight, giving him more leverage to hopefully tear through the rogue's arm, till there was no power left there—nothing but bone.

A sharp whistle and flash of silver announced the rogue was done waiting. The bar cut through the air, slashing downward toward Kol.

* * *

Her body still thrumming with unreleased energy, Kelly flipped to her hands and knees. Her back hunched, she hung her head down between her arms and heaved in breaths. She'd thought her office was filled with power during the fight there, but it was nothing like the energy that pulsed within the walls of the Guardian's Keep. A pain at her temples joined the staccato beat.

From the corner of her eye, she caught sight of something silver flipping through the air. Gritting her teeth against the pain, she pushed herself into a kneel.

Across the room, Kol, still in wolf form, had his teeth clenched deep into the arm of the man from her office, the one who had held the knife to her neck. Both had an intensity in their stances, and a determination in their eyes that screamed this was not a fight either intended the other to walk away from. The man's free arm flew up to grab the streak of silver.

A bar. He held it overhead for a second, his lips moving as he spoke some final word to Kol, then with dead resolve in his eyes, began a downward slash of his hand.

Something in Kelly screamed as the hard metal winged toward Kol. Without giving thought to why she would protect the garm she thought of as her enemy, she pulled back her arms, and with elbows bent and palms facing forward, let two solid lines of power shoot from her hands.

Some tiny bit of the human in Kol yelled for him to shimmer, to give up the fight before the bar of silver bit into his head, likely smashing his skull and ending any hope he had of leaving this struggle alive. But he couldn't. His rage at the garm who had attacked Kelly, caused her pain—to bleed—was too complete, too engulfing. All he could do was bite deeper, tear harder and curse the rogue for touching the witch.

The bar gleamed as it sliced downward. Then suddenly it glowed, and the rogue shot backward, his spine, then head smacking into the solid wall of power keeping the portal closed. Energy bounced off the bar as it spun out of the rogue's hands. With the bar no longer halting its momentum, the crackling force careened around the room, searing tables, chairs and any garm who didn't shimmer out of its path.

Kol spun, searching for the source.

Kelly knelt where he'd left her, her eyes glazed and energy flowing from her hands. She was lost, unable to separate herself from the power that surged through her. She was nothing more than a conduit at the moment—raw magic shooting through her body unchecked.

Kol shimmered, rematerializing at her side—then threw himself against the twin witch, trying to knock her to the floor, to break the stream of power. Her body swayed but she remained upright, as if the lines of energy were controlling her rather than her controlling them.

Kol shimmered again, this time a few feet away. Inhaling deep into his lungs, he lowered his head and charged at Kelly, projecting her name into her mind at the same time. He hit her from the side again, smashing into her shoulder.

The power held for a heart-stopping second, but suddenly there was a snap, the lines of energy disappeared and Kelly fell to the ground.

She lay there, pale and spent, her chest barely moving with the shallow inhale and exhale of her breaths. Behind him, the voices of the Council yelled out, as annoying as raucous laughter at a funeral. He ignored them, instead pressing his nose to Kelly's cheek, breathing in her scent, assuring his racing heart that she was tired, exhausted even—but safe.

"Kol," Birgit's voice broke through his concentration. Brushing his nose over Kelly's face one final time, he turned to face the female garm.

"Now's the time to rid ourselves of the problem." Birgit, still a wolf, tossed her nose toward Kelly.

Kol's ruff expanded. His head lowered, teeth showing, he placed himself between the fallen witch and Birgit.

Disbelief flitted behind Birgit's eyes. "Don't tell me you still believe—"

"She wasn't involved," Kol growled.

Birgit's tail stiffened. "You were at her office. She knew you weren't here to protect the portal." The female garm glanced at Kelly. "What she didn't know is that I was here."

Kol cocked a brow. "You think that would have stopped the attack? Knowing you were here?"

Birgit's tail lowered. "You may be cocky now, but wait until you lose this portal."

"I'm not the one who almost lost it," Kol replied, his own tail dropping and his ears sliding closer to his head.

Birgit stepped sideways, circling toward him.

Kol followed suit. Rage still coursed through his veins. The thought of ridding his bar of the collar of the Garm Council suddenly seemed like the ideal solution. They'd proved no help so far—why allow them to rule his decisions regarding *his* portal.

"Kol. Birgit." Magnus stood over them. He held the rogue's silver bat in one hand, then let it drop with a menacing smack against his other.

Kol kept his gaze on Birgit. Taking out the female would

prove nothing. What mattered was keeping his portal and Kelly safe. Putting himself on the opposite side from the Garm Council would accomplish neither.

Giving Birgit one last warning snarl, Kol let the forandre magic flow through him, changing him back to human form. Naked, he stalked past the female garm, and held his hand out to Magnus. "I'll take that."

The Garm Council leader stared at Kol a second, then slapped the bar against his open palm. "Birgit's right. The witch would have known you weren't here."

"It wasn't her." Not looking at any of them, Kol strode to the bar, his bare feet making a padding sound against the concrete floor. He grabbed a pair of jeans off a stack he kept hidden on a shelf and jerked them on.

Clothed, he turned to face them. "She fought for us." He couldn't say the complete truth—that she'd saved him at obvious cost to herself. That she *hadn't* fought on the side of the rogues was enough for the Council to understand.

Birgit followed Kol's example and changed into her human form also. "He's beyond—"

Magnus cut her off with a frown. "Get some clothes on."

The female garm glanced down at herself, folded her arms across her chest and stood firm.

Magnus growled.

Birgit shot both Kol and Magnus killing glances then with a roll of her eyes, shimmered. In a few seconds, her voice drifted down from the second floor, "Let me know when I'm free to return."

Ignoring their power play, Kol filled a glass with water and stalked past Magnus to where Kelly still lay.

Magnus's hand on his arm stopped him from crouching down beside her. "Birgit is right. The wise thing would be to eliminate her now, while she's weak."

Kol's jaw tightened. "No."

"There was a time I would have taken that as a challenge," Magnus replied.

Kol didn't even bother to shrug. Magnus could take it however he wanted.

"We can't lose this portal." Magnus pinned Kol with a stare.

Kol met his gaze. "I won't."

Magnus looked away first, glancing down at the still unconscious Kelly. "If she does anything to threaten the security of the portal, or shows some sign she is behind the attacks, Birgit has the authority of the Garm Council to do whatever she feels necessary."

"You hear him, Guardian?" Birgit stood in the doorway, fully clothed in jeans and a black Guardian's Keep T-shirt.

Ignoring both of them, Kol pulled his arm from Magnus's grip and turned to check on Kelly. She stirred, her fingers curling and uncurling like she was searching for the power that had shot from there moments earlier.

Behind him Magnus spoke in clipped words. "She's your problem for now. Don't let her become ours." He gave a quick jerk of his head in the direction of his goons and the four of them shimmered, leaving Kol alone, with Kelly and Birgit.

The female garm threw open the hinged portion of the bar with a bang, grabbed a broom and began sweeping broken glass into piles with quick short strokes.

Kelly rolled over, the smell of lavender telling her she was home, sleeping on sheets her sister insisted be stored with little bags of dried herbs. Lavender to calm. It seemed to work for Kara, but had never had much effect on Kelly.

Still she breathed deeply, the smell reminding her of her sister. That alone was enough to help her relax.

Kol's voice broke through her calm. "You're awake."

Kelly's eyes flew open. Her gaze darted around the room, making sure she was, as she first thought, in her own bedroom. Recognizing the sea-blue walls, she rolled back onto her back. "What are you doing here?"

"You were tired. I thought you might need a nap." Kol stretched out onto the bed beside her. Dressed in only a pair of worn denim jeans, he propped his head on his hand and stared down at her. "Feeling better?"

Kelly's eyes widened and she shifted upward onto her pillow and away from Kol. A sudden panicky thought filled her head. She glanced down and let out a relieved breath. She was fully clothed—down to her favorite black leather boots.

"How'd I get here?" She frowned. "I mean, I guess I know how I got here but…" The battle, she remembered that, and landing at the bar. Another battle. Then…

Small staccato bursts of memory zipped through her head. The attacker from her office, swinging a bat of silver down at Kol—but not Kol. Kol as a wolf, she realized. Her own overwhelming need to save the garm. She'd pulled power, but it had been too much for her to control. She'd given up and just let the magic roar through her, raw and unfiltered. It hadn't hurt—just left her numb, hollow.

But what happened next? Kol had survived, obviously. Had she saved him?

Kol reached over her body and plucked a stuffed dog off the quilt beside her.

Not sure what he was doing at her house, why he seemed so comfortable, she snapped, "Drop that."

His arm still hovering above her body, he grinned. "I didn't realize you had such a love of things…canine."

Kelly narrowed her eyes, and resisted the impulse to shove the stuffed animal out of his reach. No matter what had happened, Kol was as arrogant as ever.

"What if I said I was a cat person?"

Kol leaned forward, his arm still not touching her, but the heat of his body pressing against her. The warm pine scent she'd noticed previously when he was around filled her lungs. Something deep inside her reacted. She wanted to flip onto her side and face him, to run her fingers over his bare chest, and nuzzle the smooth strip of skin right below the stubble on his jaw.

She closed her eyes one brief second and willed the feelings away. When she opened them, he hadn't moved, but somehow he seemed closer. A light flickered behind his eyes, and he leaned in a bit more. Close enough she could feel his breath moving her hair.

A shiver danced over her body.

His mouth inches from her ear, he whispered, "I wouldn't believe you."

Chapter 7

Kelly stiffened beneath Kol. Careful not to touch her, not to spook her, he just inhaled, pulled her scent deep into his lungs. She relaxed him and excited him at the same time.

"Why are you here?" she whispered, her voice hoarse.

"I wanted to make sure you were safe," he replied.

"I am. You can go."

So tense, his twin witch. He moved his face closer, parting the hair that covered her ears with his nose. "But if I leave, how will I know you stay safe?"

She jerked her head to the side. Her eyes flashing, she replied, "It's not your problem. I can take care of myself."

Silly female. Didn't she realize that everything to do with her was his problem, his obsession? He lowered his arm slowly, his forearm brushing against the edge of her shirt. A button slipped free, revealing a strip of skin below.

She started to sit up, but he moved closer, blocking her.

He burrowed his face deeper into her hair, to her neck, ran his lips slowly from her ear down the line of her throat to the tiny pulse point at its base. He waited. Seconds ticked by, but he could feel her relaxing, giving in to what he knew was inevitable.

"You shouldn't be here," she said, but softly. The fight was finally draining out of her.

"Where should I be?" he asked, pushing the collar of her shirt aside.

She blinked as if she couldn't think of an answer.

"The Guardian's Keep is safe. I'm safe. Thanks to you," he added. He was tempted to look at her, gauge her reaction, but he didn't. He wanted to forget all his suspicions, all the Garm Council's threats, and just enjoy this moment, being with Kelly.

She shifted again. He could tell he'd said too much, reminded her of their previous battles, but he wasn't ready to deal with any of that yet. *Only one way to avoid it.*

He pushed himself high enough on his elbow so he was looking down at her face. Her lips opened, words ready to spill out, but he didn't wait for them—instead he lowered his mouth and captured her lips with his.

She gave a short gasp, and her hands flew up, ready to attack he was sure, but he ignored everything except the feel of her lips beneath his, her body tucked close, and the enticing smell of lavender and pine mixing into a heady irresistible scent.

Slowly like a belt loosening notch by notch, she relaxed. Her hands drifted to his back; her fingers traced the length of his muscles in long firm strokes and he responded, positioning his body more fully on top of hers, letting his weight push against her, pinning her to the mattress beneath them.

* * *

Kol's body pressed against Kelly's. His fingers furrowed into her hair, holding her face still while his lips assaulted hers. Somewhere in her mind something told her she should be fighting, objecting somehow, but with Kol's fingers massaging her scalp, his mouth moving across hers, then down her neck, she couldn't imagine why.

Heaving out a contented breath, she ran her fingers down the length of his back, reveling in the feel of firm muscle beneath her fingertips—and magic. She could feel that, too. He tingled with it, made her tingle.

His mouth brushed against her ear. A frisson of pleasure shot through her. She sighed and let her hands drift lower to the tops of his jeans, then lower still till she cupped his denim-clad buttocks. She pulled him tighter against her. His hardness rubbed back and forth against her mound, until she was desperate to yank his jeans from his body and wiggle out of her own. She wanted nothing more than her thin panties between them, and those not for long.

The line of buttons on her shirt slipped open one after the other, as if her clothing knew what she wanted and was doing its part to fulfill her desires. Kol's mouth moved from her neck to her chest, where her breasts poured over the top of her demi-cup bra. A snap and her bra was undone, too. Magic or Kol's fingers, Kelly didn't know, but she arched her back, loving the feeling of freedom as the confinement of her bra fell away and her breasts moved against the rough stubble on Kol's face.

Kol straightened his arms so he was staring down at her, his gaze burning as it swept over her bare breasts, then blazing as it lit upon her face.

Her lips were parted. She was panting; she knew it.

Didn't understand what was happening, but didn't want it to stop. Afraid if they paused too long sanity would return, she reached up to pull him back down. Instead, he reached under her and swept her shirt and bra from her body in one easy movement.

With a soft growl he settled back down. His hands cupping one of her breasts, he lowered his mouth to her nipple.

The magic Kelly had felt before intensified, shooting through her like an electric shot directly from where Kol's mouth touched her to her most intimate part. She squirmed against him.

He responded, moving his free hand to the front of his jeans then hers. Her thumbs hooked through the belt loops of his jeans, she tugged them down, felt his erection spring forward, pushing against her thigh. She almost screamed with need.

Then her jeans were gone, her panties soon following, and she was blessedly naked beneath Kol.

He paused, his chest moving with each breath, his erection brushing her leg, tantalizing her as it nestled against her thigh. "This changes things, you know?"

She blinked, her mind consumed with the fog of desire, her body demanding she discover just how intense this magic of his was.

"You understand?" he asked again.

She stared at him. Sex. Yes, sex changed things, always did. Wasn't like she'd never done it before.

With a short nod, she pulled his head down to hers, his lips back to hers.

He sighed and seemed to let go of something he'd been holding back. A peace settled over Kelly—a knowledge that everything would be okay, that nothing could ever hurt her. She basked in it, let her body soak up what she recognized as a new kind of magic, something that would last past the next few moments of passion.

Then Kol nudged his thigh between hers, pressed the tip of his erection against the folds of her sex and reminded her of where she was, what was happening. She inhaled, sensing this was going to be different from any other time before, knowing it might hurt.

He moved forward, his shaft sliding into her, stretching her, filling her until she thought she would scream, but not with pain—pleasure, pure and intense. He moved again, this time in and out. Her legs wrapped around his buttocks, her body pulsing with the need to be closer, filled even deeper. He gathered her in his arms and held her, both of them moving in sync.

Her fingers clung to his shoulders. Her head fell back, leaving her neck exposed for his kisses. And the movement continued.

Pressure built inside her. She could feel each and every tiny muscle inside her body contracting, preparing for one unimaginably intense release. And magic. It whirled around them, Kelly could feel it, see it, almost taste it. A warm violet glow that energized her, made her feel like she could keep up this pace forever. But then just as suddenly, she felt the shift. Her body hit the edge, and she tumbled over—every muscle performing one last gasping tremor before letting her spiral downward, exhausted and content onto the bed.

Kol's body flowed with her, both of them landing together, their limbs and breaths mingling as they lay there spent, but for once peaceful in each other's company.

His hand splayed across her bare stomach, then slipped around and under her to pull her close, nestled against his chest. Kelly breathed in; the smell of their magic and sex perfumed the room. The scent relaxed her even more. Forgetting everything but the peace that surrounded her, she pressed a small kiss to his chest, closed her eyes, and fell asleep.

Kelly awoke for the second time. Just like the first, she was in her room, she could smell lavender, and she wasn't alone—but this time she was naked, and so was the man who was draped around her body. Kol.

What had she done? He stirred slightly, his fingers brushing against her bare breasts. A tingle danced through her.

Exactly what she had done smacked into her like a cross-city bus. Sex changes things. He'd said that. Did he think...damn. She needed to think.

She sat up and grabbed the quilt, which had tumbled to the floor sometime during their...she glanced at the body beside her. Kol rolled onto his side and watched her through knowing eyes.

She was avoiding his gaze. It was obvious. As she edged away from him, Kol let out a sigh, then flipped onto his back, and tucked his hands behind his head. Things had changed. She might not realize it yet, but they had. However, if it made her feel more comfortable denying that change for a bit, he could play along.

"Why were the rogues attacking your office?" he asked, his nude body stretched out, and his legs crossed at the ankles.

She barely darted a glance at him as she picked up her clothing and began tugging it on.

He waited until she was buttoning her shirt, then repeated the question.

This time confusion flitted across her face. "Rogues?"

"Garm—without responsibility."

"Oh. I don't know." Her hand went to her throat. A trail of dried blood showed where the rogue's blade had pricked her. Kol's fingers tensed behind his head. He'd tasted her blood during their lovemaking. It had infuriated him then, but now, after…

"I'll kill him," he said.

Kelly's gaze shot to his face. She pressed her palm against the wound as if covering it would make it go away—make Kol forget.

"You really shouldn't be here," she said, her fingers fidgeting with a button.

He watched her through half-closed eyes. She was right. He shouldn't. But what was done was done. Didn't mean he didn't have to get back to his other responsibilities, though.

Abruptly, he swung his legs over the side of the bed and stood. After pulling on his own jeans, he asked, "What here is important to you?" He picked up the stuffed dog she'd tried to hide from him earlier. "This obviously." With a grin, he grabbed a duffel bag that lay on the floor and stuffed the dog inside. "What else?"

She retrieved the quilt she'd had wrapped around her and gripped it until her knuckles shone white. "Excuse me?"

He walked to a basket full of unfolded laundry and plucked an armful of items off the top. After shoving them into the bag, he glanced back at her. "That enough?"

Her mouth dropped open. "What are you doing?"

He plopped the full duffel onto the bed, jerked the zipper closed, then held out his hand. "Leaving. You ready?"

"That's the sanest thing I've heard you say. Get out." Her voice trembled, but she was getting stronger. Back to herself.

She wadded up the quilt and tossed it onto the clothes basket.

He folded his arms over his chest.

Shaking her head, she reached out to grab the duffel.

He placed one hand on it.

Her fingers wrapped around the nylon handle.

"I can make you come with me," he said.

"You can try."

They stood, staring at each other, tension vibrating between them.

He took a step forward and ran the backs of his fingers down her face, her throat, stopping at the dried spot of blood. "I don't want you hurt."

"I…" She looked confused again, lost. And he wanted to gather her up and hold her to his chest, protect her, but he knew that would be the quickest way to lose her trust.

He waited, hoping he wouldn't have to force the issue, that she would come to her senses on her own.

She frowned, then asked, "Where do you want me to go?"

"With me. To the bar."

"To the bar?" She repeated the words like the idea was foreign.

Kol picked up the duffel and held his hand out again. He was trying to be patient, but he needed to return to the portal. He'd already left Birgit there alone much longer than he knew was wise.

"We need to go," he said.

She tilted her head, cocked an eyebrow, then spun on one heel and stalked from the room.

Kelly headed to the kitchen.

What was going on? The pounding headache she had felt a few days earlier had returned. She pressed her fingers to her temple. Why were things getting so confused? Why did she have to do something as stupid as have sex with the enemy?

Sex changed things—the words added to the pounding.

Kol followed close on her heels. Her duffel with her toy dog inside was bunched under his arm. "Are you in pain?"

Kelly wanted to smack him. Concern from him was not what she wanted—it just made her head pound harder. He was the bad guy, right?

"I'm fine. I just need to be alone." She stalked to the sink to get a glass of water. Maybe if she ignored him, he'd go away and she could sit down and sort out what was happening, what she even believed anymore.

Except Kol was hard to ignore. He followed her, his steps seeming to match hers. She raised her arm to reach for a glass, just to find one already filled with water slid against her fingertips.

She set the glass on the tile countertop. "It was just sex."

He raised a brow. "Can be."

"It was." She didn't know why it was important he agreed with her, but it was.

He just stared at her.

Tired of their going-nowhere conversation, she placed her hand on the duffle and tried to yank it from his arms. He looked at her, his eyes unreadable. "You need to come with me," he said.

"I need to be alone." Kelly's nails scraped against the nylon bag, the noise loud in the otherwise silent kitchen.

Kol held firm, a calm, confident expression on his face.

Kelly wanted to yank the bag from his arms and stomp on it. Yell and tell him he was wrong. *It was just sex.* Nothing had changed. She still didn't trust him and she certainly wasn't going anywhere with him, but somehow the words wouldn't form. Something in her brain niggled at her, taunting her, telling her she was the one with the error in thinking.

The phone rang. Kelly jumped, her brain so occupied with her mental struggles, it took two more rings for her to remember where she was, and how desperately she had been waiting for a call from her sister. She dropped her hold on the duffel and jogged the few steps to the phone.

Carefully turning her back on Kol, she picked up the receiver.

"Kelly? Where are you?" a harried voice asked.

Kelly hesitated, her mind searching to identify the caller. Not Kara. She darted a glance at Kol. He leaned against her kitchen table, one hip cocked, his chest distractingly bare, and an expression of bored impatience on his face. She turned her back again.

"Kelly, are you there? Are you okay? You just disappeared. I wasn't sure what to do…"

Heather. Kelly swallowed her disappointment, and tried to focus her thoughts. Worried. Heather was worried…so much had happened in the last few hours, Kelly had a hard time sorting through everything.

Heather. The office. The attack. Kelly's heart skipped ahead. How had she forgotten?

"Are you okay? Did they leave?" The words spilled out of Kelly. Behind her, Kol moved—she could feel him, feel that he was listening. She pressed a finger to her ear and concentrated on blocking him out.

"They left right after you did."

Of course, she'd seen the one…rogue, Kol had called him…at the bar. She dropped her hand to her neck, felt Kol stiffen in response.

What was going on? Why was she so aware of everything Kol was doing, feeling?

Anxiety gnawed at her concentration. Heather said something else, but Kelly missed it.

"What?" she asked.

"Aesa. She's here. You had an appointment. Remember?"

"Terje," she murmured.

Kol snapped to a stand. Ire radiated from him.

The hairs on the back of Kelly's neck rose. She resisted the urge to squirm like a guilty child, squared her feet a bit more instead and concentrated on pretending she was alone, that she couldn't feel every breath and flicker of emotion coming from the six-foot-plus man behind her.

Kol muttered something to himself, then strode across the room and placed his hand on the wall beside her. "Who are you talking to?" he asked, his voice was low and his tone casual, but he didn't fool Kelly. She could feel his tension. She wished she couldn't, but there it was.

She had to get away from him.

"Heather, I have to go. Tell Aesa I'll be there as soon as I can." She hung up the phone and stepped away, putting distance between her and a suspiciously calm-looking Kol.

"Enjoyable as this has been, I don't have time to argue with you right now." *Ignore him. Act normal.* Kelly jerked open the drawer where she kept the phone book. She had to get to her office but she was here and her car wasn't. She could either call a cab, or ask Kol to transport her, shimmer, whatever forandre called it.

She glanced at the line of Kol's jaw, at the way he held the duffel slightly away from his body. He appeared nonchalant, but he was coiled, ready to attack.

Not a tough decision.

She ran her finger down the line of print. Taxies…

The book flipped shut on her hand.

"Who was that?" Kol asked.

Kelly clamped her mouth closed and tamped down her

first instinct, which was to yell at him for messing up her life, confusing her, and now poking his nose in where it didn't belong. Fighting with him was not the quick way out of this situation. Inhaling, she tried to keep her voice as casual as his. "My assistant. I have an appointment."

"And you think you're going?" Kol's anger pulsed into her. She placed a hand on the wall to keep from falling.

His expression softened. "You feel it don't you?"

She took a breath and held it for a second, then stared him down. "I don't feel anything, but hurried. I have to leave."

He stepped back then studied her for moment, like he was weighing various options. His mouth quirked into a smile, then a grin.

Kelly hated that grin. She was close to losing control of her resolve and telling him so, when he dropped the duffel and nodded.

"Okay."

Okay? Kelly frowned. Then before she could consider his sudden change of mind, he shimmered and disappeared.

She stared around her empty kitchen with suspicion. That was too easy. What was Kol up to now? And why did he want her to come with him in the first place?

Chapter 8

"She's coming." Heather settled the receiver back onto the phone.

Aesa stopped her frantic pacing and wrapped her arms around her midsection. "What was she doing? Leifi didn't see her leave the bar."

"She didn't say."

Aesa chewed on her lower lip. "She can't shimmer, can she?"

"She is one of the most powerful witches of all time," Heather drawled. She flicked her eyes toward the ceiling. That was one piece of lore she could skip ever hearing again.

Aesa seemed to miss the sarcasm.

"True, but I don't think witches can—"

"They can't." Heather snapped the pencil she'd been holding against the phone.

Aesa gaze turned questioning.

"Kelly can't shimmer," Heather said, her tone apologetic. "If she didn't walk out of the bar someone else took her—someone who can shimmer, or whatever." She waved her hand.

Seeing one of Aesa's eyebrows twitch upward, Heather licked her lips and tried to cover her annoyance. "What happened? I did my part. I called as soon as Kol got here."

"The Council. Somehow they…" Aesa frowned.

Heather mumbled under her breath, "You underestimated them."

Aesa's lips flattened to a straight line. Cursing her big mouth, Heather started to backpedal, but Aesa turned away and resumed her pacing. "That wasn't the problem. The problem was the guardian. He showed up too soon and he brought Kelly."

"There wasn't anything I could do to keep him here, and you said he wouldn't walk out on a fight." Heather's voice cracked in her rush to get out her side. She did not need Aesa blaming her for this latest failure.

Aesa paused in her journey back and forth across the floor. "It was very…ungarm-like."

"Ungarm-like?" Heather repeated. She was beginning to think Aesa, the would-be queen of the garm knew about as much about garm as Heather did.

"He must have…" Aesa let the words trail off. "No, that's myth."

Heather rounded her eyes, concentrated on keeping her expression innocent. "Like the all-powerful witches who somehow escaped from Jormun's world? Or the undefeatable Fenrir, who was tricked into being trapped on Lyngvi?"

At the mention of her lover, Aesa squared her shoulders. "Some believe guardians can get so in tune with whatever or whoever their charge is that they can actually sense when the person or thing is in danger. Even worlds away."

"So Kol sensed when the attack began." Heather leaned back against her chair.

"Except he didn't come right away. The Council fought alone for some time. Long enough I thought…" Aesa's voice quavered. "I thought we were going to make it. That finally I'd get to see Fenrir again."

Heather performed an inward eye roll. The whole great love story was wearing thin. The only thing more annoying was the let's-right-the-wrongs-done-to-garm-worldwide chant.

"So he isn't perfect, he has a delay or something. Maybe you can use that for next time." Heather sketched a heart on the pad of paper in front of her, then with a slashing motion, added a dagger protruding from its center.

"I don't know why there'd be a delay, but…" Aesa shook her head. "*Kelly*. He didn't want to leave Kelly. You said he was attracted to her. What you *didn't* say is that he loves her."

Heather sharpened the point on the dagger. "What makes you think it isn't just sex?"

"Guardians don't risk their charges for sex. But *love*. Love is different."

Heather could almost hear the harps playing. "Love, sex. I don't see how it matters." She placed her coffee mug on top of the drawing, hiding it from Aesa who had changed her path and now strode toward Heather's desk.

The female garm ground to halt, pressed her hands onto Heather's desktop and leaned in. "But it does. Sex is a distraction, but love is a lot more, a whole lot more. If he loves Kelly, he might love her more than the portal."

"Are you saying, we should kidnap her?" Heather

frowned. She wanted the power Aesa had promised her when Fenrir was freed, but she didn't want Kelly hurt in the process. Breaking up some office equipment was one thing, but holding Kelly against her will?

"No. That won't work. What I didn't tell you yet is how my garm were defeated."

"It wasn't Kol?" Heather asked.

Aesa pushed off the desk and folded her arms back across her chest. "No. It was Kelly. They had the guardian and the Council. It was the witch who delivered a blow they couldn't defeat."

Heather rocked her chair backward. What she wouldn't give to have someone speak of her in that same tone of reverence.

Aesa tapped her fingers against her forearm. "We've been going about this all wrong. Instead of getting Kelly to fight Kol, we need her to join him—to convince him to let us through the portal."

Heather's eyebrows shot upward. "You really think that's going to happen?"

Aesa tilted her head. "Maybe not, but if she can get close to him, it won't matter. We'll be able to use his own senses against him. If he doesn't see her as a threat, she'll be able to get close to the portal, and we'll be able to get through.

"We've been trying to batter the door down, when we should have been asking nicely for it to open. It's all in the approach."

"Where's the witch—meeting with her minions?" Birgit dropped the broken pieces of a chair into a trash can.

Kol stalked past her, to the computer behind the bar. He shook the mouse to get it out of sleep mode and began checking the settings to make sure Birgit hadn't altered anything while he was gone.

"I should lock you out," she muttered, dropping the seat to what was once a bar stool onto the bar's top.

Kol started to rise, but she held out a hand. "I'm done with this fight, for now." She leaned over the bar to grab a dustpan, and froze. Her neck tense, she turned her head to look at him and inhaled sharply. "Son of a bitch. You had sex with her."

Kol didn't look up from the computer. "It's past time to open. The regulars will be getting restless."

"You're going to do it, you know. You're going to lose this portal, and I'm going to be standing right here ready to take over when you do."

She started to turn, but Kol grabbed her wrist. "If I honestly thought I was risking this portal, I'd turn it over to you myself."

She stared at him, then twisted her arm, breaking his hold. "Well, get ready to hand over the keys, because at the rate you're going even you won't be able to ignore the facts soon." She gave the bar stool top a shove. It fell, smashing a line of highball glasses as it fell.

With a last look of disgust, she tromped to the front door and yanked it open. "All right boys and girls. We're ready for business. But don't crowd the guardian, he's still recovering from his afterglow."

Kol reached in the coffee can behind his computer and pulled out the wooden dowel he'd taken from Kelly while she slept. He tightened his fingers around it until the carvings cut into his skin. He wasn't wrong. He couldn't be. The alternative was just too unimaginable. If the portal got taken, and Kelly was behind it…

He threw the rod into the can. The clank reverberated in his head.

If the Council was right and he was wrong—they wouldn't have to worry about him…or Kelly.

Two hours later, Kelly stamped into her agency, water streaming down her coat and forming a sea at her feet. At her mumbled cursing, Heather and Aesa appeared from behind the door to her private office.

"Aesa thought she left something last time she was here," Heather explained, gesturing to the door she and their client had just walked through.

Kelly shrugged, her mind still not in professional mode.

"Did you have car trouble?" Aesa asked, a concerned light in her eyes.

Kelly, in the process of jerking off her coat, paused and looked down at herself. Her jeans were wet to the knees, and she'd barely taken time to shower after Kol left, hadn't messed with fixing her hair or redoing her makeup. Not that it would have mattered, given the deluge outside.

Her face started to fold into a scowl, but catching sight of Heather's intrigued gaze, she snapped her expression into one of calm confidence. "No, sorry I'm late. I…" Mumbling something unintelligible, she stamped her feet a few times, adding more water to the puddle. "So, let's sit down." She motioned to her office.

After angling a look at Heather, Aesa nodded.

Kelly hung her dripping coat on the hook near her desk and slipped into her chair. While Aesa settled in, she fumbled through the stack of papers on her desk. Not a single pink message slip.

"So, Heather told me you had some trouble here." Aesa picked a shard from a broken statue off the table next to her, and turned it over in her hands. "Do you think it's related to one of your cases?"

Kelly froze. She hadn't even considered who had attacked her office. Her time with Kol had totally thrown her normally organized way of thinking into a tailspin.

"Heather also said the guardian was here when it happened…" Aesa tilted her head in question.

Kelly's lip slipped between her teeth. Could Kol have been behind the attack? "But he fought them off," she said as much to herself as to her client.

"Well, that's promising, isn't it?" Aesa set the sliver of stone she held onto the top of Kelly's desk.

Kelly lowered her brows. "I don't think I get where you're going."

"The guardian. He visited you. What did he say?" Aesa edged forward on her seat, her gaze sharp.

"He…he said…" What did Kol say when he first came to her office? It seemed so long ago now, and so much had happened since. Her breasts tightened at the thought of what all had happened since. "He had a proposition for me," she blurted.

"Really?" Aesa smiled.

"Proposition's the wrong word. He asked me to…" Kelly swallowed. She couldn't tell Aesa what Kol wanted, not without telling her the rest, and then the woman would never trust her. Kelly wasn't even sure if she could trust herself.

"He wants you." Aesa's smile widened and she clapped her hands together. "This is great."

Aesa's reaction was so unexpected, so unreal, Kelly inched her chair backward and slipped her hand into her coat pocket looking for the reassuring strength of the wood dowel she kept there. It was gone.

Shaken by the discovery, she jumped when Aesa continued. "If he trusts you, you can use that to get close to him. It's brilliant. You won't have to fight him. He'll let you through the portal."

Kelly frowned. Why did something about Aesa's new plan bother her? Why did it seem so much more acceptable to battle Kol than to gain his trust and betray him?

"I don't know if—"

Aesa's hand slipped into her coat and reappeared with the same small rectangle of paper in it she'd shown Kelly before. With a sigh, she set it down on the desk in front of her. She pressed one finger to her lips, then to the face of the boy gripping the stuffed rabbit. "Soon, baby. Soon, we'll be together." Her eyes glimmering with moisture she looked back up at Kelly. "Have I told you how much I appreciate you helping me? I know you said you wouldn't take payment, but somehow, someway, I'll pay you back."

Swallowing her indecision, Kelly stared at the upside down image of the little boy. "Really. It isn't necessary. As I told you when we first met, I'd do anything to shut down the Guardian's Keep."

Raising her gaze to the hopeful eyes of the woman in front of her, Kelly forced back memories of Kol gathering her to his chest, pressing kisses to her neck. Sex changed nothing. She still had a little boy to save, and a friend's death to avenge.

The Guardian's Keep was busy. Holding the full duffel bag behind her, Kelly shouldered her way past a leering dwarf only to collide with a massive chest covered in green leather.

"Tasty," a voice rumbled somewhere north of the chest.

Kelly dropped the duffle bag on the floor and slipped her hand into her coat pocket, her fingers automatically searching for the wooden dowel. Hands approximately the size of Volkswagens had already slipped under her arms before she remembered the dowel was missing.

A second later she was staring into the glimmering green eyes of what she assumed was a giant. She glanced down at his outfit—the jolly green giant, if she wasn't mistaken.

He grinned at her. "My place or my place?" he asked.

Her feet dangling in midair, Kelly pulled back her shoulders, narrowed her eyes, and did her best to appear deadly. "Put me down."

"Don't think so." He straightened his arms and let his gaze wander the length of her body. "You're little—"

"Then throw her back." The crowd opened, revealing Kol his hip angled against the wall and the silver bat hanging from one hand in a suspiciously casual grip.

The giant's one brow lowered. "You want me to throw her? But I like her." He looked back at Kelly and gave her a little shake, like a toddler with a new toy. "Not much to her. Don't think she'd survive throwing."

"Let her go, Stumi." Kol took a step forward, the bat flashing as he rested it on a bar stool.

Stumi frowned again then shook his head. "I don't think so. I'm going to keep her."

"You can't. She—"

Tired of the two discussing her like she was a discarded doll, Kelly jerked her knee upward. As it slammed into the giant's chin, his head moved backward with a rewarding snap.

"—bites," Kol finished.

The giant lowered his head, his eyes wide, but before Kelly could gloat, his expression changed. His eyes narrowed, his face flushed to bright red and sweat beaded along his brow line.

"Move," Kol yelled and without thinking, Kelly knew he meant her. Using every bit of her strength, she swung both legs up and over her head, like a six-year-old flipping over the bar on a play set—except Kelly was escaping a seven-foot-tall giant with murder in his eyes.

She landed on her feet, but only for a second before the momentum of her flip wound down and she flopped onto her back.

A roar echoed through the bar as the giant noticed her escape. He bent at the waist one massive hand swinging forward, preparing to grab her up, and, she feared, follow Kol's first instruction by tossing her against the bar's wall.

Again cursing the loss of her dowel, she tried to pull energy from the room in the few seconds her brain calculated she had. She had barely drawn enough to thwart a gnat when Kol leaped between her and Stumi. Swinging the silver bat, he yelled, "Move her."

Again Kelly was grabbed by the arms, but this time she was jerked backward at a speed so rapid she had difficulty focusing on what was happening around her. She glanced to the side. Whatever held her wasn't visible to her eyes, but the pressure of fingers pressing into her arms was undeniable.

"Here?" a voice whispered.

"Enough," another replied. With an unceremonious jerk, Kelly's backward trip halted, and she again found herself lying on the dirty floor of the Guardian's Keep, staring at the stained ceiling.

Cursing, she scrambled to her feet.

"Can't let her past," said the first voice.

"No, no," replied the second.

Across the room, Kol swung his bat, striking the raging giant in the stomach. The giant doubled over, reaching for

Kol as he moved. Stumi's hand wrapped around Kol's neck; then with another roar, he lifted the bartender off the ground.

Kelly stepped forward, her hands flying upward, her mind automatically calling for power.

The silver bat Kol held clattered to the ground. He hung there, his arms at his side, his body limp.

Was he breathing?

Her heart pounding, Kelly drained what energy she could from the room as fast as her body could siphon it.

It wasn't fast enough. Kol was dead or close to it. He had to be. The garm would never just hang there, not fight back.

Almost screaming with frustration, Kelly threw her hands back up, and took another step forward. The skin on her palms had barely started to crackle when something hit her in the chest and she fell backward over some invisible object hovering right behind her knees.

"Leave me alone," she yelled. "I have to help him."

"Like the guardian needs your help," the first voice scoffed. "Look."

Kelly flipped to her belly on the dirty floor.

The air around Kol sparkled like a million diamonds, then suddenly he was gone. Snarling from the ground beneath where he'd dangled was the black wolf she'd first seen in her office. *Kol in wolf form.*

The midnight-tinged animal angled his body to the side, his lips pulled back in a clear warning. The giant, lost in his rage, yanked back his arm and swiped at the wolf. Kol danced to the side then, his teeth flashing, threw himself at the giant.

Another roar ripped through the bar, this one laced with pain. Kol clung to the giant, his teeth clamped around the larger being's neck. His back feet pressed against the giant's chest, Kol pulled and tore. Blood streamed over the giant's green vest coloring both giant and leather a dull angry red. Stumi swiped at Kol again, but Kelly could tell he was weakening, then with a thud, the giant's legs gave, and he crumpled to his knees. With a graceful leap, Kol jumped free of the giant, landing a few feet away as Stumi lost his struggle with consciousness and fell like a downed tree onto the floor.

Kelly's gaze caught by the unmoving Stumi, she didn't notice Kol's return to his human form until he spoke. "Get him out of here. And when he comes to, tell him the Guardian's Keep is off-limits…forever."

A murmur, like Kol had delivered a death sentence, ran through the room. Within seconds, two men almost as large as the one passed out on the floor, grabbed him and tugged him from the bar.

A half smile on his lips, a completely nude Kol sauntered toward her. As he passed the duffel, he scooped it up and kept walking. He moved like an animal stalking his prey, muscles tight, his steps smooth, light and rhythmic. Kelly's gaze dropped, unable to stop herself from admiring the way his muscles contracted with each step, the quiet power that seemed barely contained inside of him.

A few feet from her, he dropped the bag. "There's an extra room upstairs."

She pulled her gaze from his chest, still smeared with the giant's blood, to his face. He watched her, his own expression unreadable, but his eyes intense and focused only on her. Her mouth suddenly dry, she swallowed.

Then his smile returned, enticing this time. "Unless…" He stepped closer, ran his hand down the length of her neck.

Unable to resist, she tipped her head back and breathed

in the scent of him: pine, blood, and…sex. She couldn't stand this close to him without thinking about it. Her eyelids fluttered closed.

"Unless," he continued, his voice rolling over her like warm oil, "you'd rather share."

Chapter 9

Kol waited, his nostrils flaring as the scent of Kelly's arousal engulfed him. It was a bold move on his part, suggesting she sleep with him here, publicly in front a bar full of patrons and Birgit who undoubtedly was memorizing every second of this exchange to carry back to the Council. Just a week ago his offer to Kelly would have gained him a quick fist to the gut from the witch, but now?

She arched her neck, her face tilting upward. Her eyes were dark, her lips parted, her breath nothing more than tiny puffs of air.

Believing his question was answered, he leaned closer, breathing in as she breathed out, matching his heartbeat to hers. Then running his fingers up her neck, into her hair, he prepared to shimmer.

Her splayed hand knocked him square in the chest. "I'll walk. Thanks."

He glanced down at the petite fingers still spread across his chest, then back up at her heart-shaped face. Her eyes were still dark, her lips still parted, but a tiny line of determination had formed between her brows.

She was afraid...of him...or herself?

A laugh rumbled in his throat. What a pair they were. Too stubborn for their own good.

A flash of blond hair on his right caught his eye. Birgit, as he'd suspected, cataloging the scene to replay later when it suited her.

He sighed. As much he would like to push this particular issue with Kelly, now was not the time or place.

Removing his hand, he stepped backward and with a faux bow, gestured toward the doorway that led to the stairs and private section of the Guardian's Keep. "By all means. Third door on your right."

With a last tentative glance in his direction, Kelly yanked the duffel bag from his arms and wove her way through the crowd.

It had been hours since Kelly arrived at the Guardian's Keep. Kol had kept his distance—or as much distance as could be had in a 700-square-foot building. She'd come down from depositing her duffel bag in the empty room he'd assigned her, and been greeted by an overblown blonde named Birgit.

Birgit had taken it upon herself to show Kelly the ropes, meaning handing her a bucket and canister of toilet cleanser. Kol had watched from behind the bar, newly clothed in his usual jeans and T-shirt. His eyes flashed when he saw her, but he immediately turned away, apparently too busy dumping cigarette butts and filling beer mugs to bother discussing what her role at the bar would be.

Or maybe he thought his blond bimbo could handle that little task. Birgit tossed a toilet brush into the bucket with the cleanser. "A dwarf had one too many shots. I wouldn't let it sit too long if I were you."

Her eyes narrowed, Kelly set the bucket down. "I'm not here to clean bathrooms."

"Really?" The other woman stepped closer, crowding Kelly's space. "And why exactly are you here?"

Kelly's lips thinned. This was not the scenario Aesa and she had played out in Kelly's office. According to Aesa, Kol would be putty in her hands. Kelly would simply stay close to the garm and sooner or later he'd let down his guard and trust Kelly with the secret to operating the portal.

Kelly's gaze wandered to the bar where Kol bent to remove a case of beer bottles from the floor.

"Is that your only purpose?" Her arms folded over her chest, Birgit tapped her fingers against her upper arm. "Or is he just a means?"

Kelly stiffened, the hairs on her arms standing at the implied threat in the other's woman's voice.

But suddenly, Birgit relaxed, an uneasy laugh tumbling out of her. "Sorry, I didn't mean to come on so strong. It's just, I haven't been here that long, and then you show up, and it's obvious you have some…history with Kol. I'd hate to lose my position so quickly."

The change was too quick. Kelly waited, hoping the woman would continue, give Kelly more so she could decide exactly where Birgit fit into Kol's world—what exactly her *position* was.

But Birgit just stared back at her, her eyes wide, an un-intimidating smile on her lips. "Oh, don't look like that. I said I was sorry, and forget the bathrooms." She glanced around the room her nose curled and started walking toward the bar. "It isn't like anyone here will care." She stopped, her hand on the hinged portion of the bar's counter. "We're going to be friends, and roommates—almost."

Following behind her, Kelly's brows rose.

Birgit glancing over her shoulder, caught the expression on Kelly's face and laughed again. "Oh." She pulled a Guardian's Keep T-shirt from box behind the bar. "Didn't Kol tell you? I live here, too."

Her gaze on the man at the other end of the bar, Kelly replied. "No. No, he didn't."

"So, you came." Kol shoved the end of a bar towel into the top of his jeans, then dried his hands on the length left hanging free.

Kelly turned to face him, stepping away from the doorway that she knew at times doubled as the portal.

While Kol was busy breaking up the third fight of the evening, she'd ran her hands up and down the battered molding—under the pretense of dusting. Birgit had eyed her with something akin to suspicion, but then sauntered off without commenting. Kelly'd returned to her task, but learned nothing about operating the portal.

"Yeah. I did." Kelly twisted the cloth she'd been using into a spiral. She waited, expecting him to continue, but he just watched her.

She licked her lips, and stepped farther away from the doorway. "I decided you were right. After the attack…I didn't want to stay by myself."

"Really?" He picked up a bottle of gin and topped off a rather thin, but otherwise normal-looking man's drink.

"Yeah. I haven't been living alone that long. With my sister gone…I just…"

"Didn't feel safe?" he offered, sitting down the bottle and turning to stare at her.

"That's right. I didn't feel safe."

"Not many think of the Guardian's Keep as safe."

Kelly twisted the cloth in her hands tighter. "Well, I'm not alone."

"Here? No, you won't be alone here." His eyes glimmered again. Kelly's stomach constricted in response. "And maybe there's more."

"More?" Kelly repeated.

"Yeah, more." He moved to the end of the bar closest to her—his change in position so sudden, Kelly thought for a second he'd shimmered.

She let the towel drop to the floor, freeing her hands.

He leaned over the bar, his palms pressing into the top, his eyes darkening. "Maybe *I* make you feel safe."

Her pulse pounding in her throat, Kelly rested her fingers against her thighs. "You?"

He ducked under the hinged bar top and stood in front of her. His hand cupping her chin, he ran his thumb over her lower lip. "You feel safe around me, Kelly?"

She swayed, something inside her pushing her to relax against his chest, to tilt her face up to his and accept the kiss she knew would soon follow.

"Tell me. Do you feel safe around me?" he asked again.

Kelly opened her mouth, but no sound came out—just the too loud noise of her breathing.

He laughed, a low rumble that sent shivers along her spine. Pressing his lips against her ear, he whispered, "It's never good to feel too safe, little witch. The closer you let someone get, the easier it is for them to turn the knife—remember that."

With a fleeting kiss along her brow, he turned and vaulted back over the bar top.

* * *

"You don't believe her story do you?"

It was the morning after Kelly's arrival, and Kol had opened the bar at the normal predawn time. Birgit was up, looking surly as ever. Kelly had yet to make an appearance.

Kol flipped the warming plate under the coffee pot to On, then filled his cup.

Birgit continued, "Her whole, poor little me, I was scared routine. I saw her hit that rogue with a stream of power. If she's scared, I'm Little Bo Peep."

Kol took a sip.

"We haven't been attacked again," she added. "Not since she—" she gestured to the upstairs with a jerk of her head "—arrived."

"It's been less than a day."

Birgit shrugged. "Just saying."

Kol topped off his still-full cup, not even bothering to wipe up the brew that spilled over onto the bartop. "Leave her alone."

"I don't take orders from you. But if it makes you feel better, I have no intention of messing with your shiny new toy. I'm sure she can get herself into all kinds of trouble all by her little self."

"Birgit," he growled.

But the Council representative had already shoved her cup forward and walked away from the bar.

Kol picked up his cup, ignoring the pain as hot coffee spilled over his hand. Birgit was right. Kelly's story was thin at best. He had seen her near the portal, skulking, running her hands over the frame whenever she didn't think he was looking.

So, even though he would like to believe she came to the Keep because she knew Kol would keep her safe—or even because she wanted to be near him like he wanted her near—he knew it wasn't likely.

Kelly was human. She couldn't feel the connection between them as strongly as he could. Sure, she sensed it, but she probably still thought she could ignore it.

And there was her fascination with the portal. *He* couldn't ignore that—much as he wanted to.

The next day, Kelly was determined to learn the secret of operating the portal as quickly as possible. Her first opportunity came not long after opening. Kol disappeared into the beer cooler, and Birgit was arguing with a group of female dwarves who claimed she'd short-changed them.

Kelly slipped behind the counter and eyed the machine. It appeared perfectly mundane, but the PC had to hold the secret. She reached out, ready to tap it out of sleep mode.

"You know much about computers?"

Kelly, her hand hovering over the mouse, jumped at Birgit's words, knocking a glass full of dirty spoons onto the floor. She squatted and began brushing them into a pile with her hand.

Birgit kneeled beside her. "Didn't mean to startle you. It's just that Kol's a bit possessive of his PC."

"Oh." Kelly shoved a handful of spoons back into the glass. "I was just going to check my e-mail."

"Well, take my advice and do it when he's not around. I went online one day—just to check some boards—and he went all growly. I mean, I'm not a computer geek, but I wasn't hurting anything, either—you know?"

Kelly dropped another spoon in the glass and studied Birgit through her lashes. She just couldn't figure the waitress out. It was as though every time Kelly saw her she was dealing with a new personality.

Birgit sat back on her heels. Something silver flashed at her throat.

"That's pretty." Kelly reached out to tap the tiny replica of a wolf, head thrown back in full howl, that dangled from Birgit's neck. Birgit pulled back before Kelly's finger could make contact.

"Thanks. It means a lot to me."

"I can see why." Kelly placed the glass full of spoons back on the shelf. Sensing an opportunity to learn something about the other woman, she pressed on. "Was it a gift?"

The camaraderie from seconds earlier dropped from Birgit's face. "No. It wasn't." She stood, then glanced back at Kelly. "If you really want to get on the PC, you'll need the password."

"Oh." Kelly cast a look at the computer she'd been eyeing since her examination of the portal doorway had proved fruitless. "I didn't think about that. I guess I'll have to ask Kol." She waited, hoping the "we're buddies" Birgit would reappear.

After a quick glance over her shoulder to the back of the bar where Kol was arguing with a couple of female trolls, Birgit motioned for Kelly to move closer. "He doesn't have to know everything we do, does he?" She looked at Kelly. Kelly gave a short nod. Apparently satisfied Kelly agreed, she continued, "The password's howler—use the zero for the *O* and the *3* for the *E*. That will get you into everything."

After dropping that morsel, Birgit picked up a tray and strolled out from behind the bar—leaving Kelly to stare at the computer alone. The computer had to be the key, but could she trust Birgit? The woman was a big question mark in Kelly's mind. Still what harm could come of trying the password? Worst case if she got caught, she'd tell Kol the same story she'd told Birgit.

It was reasonable.

As she stood there staring at the screen saver of a pine-covered mountain, Kol snuck up behind her. "You looking for something?" he asked, his hand lowering to rest on the computer's monitor.

Kelly grabbed another spoon still left on the floor and plunked it into the glass. "No, just made a bit of a mess."

His gaze captured hers, and Kelly felt it again—the uncomfortable awareness, like he could see inside her, knew her every thought and emotion. Her tongue darted out to moisten her suddenly dry lips as she jerked her gaze from his.

"Don't listen to Birgit."

The words seemed to come from nowhere. At least they weren't what Kelly had expected him to say. She found herself edging away from the computer, and stopped herself. Lifting her chin, she asked, "What do you mean?"

He picked up a dirty mug left by one of the trolls, and replied, "I didn't ask you to come here to wait tables, or—" he grinned "—clean toilets."

Why did he ask her then? She could taste the question, but was too afraid of the answer and her reaction to it to ask. Instead she licked her lips again, and replied, "It's not like there's anything else for me to do. Unless…" She glanced at the computer. *Could she convince him to give her free access?* "There's something else I could do for you."

His pupils dilated, the ice-blue of his eyes all but disappearing. A lazy smile curved his lips, and his hand reached out to cup the curve of her hip.

With a quick breath, she continued, "I mean I do the books for my own business, maybe I could do some book-keeping or something."

His touch, soft just seconds earlier, hardened.

"As long as I'm here," she finished.

"As long as you're here," he repeated. He dropped his hand completely and stepped back. "How long do you think that will be anyway?"

Kelly frowned. He'd asked her here, and now he was acting as though she'd already outstayed her welcome. "If you don't want me here—"

"I didn't say that." He sighed and ran a hand through his hair. "I most certainly want you…"

Kelly's breath stopped.

"Here," he finished. "I just wondered if you'd figured out who was behind the attacks…attack that is, at your office."

"No." For the first time during their conversation, Kelly was able to relax knowing she was being one hundred percent honest. "I have no idea, and I'd really like to."

"Yeah." He shoved his hands into his pockets and studied her. "Me, too."

Kelly stood there, feeling completely comfortable in Kol's presence for the first time in her memory. Her hand raised. She wanted to touch him, just to cement the moment in her mind. But Birgit banged up to the bar, dropping her tray on its top and calling out a drink order.

Kelly dropped her hand and stepped back. She'd almost slipped, forgotten why she was here. Maybe she'd been wrong about Kol in the past, maybe she hadn't. She couldn't trust herself to sort things out anymore. She needed to accomplish what she came here to do—rescue Terje. Saving a little boy, that she *knew* was the right thing. Then, later, if Kol could forgive her for deceiving him, she could reassess her feelings toward the garm.

But for now, she really needed time alone with that computer.

She got her chance a few hours later. A couple of hard-luck cases wandered into the bar dragging a bag with something squirming inside. It was small—too small to hold even a child, at least a human child. So Kelly didn't feel the need to wrest the sack from their hands, although she kept a close eye on it, just in case anything yelled for help.

They approached Kol and intense negotiations began. Kol opened the sack and something long, green and most definitely not human attempted to wiggle free. After shoving the creature and bag back into its captors hands, Kol went to the computer, clicked around a bit, then waved the pair through the doorway. They disappeared and with a snap, the waving lines of power that identified the portal changed back to the mundane doorway.

No one else in the bar seemed to give any part of the exchange more than a passing glance. Kelly tried to make it appear she hadn't, either, but as she stepped away from the wall where she'd been standing, she caught sight of Birgit watching her. The other waitress quickly averted her gaze, but not before Kelly noticed the assessing look in her eye.

Birgit was watching her.

Ignoring a patron who grabbed at her arm as she passed his table, Birgit tromped behind the bar and tapped Kol on the shoulder.

Kelly's heart shot to her throat. Had she completely underestimated the waitress? Had she discovered Kelly's purpose? Was she about to expose Kelly to Kol?

Her head low, Kelly prepared to pull energy from the bar, but to her surprise, Kol didn't even glance her way. Instead, he made an angry motion with his hand, letting Kelly know whatever Birgit had said to him, he didn't like, then stalked through the bar to the front door.

His hand on the knob, he paused and gave both Birgit and Kelly a last glance. He started to turn back, but Birgit made a motion with her hand, and shaking his head, he pulled open the door and left.

Birgit's gaze swung to where Kelly still stood.

Kelly fisted and unfisted her hands. This was it. The waitress had gotten rid of Kol to confront Kelly on her own. That was fine. Kelly was tired of playing mouse to an unknown cat. Opening her hands she slowly let power drift into her body—not too fast. She didn't want to alert the waitress to what she was doing, especially since Kelly wasn't sure what Birgit was, what powers she had.

"Kelly," Birgit called with an impatient jerk of her head. "Now's the time."

Time? Kelly glanced around the bar, like one of the drunken patrons might interpret Birgit's meaning. Not a single being raised their gaze from their glass.

Birgit curled a finger toward herself.

Her hands still tingling with the power she'd managed to absorb, Kelly walked to the bar.

"Kol went to check something outside." Birgit nodded toward the computer screen, which showed Kol stalking across the street, his muscles taut, his head twisting slightly from right to left, as if scanning for some kind of threat. "He won't be gone long, but now's the time to check your e-mail, if you want to." Birgit bent down to click shut the window showing Kol, then motioned to the monitor. "The Internet's up. Just click on the icon. But don't click on anything else. Especially the window that's minimized. It…" She paused. "Just don't mess with it, okay?"

She waited until Kelly nodded her agreement, then added, "Can you handle things for a few minutes? I need a quick break." She motioned toward the bathrooms.

Before Kelly could reply, she'd already started striding toward the back.

Kelly stood there, staring at the computer. Here was her chance, all but gift-wrapped. Could it be this easy?

After a quick glance at the bar patrons, she studied the screen. A gray box at the bottom of the screen read Passages Pro, a tiny closed door image sat beside the words.

Her hand on the mouse, Kelly hesitated. Her natural suspicions flared—too easy. This had to be too easy.

Another box flanked the first. This one was titled Security Cam. Her brow lowering, Kelly clicked on it. The window showing Kol filled the screen. He had turned and was now facing the bar. He mumbled something to himself, and glanced around the street, then after shooting a dark look at the bar, began quick long strides back toward the building.

No time. Kelly had to decide now. She might not get another chance.

Sucking in a breath, she clicked on the closed-door icon. A list of words appeared on the left-hand side of the screen, to the right various options that seemed to set times or durations. Perhaps how long to leave the doorway open? Or a way to preset when it would be open?

Kelly didn't have time to sort through it all. Instead she scrolled down the list, looking for anything that looked familiar.

Nothing.

She glanced at the front door, then flipped to the security camera window. Kol had stopped, his head cocked as if listening to some noise.

Swallowing the lump in her throat, Kelly switched back to the portal operation.

It had to be here.

Then she saw it—a separate category labeled Restricted. She clicked. There were only a few places listed and the first was Lyngvi.

Chapter 10

Kelly could only stare at the six letter word. *Lyngvi*. Home of Fenrir. Most desolate place in the nine worlds.

Aesa had only asked her to figure out how to get there—not to go there herself. But knowing how to operate the portal would do them no good, would not save Terje, not without an opportunity to actually go through the doorway.

And could she count on another time as open as this?

The hinges on the front door began to squeak as someone pushed against it, ready to enter the bar.

Decision time.

Blowing out whatever fear she'd been holding inside, Kelly clicked on Lyngvi. A second window popped open. A warning—*Restricted—do you wish to proceed?*

Another mouse click—Yes.

Are you sure?

Again—Yes. Kelly's palms began to sweat. Her hands shaking she waited for the next prompt.

This is a restricted zone. You will have five seconds only. Open now?

Last chance. Kelly glanced at the space separating her from the portal. She could make it. Walking toward the portal, she held the mouse at arm's reach hoping it could still operate the computer—then clicked.

Streams of energy waved in the doorway. Kelly tossed down the mouse and sprinted through the portal.

Kol stomped back into the bar. Why Birgit insisted he check out the men she claimed were lurking outside was beyond him. This was the Guardian's Keep. There was always someone questionable lurking somewhere.

Besides, he had no desire to run anyone off. Not even would-be attackers. He wanted them to come inside. Especially right now. With Kelly so close and him feeling he couldn't touch her, his frustration level was almost beyond containment. The battle with Stumi had just whetted his desire for more.

He could use a confrontation with about a dozen rogues right about now.

Slamming the door behind him, he sidestepped a drunken Svartalfar and headed back to the bar. As he rounded the corner, Birgit appeared from the back.

"There was nothing there," he muttered.

"Really?" Birgit stopped near the portal, then glanced around the bar.

"No, you can't..." Kol paused. The computer mouse was laying in the middle of the floor. He bent to pick it up, then turned to stare at Birgit.

She widened her eyes—a look of innocence completely at odds with her personality.

Suspicion chipping at Kol's brain, he lunged toward the computer. The portal window was up, but nothing seemed to be active.

Anxiety wrapping around him like a steel band, he ran the cursor up the page, stopping on *History*.

"Did you send anyone through?" he asked, not even bothering to look at Birgit as he did.

"Not me. I've been in the back—potty break."

Her tone was too calm—too innocent.

The last place he sent anyone was a fairly common location in Midgard.

Praying that would be the name at the top of the list, he opened the file.

Lyngvi.

Good gods, no.

It was dark and cold. Something slapped against Kelly's body like wet bed sheets, but when she ran her hands over her clothing they were still dry. She took a step forward, just to stumble and fall. She slid downward, her arms flaying blindly around her, her fingers grasped for anything solid to stop her descent, but bits of shale or something smooth and hard just continued to give way allowing her body to sled down a hill she couldn't even see. Something spiny brushed against her face, scratching her. A plant, her mind yelled, with roots. Her feet scrambling to slow her downward motion, she managed to wrap one hand around the prickly plant. It held. Her heart beating so hard she thought it might shake her precarious grip loose, she made another blind grab with her free hand, driving it into a jagged rock.

The dagger-sharp stone pierced her skin. She pressed her palm to her mouth, catching the accompanying cry of pain before it could be fully vocalized. The metallic taste of blood seeped in through her lips.

Pain. Blood. She was still alive. Her feet now braced on some type of ledge, she groped in the darkness for another plant or rock that could hold her weight. She found one, then another. Slowly, she inched her way to the top and flung her body onto a flat surface. She lay there, her eyes staring blindly up at what she assumed had to be a night sky and the reassuring solidity of dirt under her back.

Then something shifted in the darkness—something she could feel more than see. An energy reaching out to her, testing her. She fought the urge to shrink back, more because there was nothing to shrink back against than any misplaced bravery. Her breath was loud in her ears. Realizing she couldn't hear anything over the sound, she forced herself to take smaller amounts of air in through her nose, out through her mouth.

Slowly the noise lessened and she was able to make out other sounds: waves pounding against hard rock, the stones that had rolled from under her feet down whatever precipice she had clung to were still falling—and she heard cries. Unearthly cries that sent shudders through her body and made her hair raise from her scalp.

Good God, what had she gotten herself into?

"Kelly. Where is she?" Kol dropped the mouse and turned to face Birgit. The bar seemed still suddenly, his attention only on the Garm Council representative. He was calm, focused. Every molecule of his being waiting to hear what she had to say.

Birgit took a step back, her shoulder going up in a one-sided shrug. "Couldn't tell you. Isn't it your job to keep tabs on her?"

Kol tilted his head. She was lying. He could see it in the way she dropped her gaze, toyed with a bar napkin. And despite her "who cares" response, she was nervous. He was making her nervous.

He should.

"Where is she, Birgit? She was here when I left—before you sent me on a wild-rogue chase."

"It wasn't—" Her voice broke. A crack in her normally strong facade.

Kol took another step toward her, his hand drifting to where his silver bat leaned against the wall. "Really? It wasn't? You didn't reset the portal? Somehow lure Kelly through?" The weight of the bar felt good in his hand— right. Less than an arm's length away from the female garm, close enough for an easy swing, an easy kill, he stopped. "Send her to Lyngvi?"

"What? No!" Birgit pulled back, her eyes and mouth rounded. "What are you talking about? Are you saying that stupid witch sent herself to Lyngvi?" She whirled around the corner of the bar, brushed past him, not even glancing at the silver bat still warming in his hand.

She picked up the mouse and slammed it onto the table next to the computer. "Damn. She did it. What the hell was that idiot thinking?"

Spinning she advanced on Kol. "You realize what this means, don't you? We are screwed. Royally. No one is allowed travel to Lyngvi. No one."

Staring blankly out into the bar, she shoved her hand up into her hair. "I should have known she'd pull something like this. I mean why try to take over a portal if you just want to go somewhere simple?"

A barrage of curse words flowed from her mouth.

Something about Birgit's rage seemed to lessen Kol's. A tiny bit of the tension surrounding him fell away. He just felt tired, deflated—shell-shocked.

"Well, there's only one answer." Birgit rambled more to herself than to Kol. "They'll have to let me close it. Now that we know Lyngvi was the target. We have to make one-hundred-percent sure no one else gets through. It will take time. Magnus will want to call all the guardians, get their input, but it will have to be done. There's no other solution."

"Can she get out?" Kol asked, his voice low, controlled.

"What?" Birgit blinked at him, like he'd just flashed a spotlight in her face. "What the hell do I care…no wait. That's a good point. Another reason for Magnus to agree to shut access to Lyngvi down. It's the only way to make sure she's trapped there. Or trapped for a while at least." Birgit shrugged. "She won't last long."

Kol grabbed the babbling female by the shoulders, his fingers digging into her muscle. "So, right now. Until access is closed. Can she get out?"

Birgit stared at him, realization making its way to her eyes. "Theoretically, yes. The portal works both ways. But on that end, the security is a lot tighter. It's protected by the gods. Chances are if she even tries to touch the controls she'll be vaporized or something."

"What if the portal was left open?"

"Can't be. It's on a timer. The most it can be left open at a time is five seconds. So unless she was just standing there, nose pressed to the doorway, there's no way she'd make it through."

"But I could open it again and again, right? Basically the same thing as leaving it open."

Birgit shook her head, her mouth falling open in disgust. "Even you can't be that directed by your…" She nodded to his crotch.

"Would it work?" He squeezed her shoulders tighter.

"I don't know. I doubt it. You may not think a lot of the gods, but they aren't that stupid. I'm sure there's some guard in place to keep that from happening. You might blow the whole portal system. And besides, you know what kind of nasties are kept at Lyngvi? You really want to unleash that on this world just so you can get a good lay?"

Kol released her, shoving her away from him.

Birgit watched him, her arms crossed over her chest, her head shaking side to side. "Would you really risk everything for her?"

Kol walked to the coffee can where he'd stashed Kelly's wooden dowel, and pulled the tool out, with his fingers wrapped around the smooth wood, he considered Birgit's question.

What would he risk to save Kelly? Why risk anything? It was obvious now she'd lied to him. Birgit hadn't sent her to Lyngvi. That was unmistakable. He'd told himself if Kelly was lying to him, he'd kill her with his own hands, but now that he was faced with the truth?

The dowel still in one hand, he grasped the silver bat with the other, then turned to walk to the portal.

His gaze on Birgit, he replied, "Yes, apparently I would."

Kelly screwed her eyes shut for one moment, her fingers digging into the scant soil beneath her. She couldn't just lay here in the dark, waiting for whatever was watching her to approach.

She needed light. Attempting to relax, she reached for power. Energy flickered around her, teasing, taunting. With a smile she pulled, eager to refill her reserves, strengthen herself both mentally and physically. The stream began, a ribbon actually, but with the promise of much more— more power than Kelly had ever felt.

She pulled harder, like tugging on a string. But just as she could feel the real power was near, the dam about to break, the stream stopped. The loss was so sudden she jerked, her eyes flying open.

Licking her lips, she squared her jaw and reached out again, but there was nothing, not even the tingle of leftover static. Heaving out an exhausted breath, she pulled herself to sit, curling her legs in to her body.

Power like that didn't just go away. It was as if someone flipped a switch, breaking a circuit. Who could have the power to do that?

Suddenly cold, she shivered and pressed her forehead against her jean-covered knees. It could be worse. She had gained some power, enough to light her way, surely. Maybe even enough to hold off anything that was out there, that might attack until…

Until what?

No one was coming to get her. No one was even looking for her. She'd made this jump all on her own, and had only herself to depend on to get out of here alive.

Shaking off the negative thoughts, she shifted her weight to her feet and pushed herself to a stand. A breeze brushed against her, causing her to sway. She widened her stance. She had to get her bearings. Time to see where she was.

Taking a deep breath, she held up her hand and willed the power she'd drawn to take form. To her relief a softball-size orb began to glow on her palm.

With light to guide her, she slowly spun in a circle. She was standing on a small flat area about five feet in diameter. Behind her she could see the ground dropped away. She edged toward it and peered over the side—nothing but the sound of the waves. With her foot she knocked a rock over the edge. She listened waiting for it to collide with something, rock, ocean, something, but the sound never came.

Suppressing another shiver, she squared her shoulders and continued her circuit. On the other side of the space a wall of stone shot from the ground. She walked forward and held the light as high as she could. The wall didn't seem to end.

But there had to be a way out of here. There had to be.

Blinking back moisture that had gathered in her eyes, she bit her lip and faced the wall again. Up or down. She'd already been down and had no desire to try that route again. So up. It had to be up.

This time as she ran the light over the wall she saw something—narrow footholds carved in the stone, not stairs, but enough, if she was careful and lucky she should be able to climb them. But not with the orb. She'd have to lose that, at least for a while.

With a murmured prayer, she closed her hand over the glow, then ran her foot up the wall until it hit the first notch. Here she went. Whatever awaited her, it had to be better than staying put or tumbling over the side into the angry waves.

Kol stepped into Lyngvi, the dowel shoved into his front pocket and the silver bat poised in front of him. The change in worlds hit him immediately—the smell of the ocean, the damp feel of the air, the pounding of the sea against the rocks, and the impenetrable darkness.

Shale shifted under his feet. He leaned forward to regain his balance. The doorway to Lyngvi was not a place to lose your footing. One misstep in the wrong direction and you'd go crashing onto the jagged rocks that surrounded the island.

Kelly. Had she…? He tightened his grip on the bat. She was fine—she had to be. He hadn't risked everything to come to this dark spot of oblivion and find her dead.

Clenching his jaw, he lowered the bat and slid his foot forward. Rocks moved under his feet. He froze again. Which direction? In human form, he could see nothing. In wolf, his vision would be sharper, but he'd have to leave the bat, and there was the issue of being a garm on Lyngvi. The island existed to contain Fenrir—the strongest of the garm. Any advantage wolf form might gain him some-where else would be taken into account here—a guard already put in place to counter it.

Besides, no wolf could scale these cliffs. It took human form to do that. And to shimmer, he needed a direction. He'd never been to Lyngvi, knew nothing about the isle. So, for now at least he would stay as he was, but there was still the problem of knowing where he was going.

Suddenly it occurred to him. *Kelly.* He didn't need to know where he was going. He only had to know where Kelly was.

Exhaling all the air from his lungs, he shook his limbs and willed his body and mind to relax, to focus on Kelly, to see her, feel her. For a few heart-stopping seconds, he couldn't sense her—nothing. Then he felt her—or more exactly what she was feeling: uncertainty, she didn't know where she was, what she should do next; sorrow, had she left everything she valued behind—for…he tried to zero in on what she regretted leaving, what she was searching

for here on Lyngvi, but the bond wasn't tight enough…
then finally determination: to live, to save…he couldn't
grasp who or what…and to make it back to… He didn't
know what, wasn't sure Kelly knew what.

Something clenched deep in his chest, like a band
wrapping around his heart. She was here and she was safe.
All he had to do was find her, a simple matter. Now that he
had Kelly to focus on, he could shimmer. His lips turning
upward in a smile, he concentrated on his goal, and started
to shimmer.

He felt the first tingles of the transformation before
some force dropped over him, interrupted his transition
and knocked him back into solid form. His eyes wide, he
spun in the small space available. No one was near, but his
shimmer had been stopped cleanly.

A bead of sweat found its way to his brow. So, he
couldn't shimmer. There were other paths open to him. He
touched the cold rock in front of him and stared up into
the darkness. Not an easy path, but a path all the same.

Exhaling, he centered every sense he possessed on
Kelly, then ran his hands over the cliff wall. If Kelly wasn't
here on this ledge, there had to be some way off of it.

Another broad swipe and he found it—small niches
were carved in the rock. He shook his head. Even with
light, he doubted they'd be visible.

The silver bat pressed against his leg. He needed both
hands to climb the wall, but once at the top odds were good
he'd need the bat even more.

With grim determination, he pulled off his shirt and belt,
and began fashioning a scabbard.

Once he was sure the bat wouldn't get in the way of his
ascent, or slip from the shirt and fall to the rocks below, he
grabbed hold of a niche and began pulling himself up the cliff.

* * *

Kelly's second climb of the evening was no more pleasant than the first, but this time something aside from fear drove her. Rock-hard determination.

She'd beaten the odds by getting this far. She'd be damned if she'd give up now.

Finally, her hand reached for another niche and instead hit air. She bent her wrists, groping for something solid and found it—another flat space. Hopefully, more than just another landing.

Praying she wasn't just pulling herself to a second pit stop on a never-ending climb, she strained upward, using her legs, fingers and pure will to lever her body over the cliffside and onto flat ground.

She lay panting on the dirt, her eyes closed.

A roar split the night air, shaking the ground beneath her. Rocks from above peppered Kelly, sharp little strikes like birds pecking at her flesh. With a gasp, she curled into herself and rolled onto her feet, into a crouch.

More rocks hit her head and back, got trapped in her hair. Cursing, she flattened her palm and called for the lit sphere. Within seconds, a softly glowing orb formed. She held up her hand and muttered a second prayer. In the dim light she could make out a path curving up a steep hillside and a small overhang at its beginning.

She half stood and sprinted, still bent at the waist, toward the small protected area. New sound broke through the night. Men yelling in a language she didn't recognize and then the ping of metal against metal. Another roar, but lower this time. More of a growl—full of menace, but blessedly lacking in the destructive volume of the first.

A few last rocks pattered down the hill, then silence.

The orb still glowing in her palm, Kelly stepped out from beneath the shelter and stared up the path.

Every survival instinct in her being screamed for her to turn and run the opposite direction.

Must mean this was the way she had to go.

Chapter 11

The path wove back and forth up the mountain, the air growing colder the higher Kelly climbed. She could have used magic to warm the air around her, but she could already feel the little power she'd pulled earlier dwindling. She needed light more than heat—at least right now.

The sounds she'd heard before: metal clanking, men yelling and some huge animal growling and sniffing grew louder. Then suddenly she hit a clearing, and she knew she'd arrived—the purpose of the place she wasn't sure, but she could tell this was the heart of Lyngvi. Lanterns hung around the space, illuminating a round, flattened piece of ground.

Hiding behind a square-cut boulder, she watched dark forms trudge forward, pulling what appeared to be a massive length of chain from a gigantic spool. Each link had to weigh more than Kelly and her sister combined.

Realizing the risk of discovery was great, she squelched the light and crept closer to the center of the clearing.

"Where are the dwarves?" a man towering over the forms fighting with the chain bellowed.

"Not here. No word when they'll arrive." Another smaller man darted a glance at the first, then back over his shoulder to where Kelly hid.

She froze, not even risking a breath, until the man looked away.

"And the gods think this new fetter will hold him?" A third man stepped forward, from a dark spot Kelly now realized was the mouth of a cave. "I'm tired of being called here to serve the beast. All because those greater—" he spat out the word "—than us, fear him."

"Why they don't kill him, I don't know." The first man gestured toward the cave.

"And what of those who still follow him in the nine worlds? He may be dangerous alive, but he'd be even more so dead." The second man gestured to one of the forms. "Bring his meal. I'm tired and want to return to my own home before the stink of this isle rots through my clothes."

There was the creak of unoiled wheels and a wooden cart pushed by four more of the shadowy shapes appeared. Something was dragged from its bed, landing on the hard earth with a thump so solid Kelly could feel the earth reverberate beneath her. The two larger men who seemed in charge strolled into the cave, giving no further attention to the shadowy figures or the burden they tugged behind them.

When the group had disappeared into the dark opening, Kelly crept closer, her heart thumping in her chest. Fenrir. It had to be the great garm housed inside the cave. Was Terje there, too? Nothing in the men's conversation had appeared to reference the boy. But if he was here, he'd be near Fenrir—at least that was what Aesa believed. Kelly couldn't come so close and not at least check.

Even with the cool temperature of the air surrounding her, sweat beaded on Kelly's torso. The massive chain stretched in front of her. She stopped, unable to make her feet move past it. The metal was thicker than her waist.

What kind of beast was Fenrir that even contained by *that*, the gods still feared him?

A shiver shook her. She wrapped her arms around her middle and forced her legs to move. With a leap, she left the chain behind and crept closer. Only a few feet from the mouth of the cave, she stopped.

"Ah, and doesn't he smell foul?" The man who'd voiced a hurry to leave the island stepped into the light cast by a lantern that swayed overhead. "Bring the meat."

The shadows trudged ahead. As the light hit them, Kelly captured a cry that threatened to spill from her lips. They were like nothing she'd seen before, globs of mud in the rough outline of men. Two more joined the four she'd seen outside. Together they gripped the carcass of what appeared to be a two-headed ox by its legs, tail and horns. With labored steps they pulled the lifeless animal forward.

Once they reached the man who had called them, he held up one hand. "Enough. He can reach it from here— if he's eating today."

"Fenrir, would you deign to join us this lovely spring afternoon?" he called.

Something shifted deeper in the shadows. Chains clanked, and a grumbling growl sent a new set of shivers tripping down Kelly's body. Then with a shake of its fur, the creature stood, releasing a whiff of wet fur and rancid breath that almost sent Kelly to her knees.

"Ah, feeling sociable today? What's caused this change of state?" The man bent down to pluck up the massive chain as if it weighed no more than a breeze. Stepping backward, he held it out of Fenrir's way, so the mighty garm could step forward toward his meal, and into the light.

The size of a Percheron stallion, Fenrir stood, his head low, his nose moving back and forth. His fur was silvery gray, beautiful even in the dirty matted condition it was. And his eyes were a brilliant green, almost phosphorescent. He looked up, his gaze pinning Kelly. She felt it physically just as if he had reached out and poked her in the stomach.

This time she couldn't stop the gasp that rushed to her lips. She clamped her mouth closed and pressed her hand to her lips. But it was too late.

All heads turned toward her.

Before her brain could even offer the options of fight or flight, the mud men raced toward her. No longer in any way human in appearance, they formed one solid curtain, pushing up from the ground as they zipped toward her— like a wave curling out of the ocean.

"Catch her," the first man she'd seen, the one not occupied with Fenrir, yelled.

Fenrir lunged, a roar exploding from his black gums.

"Aesa, is she here?" a rough voice yelled in her head.

Kelly spun, her gaze darting from the advancing wall of mud, to the mighty garm, to the man who held Fenrir's chain. Who spoke to her?

The wave was almost on her, she could feel the slippery cold of its touch. No time to sort things out. Survival finally clicked in, and she sprang forward toward the path and, she hoped, the portal.

Behind her, the wave made no noise, but Kelly could feel them as they edged closer, split back into individual forms. She ran, her feet pounding on the hard packed dirt of the clearing, her breath coming in puffs. Her eyes accustomed to the little bit of light that illuminated the clearing failed her now. She had no choice but to run blindly into the darkness and pray she found the path.

Even with the thought in her head, she hesitated, some tiny bit of survival instinct telling her falling off the side of a Lyngvi cliff would be just as deadly as whatever the mud creatures planned for her. She needed time and light.

Let her have enough reserves left for both. She called for power. Both hands began to glow, one with the orb of light and the other with a crackling ball of energy.

She spun, tossing the energy ball toward the creatures. Then without even pausing to see what if any damage the missile caused, she hurried forward, searching the darkness for the path.

"Here." She felt as much as heard Kol's voice call to her. A dream? Some trick of Lyngvi to lure her to her death?

"Kelly." This time the voice was louder, annoyed. Her heart skipping, she raced forward and collided with a familiar broad, bare chest.

Kol wrapped one arm around Kelly and held her pressed against his chest. Her teeth were chattering, and her heart was beating like a hummingbird's but she was alive. Murmuring a prayer of thanks, he pressed a kiss onto the top of her head and ran his cheek across her hair.

She shuddered out a breath, then pulled back, her face jerking back the direction she had dashed from. "They're coming. I can feel them."

"What? Who?" He lifted his arm overhead and pulled the silver bat from the makeshift scabbard on his back.

"Them," she replied, her voice cloaked with horror.

He had little more than seconds to glance at their attackers before they were almost surrounded by black, oily-looking shapes. The feil. Beings created from the very earth of Lyngvi to serve and protect those who guarded Fenrir. Kol had never seen one before, never thought he'd have reason to. They could only exist in one place, Lyngvi. But from what little he'd heard, there was no mistaking them and he also knew—no destroying them.

"Go down the path," he ordered Kelly.

She turned, started to comply, then stopped. "Aren't you coming?"

"When you get to the portal, wait. I'll try to get there as soon as I can." One edge of the feil shifted, sweeping over Kol's head. He ducked. Still a dark tendril slid across his shoulder, tried to curl its way into his skin. He jumped back, jerking away from the feil's hold. There was a pop, and he realized the feil had sunk its first hook. He'd managed to jerk free, but not without cost. Blood streamed from the wound.

Around him the feil sighed and began throbbing like a giant hungry heart.

His free hand pressed to the wound, he realized Kelly still stood beside him. "I said to leave."

She stared at him a second, her eyes huge in her face, then glanced at the menace around them. "I don't think so."

The feil reached out again. Kol bit back a curse and tried to shield her body with his, but she stepped forward, balls of energy crackling in her hands. "You go. I can't operate the portal anyway, and I'm the reason we're in this mess."

She twisted her body, feinting one direction and then the other. To Kol's surprise the feil seemed to retreat—not much, but some. The feil couldn't be killed, but was it possible they could be hurt, intimidated?

"Leave now. I don't have much left in me." Kelly

twisted again, the balls of energy still blazing, but almost as the words left her mouth, one sphere sputtered—its light dimming to a low glow.

Muttering a curse, Kol grabbed her by the back of her shirt and jerked her back behind him. In the same movement he swung the silver bat one-handed like a sword around them.

The feil wavered, pulling back where the silver would have brushed them.

Something sizzled in his ear. Kelly with the powerballs still held overhead pressed against his side. "Can we hurt them?" she asked her voice low.

He shook his head. "I don't know. But they seem to retreat when we attack."

"Then let's chase them back to the cave, block them in somehow," Kelly murmured.

The cave. Kol slid a quick glance her direction. *What had she seen?* No time to wonder about that now. "Look at them. They are the feil, made from the very earth we stand on. Do you think we can trap them inside some cave? Besides, I'm sure there are other things we don't want to encounter back at *the cave.*"

The way her lip slipped between her teeth was answer enough for him. He continued, "We just have to keep them at bay long enough to make it to the portal."

She nodded. "I'll do my best, but this…" Her gaze rolled to the quickly dwindling blue fire in her hands.

"Here." Kol dug into his front pocket and pulled out the dowel. "Will this help?"

Kelly stared at it, then Kol. "That's my—"

"Take it," he ordered. They didn't have time for an argument now. He could only pray they'd have time and opportunity for one in the future.

Biting back whatever other words were on her lips, Kelly dropped one hand and curled her fingers around the wooden dowel. Instantly the sphere she still held overhead glowed brighter.

With a grim nod, Kol stared back at the feil. The servers of Lyngvi seemed to be waiting, the mud they were made up of thin and fluttering as if caught in a light breeze. They looked harmless at the moment, peaceful even, but Kol knew better. The stinging wound on his shoulder told him better.

"To the cliff," he said.

He could feel Kelly nod beside him, feel her draw on the reserve of power in the dowel he'd given her. "To the cliff," she replied.

Their sides pressed against each other, their weapons held out in a protective manner, they began the slow backward walk down the uneven path and toward the pounding sound of the sea.

Kelly and Kol walked side by side back toward the cliff. The constant view of the mud creatures circling them, occasionally darting forward to snap a whiplike length of darkness at one of them, should have made the trip back a million times worse than the trip to the cave, but just feeling Kol's warmth against her, the occasional touch of his hand when she stumbled, gave Kelly a strength she'd lacked alone.

However, when they reached the spot where she'd climbed up, clinging to the tiny slits notched in the cliff-side, her calm wavered.

"We can't hold them off and climb," she said to Kol.

His lips thinned as if he'd had the same thought himself.

"I won't leave you," she stated, cutting him off before he could insist she climb alone, leaving him at the top to hold off the feil.

"There's no time to—" he started, but then stopped, his head angling to the side.

"Kol?" she asked a furrow forming between her brows. His only reply was to twist his head again.

"What is it?" she whispered. The feil edged closer. She pulled as much power as she dared from the dowel and shot a stream of energy from her palm, knocking them back, regaining the foot or so the creatures had encroached upon.

Shaking his head as if leaving a trance, Kol stared at her, a look of disbelief on his face. "Maybe we won't have to."

"What?" she began, but was cut off by a roar even louder than the one that had sent stones scurrying down the hill earlier. This time she almost lost her footing. She grabbed Kol's bicep to keep from falling.

"It worked," Kol murmured.

Realizing at some point during the roar she'd closed her eyes, Kelly opened them and glanced around. The feil were gone.

"Where'd they…?"

"No time. They'll be back. We have to get to the portal, now." Frowning, Kol leaned over the side of the cliff and studied the notches. Pulling himself back up, he sat in a crouch and shifted his analysis to her. "Do you trust me?" he asked.

Kelly stared at him. *Did she trust him?* That was kind of what got her into this situation to start with. Did she trust him now? Swallowing the lump that formed in her throat, she nodded. God help her. She did.

"Good. Climb on my back."

Kelly gave him an incredulous look.

"I can't shimmer. I tried earlier. We have to climb. If we climb as one, it will cut our time in half and leave you freer to use your magic if we need it."

She hesitated.

"Now, Kelly," he ordered.

Hating that it had come to this, that she was so dependent on another being to get out of a mess she got herself into, Kelly blinked back tears of exasperation and wrapped her arms around his neck. Once her legs were also wrapped around his waist, Kol lowered them both over the side and began the climb down the cliffside.

Any other time, Kelly's breasts flattened against his bare back, her legs squeezing his waist, and her lips just inches from his neck would have been more temptation than Kol could have resisted. But knowing the feil were sure to return any second managed to put a damper on his libido. For now at least. He had no doubt this moment would come back to him with a multitude of erotic possibilities, as soon as they were safely off Lyngvi.

If they got off Lyngvi.

He was still amazed they had gotten this far. They'd only managed it with help from Fenrir. Fenrir. The mighty garm had spoken to Kol. Asked if Kol was there to free him, then realizing Kol couldn't respond in his human form, he'd gone on to tell Kol to get his mate—mate, he'd been referring to Kelly. Kol hadn't had time to work that out yet, either. To get his mate and go back to the portal, that Fenrir would cause a distraction.

It had worked. The feil's main reason for existence was to guard Fenrir. One sign he was resisting his captive state and they'd whisked themselves back to his cave.

But Fenrir, the garm Kol had always thought of as the ultimate sign of chaos and destruction, had saved him and Kelly. Kol would never forget this favor.

Kelly shifted, her hips slipping down his, her sex

rubbing against his backside. What Kol wouldn't give to be on solid ground, to be able to spin around and press against her, chest to breast, and push into her.

She shifted again, her lips brushing against the side of his neck as she grappled for a stronger hold. He swayed a little more than necessary, forcing her to cling even tighter. Then suddenly the tempting press of her body was gone, and Kol realized they'd reached the bottom of the cliff.

"Thanks."

He could hear her fidgeting with her jeans, brushing off dirt, and in general trying to ignore the attraction he knew she had to feel, too.

"Not a problem," he replied. The air vibrated between them, the sweet mix of danger and adrenaline increasing the pull she had on him.

He could feel her nod, then heard her murmur something under her breath and a low glow formed in her palm—a ball of energy big enough to illuminate the small space around them, but no more.

"So, we're back at the portal." Her gaze darted around the clearing, toward the sea, back up the cliff, everywhere but at Kol.

He wanted to pull her to him, tilt her chin up and force her to admit she felt what he felt, wanted what he wanted, needed—

Another roar split through the darkness.

Fenrir. The feil must be coming.

A curse forming on his lips, he tucked Kelly closer to the cliff where perhaps she wouldn't be seen, at least not immediately and went to investigate the portal.

Portals predated everything except the nine worlds themselves. No one really knew if they were formed with the worlds or after, or who created them. But for millennia, garm had operated and protected the doorways.

It had only been in the last twenty years that computers had been brought into the equation. A bleep in time. Kol had been a guardian for decades before that. He could still operate a portal without the extra convenience of a computer monitor—hopefully.

First, he had to find the thing though. Taking a deep breath, he concentrated on the energy flow around him. Unless they were actually in use, portals had an almost negative impact on the normal magic that was present in every world, a dead zone, like standing in a well.

Raising both arms, he turned slowly waiting for his senses to zero in on the doorway. Halfway back to where Kelly stood watching him, he felt it. A cold spot. A void in reality.

Smiling, he stepped forward and began running his hands over the rocks in front of him.

Chapter 12

"Is it working?" Aesa looked over Heather's shoulder as she tapped on the portal computer's keyboard.

Heather kept her gaze on the screen. "It's on. But I can't get into anything without the password. And there's some kind of security system in place. After every five tries it goes into some kind of sleep mode. I think it's sending a message to someone." She licked her lips and glanced at the front door of the Guardian's Keep.

Thankfully, she'd missed out on most of the battle that Aesa and her pack of rogues had waged on the bar, ousting the Garm Council, and gaining control of the portal— they'd thought. Unfortunately, the blond garm, a Council member apparently, had managed to slap off the computer's power strip.

When the machine rebooted, Heather discovered, not surprisingly, that the system was password protected. And, as much as Aesa wanted her to be, Heather was no hacker.

"Isn't there another way to operate that thing?" She gestured to the doorway where Leifi and another garm stood, running their hands over the molding. "Computers haven't been around that long. Isn't operating portals what garm do?"

"Garm are guardians. Running a portal takes special training. Something…" Aesa's lips turned down. "None of us have had."

"So, you attacked the bar because…" Heather knew her true feelings were starting to show, that she sounded pissed, but damn it, she'd been made promises. She'd done things she wasn't proud of—like deceiving Kelly, a woman she actually liked—and now it looked as if all of it was for nothing. It was one thing to sell out, but for pennies?

She shoved the keyboard back against the computer causing the monitor to teeter.

"Careful." Aesa jumped forward, placing a hand on the computer monitor.

"It's fine." Heather crossed her arms over her chest. "So, are they going to figure this out?"

Aesa chewed on the tip of her finger. "Karl worked near a portal." She nodded to the garm standing next to Leifi. "He's just never actually…"

There was a hum, a shift in energy in the bar and the space in front of the two garm changed from a normal doorway to waving lines of power. A cheer went up from the rogues gathered in the bar.

"Finally," Heather murmured, following Aesa as she hurried toward the portal.

"It's working." Aesa clasped her hands in front of her, her lips disappearing into her mouth.

"Yes, but—" Leifi began, only to have his words drowned by a piercing shriek that broke through the portal.

Heather threw herself to the floor.

Suddenly a huge wind ripped from the portal into the bar sending Karl, Leifi, and Aesa smashing into the wall behind them. The three hung there, pinned by the wind against the plaster.

The wind stopped. Using the bar's edge for leverage, Heather pulled herself back up, just missing the sight of the three released garm falling to the ground.

"What was that?" she asked. Her gaze darted to the three garm now slumped against the wall, but they didn't seem to hear her. Instead their eyes, rounded and colored with various shades of horror, were turned to the portal.

Stiffly, as if her body knew what her mind didn't yet, Heather turned to look.

A giant, hooked beak poked through the doorway and began digging troughlike gouges in the cement floor.

"*Helheim!* You opened the doorway to Helheim!" Aesa screamed.

Helheim. The word registered somewhere in Heather's brain—land of the dead, no way back.

Good God. What had she helped the garm do?

One minute Kelly was shivering under an overhang on the dismal isle of Lyngvi watching Kol twisting stones and mumbling to himself, the next she was being yanked through the suddenly shimmering portal.

Cradled in Kol's arms, she felt herself falling, tumbling head then feet down to where she had no idea. Her fingers clawed at his chest. Morbid thoughts raced through her head... *Had they missed the portal, and catapulted off the cliff instead?*

Then just as panic was beginning to take over, a scream finding its way out of her lungs, they hit. Kol rolled them both, his arms under her head, protecting her. Kelly just lay there, panting, praying wherever they'd landed it was worlds away from the misty isle of Lyngvi.

Nothing could be that bad.

"Well, what do you know? He made it." A high-heeled boot stepped into Kol's view. With a grunt, he looked down at Kelly and swiped his cheek against hers. Then slowly, he pulled them both to a sit.

Birgit stared down at them.

Apparently still in a daze from everything she'd survived, Kelly simply returned her look.

"I can't believe you brought her back," Birgit continued. Then over her shoulder to someone he couldn't see, "I told you. He cares more about her than the portal. He's the reason we lost it."

"Lost it?" Kol stiffened, but kept his arm curled around Kelly. Realizing they weren't at the Guardian's Keep where he'd planned to return, he glanced around. Instead of the bar, they were in a small room, furnished only with a desk, computer, couch, and bookshelf. Standing near the door was Magnus. He kept a steady gaze on Kelly. Somehow they'd come through another portal, one he wasn't familiar with, but judging by his surroundings at least in the human world.

"That's right. After you insisted I let you through to…" Birgit glanced behind her. "After you deserted your station, the rogues attacked. I barely had time to disconnect the terminal before shimmering out."

"You let them have the bar?" Kol leaped to his feet, pulling Kelly to a stand beside them. She followed his move easily, but he could tell she was still disoriented. Her forehead was creased and her gaze darted around the room as if trying to place what was happening.

"You didn't fight?" he asked.

Birgit stepped closer. Close enough Kol could smell the woodsy garm scent of her. She stood with her back rigid and her eyes fixed on Kol. For a second, he thought she was going to strike him, but she just spun on her heel and stalked to the other side of the room.

Magnus dropped his arms to his sides, and let out a breath. "Rogues broke in as soon as you were gone. They must have had spies inside." His gaze wandered to Kelly again.

Kol took a sideways step, moving between Kelly and the two Council members.

The other man shook his head slightly, his gaze moving back to Kol. "Lyngvi?"

Birgit stiffened.

Without glancing at her, Magnus continued, "That's right. I know, Birgit. Did the two of you think you could open the portal to one of the most protected spots in the nine worlds, and word not get back to me? The two of you, for reasons I couldn't possibly fathom, endangered not only this portal, but the entire guardian system."

Birgit's already pale complexion, lightened another degree. "So, the gods—"

The man exhaled loudly through his nose. "For some reason, Tyr chose not to inform them. At least for now."

Birgit licked her lips.

Kol didn't care about the gods or the Garm Council. He only cared about two things—his portal and Kelly.

"Why didn't you regain it?" he asked.

Birgit let out a little laugh. "There were at least a hundred of them. Whoever's behind this has been very busy gathering forces. I didn't know there were that many rogues in existence."

"You've spent too much time behind a computer screen, then," Kol drawled.

Her gaze sharp, Birgit lifted her chin. "Maybe that's about to change."

"Meaning?" Kol stared the female down.

"Meaning nothing." Magnus glared at both of them. "Right now neither of you qualify as portal guardian material. When…*if* we regain the Guardian's Keep, the Council will be called, and a decision will be made.

"Until then, both of you are on notice."

Birgit spun toward him. "You can't be serious?"

"As serious as what you two may have unleashed on this world." He reached in his jacket, pulled out a stack of photos and tossed them on the desk. "Got these a few minutes ago. Looks like whoever has the portal is trying to use it."

Neither Kol nor Birgit moved, but Kelly, after a quick glance at all of them crossed to the desk and fanned out the photos. Her quiet gasp told Kol he wasn't going to like what she saw there.

"What is it?" she asked, a photo in her hand and her gaze on Magnus.

"Which one?" he replied. "So far we've heard tales of everything from Valkyries to Hraesvelg. This keeps up…" He pinned Kol and Birgit with a look. "There won't be a world, never mind a portal to fight over."

With a look of disgust, he shook his head and folded his arms back over his chest. "You two are officially out of this. You're banned from anything to do with *any* of the portals unless I tell you otherwise. Until then, just keep out of my sight." Without another word, he shimmered.

"I can't believe he left without…" Birgit shot Kelly a killing look.

"Without what?" Kol asked, arching a brow.

"Don't play cute. We all know this mess is her fault." Birgit fisted her hands at her sides. She wanted to change. It was obvious from the way she flexed her fingers and angled her neck.

Kol stepped between the two females, keeping his eyes on Birgit. "Obviously, he blames us, more than her. That tell you something?"

"That Magnus is as easily charmed as you?" Birgit cocked her hip and leaned forward, her body language screaming "let's fight".

Kol was tempted to comply. "I don't know what happened—how Kelly got through that portal, but I do know she didn't do it alone. You're every bit as responsible."

Birgit snorted, but dropped her gaze. "I didn't send her to Lyngvi. I'd never do that. And…" She looked back up, met his gaze. "I wouldn't have gone after her and you shouldn't have, either. You deserve to lose that portal."

"And you never deserved one to start with. I'll give that to Magnus. He was smart enough to realize your limitations."

Birgit sputtered, anger and frustration stealing her words.

Kol started to push her further, but stopped. He had nothing to gain from provoking her, and to be honest what she said was true. A guardian shouldn't choose anyone or anything over his charge. He had, plain and simple. He didn't deserve his portal.

And why? For what? For Kelly? He balled his fists. She had gone through the portal—of her own accord? Had she planned it all along? He'd had some slim hope that Birgit had somehow tricked her, forced her through the portal, but now standing in the room with both of them, he knew that couldn't be true. If Birgit had forced Kelly to do anything, much less visit Lyngvi, she wouldn't be standing behind him calmly staring the Garm Council representative down, would she?

No. He couldn't see that happening.

Which meant one thing—he'd given up everything he'd ever valued for a woman he couldn't trust.

Kelly couldn't believe what had happened, what she'd seen on those pictures—horses with eight legs, dragons, and sword-bearing Valkyries.

What was Aesa doing?

She glanced at Kol. He sat crouched near the floor, his head on his knees. He still hadn't asked her about Lyngvi—how she'd gotten there, why she'd gone there.

She ran her hands up her arms, her skin tingled just thinking about Kol. He'd saved her. She knew that. There was no way she would have made it off Lyngvi without him. And he'd done it at the cost of his bar and his portal. Maybe even his life as a guardian.

Why?

Tension clutched at her chest. She puffed air out her mouth forcing herself to relax, to breathe.

She had never been more confused in her life. She picked up the pictures Magnus had left, then dropped them. They fell onto the desktop, then slid over the side onto the ground next to Kol's feet. He still didn't stir, hadn't since Birgit left.

The waitress, Kelly still thought of her like that although she now knew better, had shimmered, too. Left Kol and Kelly alone in the room, which Kelly gathered was in some kind of official garm building. Birgit had at least taken the time to let them know how they wound up here.

After Kol followed Kelly through the portal, a group of rogue garm had shimmered into the bar. Birgit had dived for the power strip connected to the computer and managed to shut down the terminal, but that didn't shut down the portal. Made it harder to manage, yes, but it could still be run manually—just like Kol had operated the one on Lyngvi.

So Aesa and whoever was helping her were playing with the portal—letting all kinds of creatures into the human world, some of them harmless…Kelly stared at the open mouth of a fiery red dragon…some not.

Knowing she couldn't hold the bar on her own, Birgit had gone for help, but the rogue forces were too firmly entrenched for an easy defeat. The Garm Council had backed off to regroup. Birgit's part of that was monitoring movement through the portals. She couldn't stop travel to or from the Guardian's Keep, but she could still watch it. That's also how they had known when and where Kol and Kelly would appear. He'd been shooting for the bar, but had miscalculated some and wound up at a portal about a hundred miles away.

Something for which Kelly was very grateful. She needed to sort out how she felt about Kol, and she needed to talk with Aesa, but she didn't want to do the two things at the same time. In fact, she wasn't even ready for Kol to know about Aesa, or Terje, or any of it. Kelly had a very sick feeling she had been played majorly.

And not by the man whose life she had just had a gigantic hand in ruining.

Magnus had ordered Kol and Kelly to stay away from the bar, but Kol didn't exactly have a lot Magnus could take from him right now. So, when Kelly asked about getting her car, he hadn't hesitated, he'd grabbed her hand and shimmered them both to the Dumpster across the street from the Guardian's Keep.

He glanced at Kelly, then let his gaze wander past her to the still-wet streets glimmering in the midday sun. He inhaled, filling his lungs. Everything smelled fresher after a rain, even the streets in this decidedly unsavory part of town. At his feet, a few straggly pieces of grass poked their way through cracks in the pavement, green and full of life—cheery. One side of his mouth twisted upward at the irony.

A loud bang drew his attention from his immediate surroundings to the area across the street, outside the Guardian's Keep.

Five rogues burst out the front door, liquor bottles in their hands and Kol's shirts on their backs. Kol growled under his breath. He took a step forward.

Kelly placed a cool hand on his arm. "Can you take them?"

Ten more rogues immerged from the bar, stretching and strutting like victorious warriors.

Kol wanted to leap forward, swing his silver bat and smash the self-satisfied smirks back into their brains.

"Magnus said there were over a hundred. You can't fight that many. Can you?"

His gaze focused on his bar, his portal calling to him, all Kol could think about was how many he could take out, take down. How sweet the blows would feel.

"Kol. Think."

His eyes narrowed, Kol tried to ignore her words, but she wrapped another hand around his forearm. "Getting killed won't save your portal. Let's go."

He stared down at her. "Where? I have nowhere but here." He nodded to the bar, where even more rogues had appeared. A fight broke out, two of the men grappling with each other while the rest formed a circle around them. "Maybe I should join them."

Her eyes round, Kelly stared back. "You aren't serious."

Then she puffed out a breath. "With me. Come home with me. It's the least I can do."

Kol tilted his head to study her. Guilt. Was she admitting guilt? Offering an apology of some sort? He should hate her, he knew that. Should want to kill her as much as he wanted to kill each and every garm standing in front of his bar right now, but, the gods help him, he didn't.

He loved her. He'd known it all along and ignored it, but he couldn't anymore. He'd given up his portal to save her and couldn't deny he'd do it again in the flutter of an eyelid.

But he also knew he couldn't trust her.

"Why?" he asked.

She shrugged and dropped her gaze to analyze a puddle a few feet away.

She was so little, barely came to his shoulder. And while the Garm Council was occupied right now chasing down dragons and drunken marauding dwarves, they hadn't forgotten about Kelly. Kol knew them better than that—in fact, he suspected they had left her free so they could watch her, maybe even watch him with her.

At any moment they might decide to bring her in, question her or just eliminate her.

Kol had lost his portal. He wouldn't lose Kelly, too.

A howl sounded from the bar. One of the men fighting fell to the ground and didn't get up. The other raised his arms in victory, picked up a deserted bottle and took a swig.

Something squirmed in Kol's stomach. He would get his bar back, but for now he had to make sure he didn't lose something even more important.

He reached down and placed his hand over the one Kelly still had on his arm.

"Let's go."

* * *

Kelly flipped on the light as she walked into her house. Her gaze darting around her living room, she picked a sweat-shirt off the floor and shoved it behind a couch cushion. Kol ambled in behind her, the silver bat tucked under one arm. His blue eyes scanned the room with an intensity that made Kelly glance at her own home with suspicion.

"Do you sense something?" she asked, her hands slipping into her jeans' pocket where she had tucked the dowel earlier.

His eyes widened, as if surprised by the question. "No, why?"

A nervous laugh bubbled to the top of her throat. "No reason." She smoothed her hands down the front of her jeans. "Well, there are two bedrooms—mine, which you—" She paused, memories of the last time he was in her house flooding back to her.

His eyes glowed blue fire. "I've seen. Yes, I remember."

"And Kara's. You can have Kara's." She spun and started down the hall, the heels of her boots making a clicking noise against the wood floors as she went.

She could feel Kol following her. When they reached Kara's room, Kelly shoved open the door with the flat of her hand and stepped back. "Well, make yourself at home. I'm going to…"

Kol dropped the silver bar onto her sister's flowered carpet and reached his hands over his head, his back muscles flexing as he stretched. He moved left then right. The lines of his back called out for Kelly to step forward and trace them, taste them. She licked her lips, and forced her gaze to the floor.

Eyes downcast, she puffed out a breath and ordered her feet to step backward. "Shower." Then she spun on her heel and hurried down the hall to her room.

Once inside, she shoved the door shut behind her and pressed her back against the wood. Her heart hammered in her chest. What was she doing? What possessed her to invite Kol to stay at her house—with her?

Guilt and…a cloud of confusion overtook her, causing her knees to bend. She slid down the length of the door until she was curled in an upright fetal position, spine against the door, arms wrapped around her legs in front of her.

She sat there, much like Kol had sat at the office they'd just left—exhausted, drained, like every bit of energy she had, mental, physical, and magical had all just poured out of her.

The bed in Kara's room creaked.

Kol was staying at her house and she could hardly stand to be in the same room with him right now—too much guilt and confused feelings.

Kelly knocked her head back against the door with a groan. She had to get herself up and moving. Pull herself together and get to Aesa. Find out what was going on.

She pushed herself up and dragged herself to the small connected bath. Her hands shaking, she turned the water to warm, pulled off her clothes and stepped under the stream.

The pulsing water seemed to release something inside of her. Tears flowed down her face. Her palms braced against the shower wall, she hung her head and let them come.

At the sound of Kelly's heels retreating down the hallway, Kol turned. She was inside another room, the door closed behind her before he could follow.

He walked back into the room she'd assigned him, picked the silver bat up and dropped it on the bed. It bounced twice before settling into the puffy down comforter. He stared at it—all he had left, that and the clothes he wore.

But not for long. He would get his portal back. He couldn't tolerate even thinking anything else. His hand drifted to the reassuring coolness of the silver bar. He sat there, letting the stillness settle over him, willing his mind to form a plan, but suddenly he felt something. Sadness. Tears.

Kelly was somewhere crying.

Thinking of nothing but her, he shimmered and found himself standing in a steam-filled bathroom. Soft sobs sounded from behind the plastic curtain, piercing him like six-inch needles.

Without pause, he grabbed the plastic sheet and yanked it open. Kelly stood facing the wall, her hands pressed against the sea-green tile, water sluicing over her perfect naked body.

Kol inhaled, his nostrils flaring, then stepped into the shower.

Chapter 13

Hands cupped Kelly's breasts, a bare male chest pressed against her back. She didn't even jump, just knew it was Kol. She blinked her eyes, trying to stop the tears, but his hands slipped lower, around her waist, and pulled her against him.

"Shh," he murmured into her ear. "Everything's fine. It's going to be fine."

"But…" She couldn't reply. What could she say? He knew what she had done, what she had cost him.

"But nothing. Don't think. Just feel." His hands rose again, skimming up over her stomach, stopping at her breasts. His thumbs ran over their sides, his fingers playing with the hard buds of her nipples. His mouth lowered to the side of her neck and he lapped at the water that beaded there.

Even with the steaming water beating against her, Kelly shivered. Just feel? How could she not when being this close to Kol felt so right?

She started to turn to face him, but he stopped her with a whisper in her ear. "Not yet. Just feel. Enjoy." His right hand drifted down, over the curve of her hip, down the side of her thigh.

Her legs began to part, a silent plea for his hand to find her sex. His left hand moved lower too, skimming the outside of her other thigh. Still he didn't move to accept the offer of her parted legs. Instead he traced the line of muscle that ran from her neck to her shoulder with his mouth.

She groaned, blood rushing to her core, moisture gathering there, ready…waiting.

She pressed her buttocks back against the shower-soaked material of his jeans. Even through the thick denim, she could feel his hardness, that he was ready, too.

He rubbed against her, a soft groan escaping his lips as they traveled back up her shoulder to her ear.

"Do you feel it? Are you with me?" he murmured.

Kelly squirmed against him, willing the denim separating his hardness from her to disappear.

His hands returned to her breasts, and he squeezed her nipples.

Kelly panted. Her hands still pressed against the shower wall, she had yet to touch him. The need became overwhelming. She lowered one arm, reached back to feel his body, but he stopped her again.

"No, let me." He carefully replaced her hand to where it had been, then slowly squatted behind her, his lips following the flow of water down her spine. At her hips, he paused. His thumbs found the tiny indentations at the top of her buttocks as he kneaded the flesh.

Panting so loudly she could hardly hear the water beating against the tiles, she arched her back, shoving her buttocks back, begging him with her body.

His hands slipped back to the front of her thighs, and he rose until he was again standing behind her, his chest pressed to her back, his erection teasing her through his jeans.

He lowered his forehead to her shoulder, letting out small pants of his own, then slipped his hands farther forward and between her welcoming thighs.

His finger found the nub there. Her head flinging backward with sheer pleasure, Kelly's hands left the damp surface of the tile then, with a slap, reconnected.

Kol rubbed his finger over the most sensitive part of her so lightly, teasingly, she pushed against the shower wall. Her hips tilted upward to increase his access, encourage the slow torturous play he had begun.

His finger swirled around, the pressure increasing both on the nub hidden in her folds and deep inside her. His other hand moved back to her breast, his fingers finding her nipple and squeezing, rolling it between the pads of his thumb and index finger.

Kelly gasped and, ignoring his earlier demands, lowered her hand to reach for the zipper of his jeans. His erection moved free, the tip nudging her buttocks as she bucked against him.

He suckled her neck, his hands still busy teasing her breast and sex.

The denim, wet from the stream of water beating down on them, was too heavy for her to pull down completely. She moaned with frustration, her head tossing to one side and her hips tilting even higher.

As she spiraled upward, almost as if leaving her body, she felt the denim give and his erection become completely free, the silken tip bobbing against her bare buttocks.

"Now," she begged, forcing herself to arch her back,

pulling away from his hand, but tilting her buttocks toward the hard shaft behind her.

His hand still claiming her nub, he edged his erection between her thighs and began rocking back and forth against her, his slow deliberate motion almost making her scream for release.

Kelly's breast heavy in his palm, his mouth pressed against her neck, and the scent of her need calling to him, Kol urged her thighs closed. His erection hugged between them, he closed his eyes and moved his hips with a slow deliberate motion.

So close. His want was almost unbearable, but he wouldn't rush this, lose this moment.

"Kol," Kelly urged.

His name falling from her lips, brought a new intensity to his movements.

"Please," she panted. "Now." Her hips wiggled backward in an invitation he could no longer deny. Removing his hands from her body, he jerked his wet jeans down and off his body. Crouched between her open legs, he rose, running his hands up her calves, then thighs, until he cupped her buttocks. His knee holding her legs apart, he positioned his shaft between her cheeks, pulled her buttocks back against him and plunged his pulsing erection inside her.

Her fingers splayed over the wall in front of them, Kelly bent at the waist, increasing his access. His hands still on her hips he plunged in and out, each thrust harder than the last.

Her body started to quiver, a whimper escaping her lips, as the beginnings of her orgasm swept over her. He held his own release, enjoying the sensation of her body tightening around him, pulling him along until he could resist no more. Pulling her even more tightly against him, he threw back his head and joined her in the whorl of release.

The tremors of her orgasm still shaking her body, Kol spun Kelly in his arms and cradled her against his chest. Snuggled against him, his heart beat seemed louder, more real than her own. As he twisted off the stream of water, and pulled her from the shower, she didn't resist, just let her guard down and enjoyed feeling safe, cherished.

His eyes glimmered as he stared down at her face; Kelly's eyes widened in response. It was as if he could see into her soul, knew her better than anyone knew her, better than she knew herself.

His thumb grazed her lower lip. With his gaze still holding hers, he tugged a towel from the lone bar, and dropped to his knees in front of her. Slowly, he worked the cloth up her body, rubbing every square inch of her dry with almost worshipful care.

Pulling in a shaking breath, Kelly placed her hands on his shoulders and sucked the lip he'd just caressed into her mouth. Once he was finished and standing, he wrapped the towel around her and tucked the end in between her breasts.

His eyes were beautiful, blue, and clear, his gaze full of adoration. Kelly swallowed, hard, then pulled the towel from her body and knelt at his feet. The cloth bunched in her hands she ran the material up his calves, then thighs. Rubbing the muscles of his leg, marveling at how a man could be so perfect, so masculine and beautiful at the same time.

At his abdomen she stopped. His shaft stood rigid in front of her. Tentatively, she ran her fingers along its length.

Kol groaned in response, but made no move to touch her, to stop her.

Her tongue darted out of her mouth and tasted the pearl of salty fluid that appeared at his shaft's tip. She glanced up; Kol stared down at her, neither saying anything to interrupt this moment. She flicked out her tongue and circled the soft end of his erection again.

A low moan rumbled from Kol's chest. He placed his hands on opposite walls of the small bathroom, bracing himself.

Slowly, with the same deliberation and attention he had given her, she opened her lips and inched his length into her mouth. He moaned again. She found a rhythm, pulling him deeper into her throat, then letting him slip away. Her hands crept up his thighs, found the sensitive sacs beneath his shaft and stroked them.

Kol moaned again, this time with a new intensity. His head tilted back; his muscles clenched as if fighting against his release. Then he reached down, pulled her up his body. Her bare breast brushed over the planes of his chest, his hair there teasing her nipples.

With a murmured word she couldn't hear, he turned and placed her on the cabinet counter. Her legs opened to accept him; her hands gripped his shoulders, her fingers digging into the hard muscle. He stared at her for a second, the reverence in his eyes sending a shiver of anticipation dancing over her fevered skin.

He captured her lips with his. Pulled back to press a series of smaller ones around her mouth, along her jaw.

She edged her buttocks closer until she could feel his erection nipping against her folds.

His hands slipped behind her, tilting her. Then, with one last murmur against her ear, he thrust inside of her.

* * *

Kol pulled the comforter up and tucked it around Kelly. She was so tiny, so vulnerable looking in sleep. More vulnerable than she wanted to admit when awake.

She needed him—maybe as much as he needed her. He'd lost his portal, but gained Kelly. Was it enough? A fair exchange? A fist squeezed around his heart.

Even with Kelly by his side, could he face life without his portal? As a rogue?

He fisted his hand, hit the bed beside where he sat.

Kelly stirred, her fingers moving as if feeling for something…someone. He slipped his hand under hers. Her fingers curled around his, and with a tiny upward curve of her lips she drifted back to sleep.

Did he have her? Nothing was sure until she woke up, said the words herself. He knew they were bonded, but she could still reject him.

Then where would he be? With no portal and no Kelly, he knew he couldn't survive.

When Kelly awoke, she was alone. She pressed her face against her pillow. The scent of pine she now associated with Kol filled her nostrils. She burrowed deeper, letting the smell engulf her.

Kol. How could she ever have seen him as evil? No one could give up what he did for her, make love to her with such selfless adoration and be evil—could they?

One small doubt still niggled in the back of her mind.

How she wished Kara would call her back. She needed her sister's advice more than ever now.

She sat up, gathering the down comforter around herself. Trust her heart or her brain? That was the question.

Did she even need to talk to Kara? Her twin had always

been the one to follow her heart—while Kelly doggedly traveled the path dictated by logic.

She picked up the pillow and breathed in the piney scent again.

Maybe it was time she let her sister's example be her lead.

Kelly stood outside the Guardian's Keep. At seven in the morning, the place seemed quiet. Her hand slipped into her coat pocket. Assured the wooden dowel was back where she needed it, she pulled open the door and stepped inside.

What she saw brought her to a grinding halt.

Heather, her assistant, stood behind the bar, ferverently pecking away at the computer. She looked up, saw Kelly and staggered backward.

At the same instant the space around Kelly shimmered and five burly men formed a semicircle around her, each with a silver bar like the one Kol carried gripped in his hand.

Kelly's eyes darted from the men to Heather.

Her assistant took a cautious step back toward the computer and glanced at the men. "It's fine. You can go."

The men didn't move.

"I said go." Heather's voice took on an impatient edge.

The man directly in front of Kelly cast a sideways look at Heather, who widened her eyes at him in some secret dialogue. Then, shaking his head, he signaled the others and all five men shimmered away.

"Kelly. You're safe." A tremulous smile curved Heather's lips.

Her brows lowered, Kelly glanced around. The rest of the bar appeared empty.

"Yes." She wrapped her fingers around the dowel and strolled toward the bar. "Some welcome. Who were they?"

Heather shrugged. "Friends of Aesa."

Kelly waited for her assistant to explain more, but the other woman just licked her lips and stared back. Deciding to pursue another issue, Kelly asked, "What are you doing here?" She pulled out a stool and sat down. Placing her left hand casually on the bar, her right remained in her coat pocket.

"Trying to find you, of course. When you didn't check in. I came by here and found out what had happened. Aesa was just as worried as I was. We've been trying everything to find you so we could bring you back."

Kelly's fingers tapped against the bar top. "Well, I'm back."

"Yes." Heather's lips angled into a smile, but her eyes remained wary.

"So, what exactly been's happening-here? I've heard rumors."

"Rumors?" Heather took another step backward until her ponytail was brushing the mirrored wall behind her.

"Yeah, rumors. Kind of disturbing ones."

Heather shot a sidelong look to the doorway that doubled as the portal. "Disturbing how?"

"I heard—"

"Kelly. You're back. This is great." Aesa appeared in the doorway that led to the rooms upstairs and hurried to where Kelly sat. Without waiting for a response, she pulled Kelly into a hug.

For the first time, Kelly noticed the distinct smell of the outdoors coming from the other woman—the smell of a garm.

"How did you do it? Did you figure out how to work the portal?" Aesa lowered herself onto the stool next to Kelly.

Heather interrupted. "I was telling Kelly, how we've been working to bring her back."

With a quick glance at Kelly's assistant, Aesa nodded. "That's right. We had about given up hope. Heather's tried, as have…others, but we just can't operate the portal reliably without the computer." She frowned. "There's a password." Her lips pursed, then she glanced at Kelly. "But you got through. How'd you do it?"

"Does it matter now? I'm here." Kelly kept her gaze steady, unconcerned.

"Of course, but there's still Lyngvi. I still need to get there." Aesa leaned forward and placed her hands on Kelly's legs.

"To save Terje you mean?" Kelly replied.

Aesa blinked. "Yes, Terje. Everything is for Terje."

Kelly stared down at the other woman's pale hands resting on Kelly's thighs. "Terje. How long did you say he's been gone?"

Aesa pulled back, removing her hands. "Too long. Why do you ask?"

"Just wondering if maybe he could have been taken somewhere besides Lyngvi. How long could they keep him there? Where would they keep him? There's really nothing there."

"You were there? You made it to Lyngvi?" Excitement sent Aesa to her feet. This time she grabbed Kelly's arm—the one partially hidden inside her coat pocket, the one connected to the hand clasping the dowel. "Did you see him? Was he okay?"

"Terje, you mean?" Kelly paused to study her client for a second.

Aesa hesitated, too, then nodded. "Of course, who else?"

"I wasn't there long," Kelly replied.

"But you made it there and back. It can be done." Aesa spun, a smile lighting her face. "I knew it. I just knew it."

Before Kelly could respond, Aesa twirled again. "And you can show us how." This time her eyes glimmered with an emotion Kelly couldn't peg—desperation?

Moving to stand, Kelly replied, "No, I can't. The first time I kind of…fell through. The second Kol brought me." The first part was a lie, of course, but Kelly needed time to sort out exactly what was happening, to plan.

Aesa frowned. "Fell through? How—"

"I don't really know. One minute I was here, the next I was on Lyngvi."

"Interesting." Heather dropped ice into a glass and filled it with soda.

"I was very lucky Kol came through to save me."

"Very," Heather agreed.

"So, do you think he trusts you?" Aesa asked.

Kelly licked her lips, her thoughts on Kol's eyes as he wrapped the towel around her nude body. "Yes, I think he does."

God knew why.

Seconds after the bar's door closed behind Kelly, Heather plunked down her glass. "I think she's on to us."

"What do you mean?" Aesa was still atremble over the news Kelly had made it to Lyngvi and back.

"She knows." Heather stared at the other woman. *Why had she trusted her?* She was obviously guided way too much by her emotions—how she wanted things to be.

"Knows what? We're not doing anything wrong." Aesa perched herself back on the bar stool, her eyes dreamy.

"Terje? The son who Kelly thinks is a cute little eight-year-old snuggling his stuffed bunny? Or how about the last five—" she glanced at the portal, a shiver shaking her "—things we let through that portal?"

Aesa frowned.

"Or your real goal—freeing Fenrir, the most guarded prisoner in the nine worlds?"

"Unfairly imprisoned," Aesa snapped out.

Seeing the female garm was about to go off on another fight-for-what's-right tandem, Heather held up a hand. "My point is, she finds out about any of those things and she's going to want blood. *Our* blood."

"I'm not worried. We just need her to open the portal for us. You can keep her on our side that long."

"Me?" Heather began to shake her head. The entire situation was beginning to smell, and not like victory. She'd been having doubts for a while, and now looked like an opportune time to pack up her ambitions and head to safer pastures.

"Yes, you." Aesa's upper lip curled, revealing petite white teeth. "That's your job—don't forget it."

Heather edged a glance to the door. She was tired. Tired of lying, tired of wanting something more, and tired of feeling like the outsider. She turned back, ready to tell Aesa she was done, but the dainty Aesa was gone. In her place, front feet on the bar, stood a silver-gray wolf.

With a snarl, the animal lunged, revealing teeth that were anything but petite.

Heather hopped backward, but the wall kept her from going too far. The wolf hit her full force in the chest, sending her to the ground.

Jaws snapping, the wolf stood on her, stared down at her.

Aesa's voice spoke in Heather's head. "We all have a part to play. You play yours, or I may be forced to forget mine." Aesa lowered her head and ran her cold nose along Heather's throat, pausing where Heather's pulse hammered through an artery. She inhaled loudly, then raising her head, looked Heather in the eye. "Understood?"

Heather nodded. Nothing had ever been more clear in her life.

Chapter 14

Kol stood, hidden in the shadows cast by the early morning sun as it peeked over the top of the Guardian's Keep.

Kelly had spent a half hour or so in the bar.

Doing what?

He hadn't meant to spy on her, but this morning when he awoke, he'd needed time alone and inevitably he'd found his way back to the bar. The place seemed quiet, but he could sense the rogues were nearby. Still, he'd considered shimmering into the bar and fighting till all of the challengers or he were dead. But then, he'd seen Kelly walk boldly through the front door, and he'd waited. Unsure.

Now she was gone and he still hesitated. He wanted his portal back, that was true enough, but he also wanted to know exactly what was going on with Kelly. He wanted to know how involved she was in this mess.

So, instead of claiming what was his, he was waiting to see if the woman he loved would betray him—again.

Kelly stepped into her office and flipped on the light. The place practically echoed with abandonment. It was obvious no one had been there since she'd made her trip to Lyngvi.

She wandered around, running her fingers over Heather's dusty desktop, cataloging what she saw. The answering machine was on and blinked incessantly with unheard messages. Mail was overflowing from the mailbox and a mandrake plant she'd been trying to grow from seeds was wilted and sad looking.

Plainly, Heather had not entered the office once—or if she had, she'd done nothing involved with her job.

Kelly picked up the plant and carried it into the bathroom for an overdue drink.

Heather. What was she up to? Was it possible she had told the truth? Could she just have been helping Aesa find Kelly?

Kelly sincerely doubted it.

Back in the main office, Kelly hit the button on the answering machine and fell into a chair.

The first message was her sister returning Kelly's call. She would try again later. Kelly groaned.

Next were a few crank calls, something Kelly's office seemed to get frequently.

Then the bed-and-breakfast who had hired her to investigate the giant wolves driving away their business. They thanked her for her help, said they hadn't seen a wolf in days, for her to please send them a bill, and if she had a chance they'd appreciate a call. They were just curious where the wolves had come from and more importantly where they'd gone.

This time Kelly slapped her hand against her forehead. The rogues. Aesa. No wonder Heather had discouraged her from going to visit the bed-and-breakfast. She'd known exactly what Kelly would find there.

But why? Why would her assistant be helping Aesa and the rogues?

The machine beeped again. This time the voice on the other end was rough and panicked. The man's garage had just been knocked down by a rampaging giant. He'd called the authorities, but been accused of somehow plowing down the structure himself. Did Kelly believe him?

Unfortunately, she did.

The remaining calls were all from terrified citizens looking for someone to reassure them they weren't losing their minds as much as anything else. Could Kelly call them back?

She leaned forward and rested her head on arms. She had made quite the mess, and she had no idea where to even start to clean it up.

The phone rang. She heaved out a breath, then picked up the receiver.

Silver bat under his arm, Kol strode down the artfully casual stone path that bisected the city's botanical garden. The gardens were famous for their statuary and roses. Too bad today the sweet perfume of the flowers was completely drowned out by the even sweeter stench of death.

Draugrs—the corporeal undead. Zombies with magic. A nightmare.

Beside him a ribbon of smoke rose, twisting from the ground, then quickly expanded and gained in solidity until the blue-white body of a draugr towered overhead. The draugr leaned down and stretched out toward Kol, the fingers on its meaty hand curling as if planning to pluck Kol up.

Kol shimmered, reappearing just outside of the creature's reach. The draugr's mouth opened, releasing a tidal wave of stench, then screamed. The bushes around Kol shook as the last few terrified animals that called the gardens home dashed for the safety of the streets beyond the iron gates.

"Not too pretty is he?" Birgit shimmered into solidity at Kol's elbow.

"What are you doing here?" Kol asked, his gaze never leaving the draugr.

"Same as you—cleaning up after your girlfriend."

Kol growled, but didn't argue. There was no denying Kelly had a major hand in everything that had happened.

"Can't kill him, you know. Not unless you went and turned into a certifiable hero since I last checked."

The draugr took a stumbling step forward, crushing an iron-and-marble gazebo to rubble.

Kol cursed under his breath. Being dead already made draugr nearly impossible to destroy. Only a select few carried the bloodlines that made it possible. Kol was not one of them.

"You have one handy?" he asked.

The draugr picked up a particularly lifelike rendition of the city's founder and popped it into its mouth. With a roar of disgust the creature promptly spewed it back out, showering the garden with bits of statuary shrapnel. Before he could shimmer or duck, a piece struck Kol in the shoulder, right where he'd been wounded the day before by the feil.

The entire right side of his body burning with pain, Kol switched his bat to his left hand. "So, no hero. What else?"

Birgit darted a look at his wound, but at Kol's warning

gaze said nothing. Instead, she waved her hand to the garden past the staggering monster.

As Kol watched, ten more garm shimmered into the garden, forming a circle around the draugr.

"We take it back to a portal. That's what. It's the best we can do."

"Where?"

Birgit named a portal located in a sparsely inhabited section of the human world. "You know it?" she asked.

Ignoring his throbbing shoulder, Kol nodded.

Birgit raised her hand with three fingers held up. Slowly, she curled each back into her fist. When the last had disappeared, all twelve garm shimmered as one, reforming within arm's reach of the draugr. Birgit nodded, and the twelve each placed one hand on the draugr. Before the creature could react, they shimmered again—this time taking the undead monster with them.

One drunken giant, three angry dwarves, and a herd of stampeding stags later, Kelly collapsed on the steps of the city library. She'd answered every message on her answering machine, even the cranks—just in case. Right now Kelly didn't think she could afford to take anything for granted.

She'd told the bed-and-breakfast owners she couldn't take payment for something she hadn't done, then dialed her sister only to get voice mail again. But the other callers had all been huddled inside their homes and more than willing to tell their tales.

Kelly had grabbed her dowel, staff, and a backpack filled with every magical tool she could fit inside and headed out for clean-up duty.

She had never been more exhausted in her life and still one more creature to take care of today. According to a frightened librarian something large, smelly and foulmouthed had taken up residence in the back stacks. She had a feeling this time neither the promise of a few kegs of beer nor animal control were going to be any help to her.

The library was empty. A Closed Till Further Notice sign dangled from the front door. After retrieving the key from under the stone gargoyle where the librarian had told Kelly she'd find it, Kelly opened the door and crept inside.

The place was perfectly still—crypt still.

Her staff gripped in both hands in front of her, she moved quietly past the check-out desk and headed toward the darkest part of the library, the back stacks.

Something glimmered in the corner of her eye. Not waiting to see what the latest creature to escape the portal might be, she spun, her staff held in front of her like a bat, power sizzling from its tip like a souped up sparkler.

The blue glow of Kol's eyes registered seconds before he dove and somersaulted over the dancing stream of energy.

Kelly dropped the staff and ran to his side. He lay still, his eyes closed. She pressed her hand to his chest and felt the reassuring up and down movement, but then she felt something else, something warm and sticky. She jerked her hand up and stared in horror at the red stain smeared across her palm.

"Looking for me?" he asked, his voice tired.

Kelly shifted her gaze to his face. "You're okay."

"Disappointed?" he replied, his tone noncommittal making it impossible for Kelly to tell whether he was serious.

"Of course not." She balled her hand closed over the blood and stood up.

"Really?" He moved to sit, one arm balanced on his knee.

"Really." She frowned. In fact her heart had just started to pump again after the fright of seeing him laying on the ground, blood oozing from an obviously fresh wound. Her tension made her snap, "What are you doing here?"

"Hunting." He grimaced. "Not something that's natural to garm, but unfortunately it's become necessary."

Kelly's brows dropped lower. *Because of her.* She opened her hand and stared down at his blood. How much more literal of a sign could she get that she'd screwed up?

He nodded to her hand. "You should clean that off."

She pressed her palm against the side of her leg, hiding it. "No big deal."

"Yes, it is."

Kelly stared at him. Despite last night, he hated her. Who could blame him? And just when she was beginning to realize—she spun turning her back to him so he couldn't read the expression on her face, then squatted down to pull out a package of wipes she'd seen shoved into the bottom of her pack.

"I'm sorry. I didn't know…" she whispered. She couldn't bare to say it any louder.

"For what?" he asked.

She glanced over her shoulder at him. "For—"

A roar drowned out the rest of her words and energy rippled through the library.

Kelly leaped to her feet, the wet wipe balled in her fist. "What was that?"

"That is why you need to get the blood off your hand." Kol stood. "Holi, the roarer. He has a fondness for blood."

Kelly glanced at the still-oozing wound on Kol's shoulder.

"Garm." A deep voice bellowed.

Kol picked up his ever-present silver bat, and before Kelly could object, shimmered.

Back in the stacks, something laughed, a low deadly

rumble like the earth breaking open. After scooping up her staff, Kelly took off at a run toward the noise and Kol.

"Long time no meet, Guardian. Or should I say *meat?*" A huge gnarled creature made of what appeared to be rocks and lumps of earth tapped fingers as thick as one of Kelly's thighs onto the floor. Then as if just getting his joke, he threw back his head and laughed.

"You don't belong here, Holi," Kol stated, his silver bat hanging casually at his side.

"No? Many of my kind have come here. Why not me?" The creature reached behind him and began pulling what Kelly recognized as a long bony tail through his fingers. With a whack he let his tail drop.

Troll. Kelly shivered. She'd met trolls, but none as inhuman appearing or large as this one.

"I need my kind around me," Holi continued. "Take me to them and I'll leave you alone."

"They live in the human world for a reason, Holi," Kol replied.

"Meaning they won't welcome me?" A half-moon of an eyebrow arched. "Surely they'll be thrilled to see their king."

"You're not their king." Kol circled to the left, away from where Kelly stood.

"I am," the creature roared, his tail snapping so hard against the floor boards broke where it hit.

"One of thousands. They owe you nothing and you'll gain nothing by being here. I can call other garm. Shimmer you to a portal. You can be back in your cave before first light."

"Light? What time be it here, garm?" The troll lumbered to a squat, his head even with the top of the shelves.

"Noon," Kol replied.

"That true?" Holi turned, his backing hitting a bookcase and knocking it to the ground, directly toward Kelly.

She raised her staff to erect a shield, but before she could, Kol shimmered, wrapped his arm around her waist and shimmered again.

"Where you go, garm?" Holi knocked down another book shelf, this time with his fist. Before Kol could move them again, Kelly stepped away from him and lifted her staff. Energy shot out the end, colliding with the avalanche of books tumbling toward them. As books slid off the umbrella of power, Holi leaned forward.

"There you be. What's that you have with you?" He reached out a finger as if to tap Kelly on the head. She held the staff up again and let a warning zip of energy shoot from its end.

Holi jerked back his hand and frowned down at her. "It bites. I don't like things that bite." He folded his fingers toward his palm and, with a roar, sent his fist crashing down toward them.

Kelly glanced at Kol, but he was too far away to reach her and shimmer before the troll's fist smashed them both. Behind him she saw something else though, something that if the lore she'd learned of trolls was true should save them both.

Mumbling a prayer, she pointed her staff at Kol and willed as much velocity through the magical tool as she thought they could survive. The force knocked him ten feet to the troll's left, the recoil shooting her an equal distance the opposite direction.

Holi's fist blasted through the floor between them.

Heaving, Kelly rolled to her knees to follow through with the remaining part of her plan. Twenty feet away, Kol stood, too, his eyes snapping with anger. She ignored him and pointed her staff at the library's windows. Windows covered with thick light-blocking velvet curtains.

Power again coursed from her staff, the window erupted, millions of glass splinters shooting out into the parking lot. Leaning heavily on the staff, Kelly waited. Daylight. A troll's nemesis.

But no light broke through the now gaping windows. Instead just the artificial yellow glow of the library's outside security lamps.

"You lie, Guardian." Holi bellowed. Then with a gravelly chortle, he shoved his way through the window, taking a large chunk of wall with him, and disappeared.

Kelly ran to the window and looked out. "What happened?"

His hand pressed to his shoulder, Kol followed. "He left."

"But…?" She stared at the hole in the library wall, the darkness outside. "I thought it was light. It was light when I came in."

Kol didn't reply.

She gripped the staff until her fingers turned white. "Where will he go? I'll follow him."

Kol placed a hand on her arm. "No. Not tonight. A troll Holi's age and size is too powerful at night." He shrugged, a stiff movement that made the material around his wound gape, revealing the ragged wound more clearly. "Maybe he'll decide to take my advice and go home."

Kelly bit the inside of her cheek, unable to even look at Kol.

He sighed, a tired but resolved huff of air. "We can't do anything more tonight. We might as well go…"

She glanced at him then, knowing he wanted to say home, but that she'd taken that away from him along with his portal. Tears she wouldn't let fall crept to the inside corners of her eyes.

He reached up and ran his knuckle under her lashes. "No tears. Anything but tears." Then held out his hand, palm up.

She hesitated, wanting to place her hand in his, but somehow feeling she shouldn't...couldn't.

"Kelly," he whispered, then tipped her chin up so her eyes met his.

Her eyes caught by the intensity of his blue gaze, she slipped her hand into his.

Chapter 15

Back at her house, Kol moved to pull Kelly toward him, but she pressed a hand against his chest. It was time to come clean, to tell him everything that had happened and give him the chance to do the same. She trusted him now. He'd proved himself to her too many times not to, but she'd still like to hear his version of what had happened with the portal…and between them.

He met her gaze and understanding seemed to pass between them. With a nod, he led her to the sofa.

Knowing she couldn't say what she had to say with his body so close, calling out to hers, she edged away and sat with her back stiff against a cushion. "I blamed you for my friend Linda's death." At the other end of the couch, Kol didn't move, but she felt the need to explain anyway. "She's the witch that I was looking for when I came to your bar that first time. The one I wanted to follow through the portal. The one that wound up dumped back in this world dead." She pressed her palms down against the cushion beneath her, trying to keep control of her emotions.

Her voice cracked, but she kept going. "I'm not saying it was fair to blame you, but I guess it helped keep me from blaming *myself* quite as much."

This time she risked a glance at Kol. He sat perfectly still, only his eyes moving as he seemed to take in every aspect of her posture.

She tucked a strand of hair behind her ear, and glanced away, staring instead at a ring some damp glass had left on the coffee table. She corrected the thought—a ring caused by a glass she had left. Another thing that needed cleaning up because of her.

She wrapped her arms around herself and continued, "A few weeks ago I got a call from a bed-and-breakfast up north. Wolves—giant wolves—had moved into the area and were scaring off their customers."

She felt Kol shift on his end of the couch. Her gaze still fixed on the scarred coffee table, she went on. "I used that as an excuse to come after you. Wanted to blame you for everything, and…" She frowned. "Heather, my assistant, she seemed to think I was right. She encouraged me to focus on you and the bar." The last came out almost a mumble, Kelly working out what had happened as she spoke.

"Then the night you tossed me out." Kelly flushed and fiddled with her hair. "When I was standing outside the bar, watching, that's when I met Aesa." The name fell from her lips with leaden finality. She'd believed everything the woman said to her, not because there was any solid reason to believe her, but instead because it kept Kelly focused on Kol as being guilty. If he was guilty of taking the boy, then he could be guilty of Linda's death. She shook her head at her own stupidity, spinelessness.

"Kelly," Kol leaned forward, his hand stretched out toward her. She stared at the strong palm and long fingers that she knew would offer comfort, then shook her head. Not yet. She didn't deserve his understanding yet.

"She told me her son had been kidnapped, wanted me to find him."

"Terje," Kol murmured.

Kelly glanced at him, surprised. "That's right. Is he real?" She didn't even know that now. Did the boy even exist? Had he ever existed?

Kol twisted his palms up, in a gesture of not knowing. "I'd never heard the name until you said it to me." A flicker of emotion passed behind his eyes. "I thought he was someone you'd met in Jormun's world, a lover."

Kelly shook her head. "So, he didn't go through the Guardian Keep's portal?"

Something close to embarrassment colored Kol's face. "No, no children have ever been taken through the Guardian's Keep." He glanced down at his hand, which he'd returned to his lap, then back up. "I guess that's what you were talking about when you asked about a child that day." He shook his head. "I was being a smart-ass, taunting you."

Kelly shrugged. She'd come flying at him with accusations, how could she blame him for reacting the same way she would have? She turned back to the coffee table. "She told me his father was…Fenrir, that she thought the boy had been taken to Lyngvi."

This time Kol's movement was unmistakable. His eyes blazing, he leaned forward. "You went to Lyngvi on purpose?"

She nodded.

"How?" he asked, his body rigid.

She could feel his anger washing over her, like a red wave. Placing her hands on her thighs she turned to face him. "When you were outside, Birgit pulled up the program that operated the portal, then she left, too. It wasn't that hard to get through to Lyngvi."

"Not that hard?" He snorted. "She did it on purpose. She set you up. You could have been killed." His eyes narrowed.

Birgit. He blamed Birgit. Kelly stared at him, her mouth falling open in disbelief. "She didn't make me go there."

His gaze distant, he didn't respond. "Kol." Kelly scooted across the couch and grabbed his hand. "It isn't Birgit's fault. It's mine."

Kol could barely hear Kelly talking, hardly feel the smooth warmth of her hand, his mind was so focused on Birgit—what she had done. In her greed to raise her position with the Council, she'd purposely endangered his portal and Kelly. Because of her, he'd lost one and almost the other.

"Kol," Kelly's voice was urgent. She ran her hand over his cheek, turned his face to hers. "Did you hear me? It's me you should be angry with, not Birgit."

Kelly's eyes flashed violet, her emotions so intense, power was building inside her.

He shook his head. "I understand. You wanted through the portal to go somewhere you never should have been allowed to go. It was my responsibility, or in my absence, Birgit's, to make sure that didn't happen. Not only did she not stop you, she opened the gates."

Kelly blinked. "True, but…"

He wrapped her hand in his. "You can't make me hate you. It isn't possible."

"Because of me you lost your portal."

He laughed. "No, because of *me* I lost my portal. You say Birgit didn't make you go to Lyngvi? Well, no one made me follow you there. I could have stayed where I was, shut the portal behind you and never looked back. I didn't."

Kelly licked her lips, shifted her gaze as though the truth was too much.

Kol wouldn't let her hide from it, not now. Not when she was all he had left. He grabbed her chin and pulled her face back to his. "And you know what else? I don't regret it, not for a heart beat."

Kelly inhaled a tiny "ah" of a sound. With an intensity born of knowing she was all he had left, Kol leaned forward and pressed his lips to hers.

Only a tiny peep of objection made it past Kelly's lips when Kol scooped her up and carried her to her bedroom. She'd told him everything, and he didn't care. Said he didn't regret losing everything to save her.

How could that be?

Kol paused, one knee on Kelly's bed, his gaze locked on her. She could feel his heart beat: slow, steady, reassuring—telling her everything would be okay.

She wanted to believe him—just for a while.

With a sigh, she wrapped her arms around his neck and pulled his mouth to hers. He leaned lower, her body sinking into the feather comforter, Kol's weight settling down on top of her.

"I…I'm sorry," she whispered.

He brushed hair away from her face and pressed a small kiss at the corner of her mouth. "Me, too."

She turned her head in surprise. "For what?"

"Your friend, taunting you about the boy. Everything you've gone through."

"But that's…" She stopped, thought for a second. She needed to talk about this, to hear his explanation, otherwise it would never be behind them. "I blamed you for letting someone take her through the portal. Why did you?"

He stared across the room, his gaze somewhere else. "It's what guardians do. We aren't allowed to make individual judgments as to who can or can't go through the portals. Those decisions are made by others—gods, the owner of the portal in the other worlds. All we do is enforce the rules."

He glanced down at her, regret visible in the tiny lines around his eyes. "I can try to make it harder, try to talk people out of doing what I think is a mistake, but I can't just stop them. It's not part of the deal."

"Why not? Why can't you just refuse to operate the doorway?" Kelly wasn't angry, wasn't trying to provoke him. She just really wanted to know, to understand.

A furrow appeared between his brows. "How do I know my judgment is the right one? The one time I believed someone's story and bent the rules, might be the time—"

"You unleashed all the inhabitants of hell?" She moved her head back and forth on the pillow. *Kind of like she'd just done.*

He smiled. "It isn't *that* bad. It will sort itself out." He captured her lips, then pulled back to stare down at her again.

"Promise?" she asked.

"Promise." Then he leaned down again and this time she locked her arms around him and kept him there—wishing there was a way to keep him with her right there, safe from everything raging its way through their world, things she knew they'd have to deal with way too soon.

* * *

Kol could feel the change in Kelly—acceptance. She'd finally accepted him, them. Did she love him? She hadn't said it, but neither had he, and he had no doubt of his feelings.

He pressed kisses down the side of her face to her ear, blew a tiny puff of air there and then along the line of her neck. Her fingers stroked his sides, her hands finding where his shirt was tucked into his jeans and tugging the material free. Cool fingers brushed against his bare skin. He shivered with pleasure, not cold.

He wanted to be inside of her so badly his body ached, but this time was special. He wanted the sex to be special, too.

He let her pull his shirt higher; then he lifted up to finish yanking it off his body. Her eyes were huge and violet. Her body brimming with power and passion.

He ran his hand down her throat to the top button of her shirt. As she watched, he slipped the first free, then his fingers brushing the skin over her heart, the second and on down until her shirt fell open, revealing a lacy pink bra.

He smiled. Leave it to Kelly to hide her softness in this way.

He placed a finger inside the cup, plumping her breast until it spilled out of the top of the tiny piece of lace-covered silk.

Kelly inhaled, and he leaned down, caught her nipple in his mouth and sucked, swirling his tongue around its peak. Her hands gripped his shoulders, and her body arched. He slipped his own hands behind her, releasing her bra so her breasts fell free.

His mouth still on one breast, he cupped the other with his hand, squeezing her soft flesh, then finding her nipple and flicking his thumb over the hardened peak.

Her hands moved lower, roaming over his back, down

to his buttocks. She followed his example, squeezing until he thought he would explode with the need to escape the confines of his jeans. He flipped to his side, giving her access to the front. She slid down his zipper and his erection sprang forward.

Her hand wrapped around him and he groaned from the sheer intense pleasure. Her thumb mimicked the actions of his, swirling over the end of his penis, spreading the moisture beading from its tip.

Inhaling sharply, he willed his body to slow down, relax, extend the pleasure. Beside him Kelly moaned, her hips squirming in invitation. Unable to resist, his hand drifted to the top of her jeans.

Her hand still wrapped around him, threatening to send him over the edge, he lowered his forehead to her breast, then unwrapped her fingers. Able to think, he pressed a kiss to her forehead and unsnapped her jeans. His eyes taking in every beautiful tempting bit of her, he peeled the denim down her thighs inch by delectable inch.

Beneath the denim she wore only a teeny strip of pink lace. Unable to resist, he grabbed the material in his teeth and snapped it from her body. The lace slipped down to reveal the auburn triangle of curls beneath.

The elastic strip that made up the side of Kelly's panties snapped against her hip, but she barely noticed the sting. Her body thrummed with the need to feel Kol, his touch, his kisses, his hardness inside her. She wiggled her hips. Kol's fingers danced over the curls at the apex of her thighs, brushing against them, teasing.

She raised her hips, begging his fingers to explore more.

She ran her hand down his side, reveling in the valleys and planes of his body.

His mouth back on hers, his fingers parted the hair covering her core. He stroked along her folds, his thumb finding the nub and his finger slipping inside her. In and out, just a taste of what was to come.

Her hands tightened on him, her hips bucking. She moaned and felt his penis pressing against her thigh. She turned her head and nipped at his shoulder. He tasted of salt. She swirled her tongue over his skin.

His fingers still playing with her, he pressed his lips to her neck and suckled. Wanting to scream her need, Kelly reached out and stroked his penis, felt the liquid pearling on its tip, felt it quiver in her grasp.

Done with patience, she turned to her side and guided his erection to where she needed it most.

With a low laugh, Kol slipped onto his back, bringing Kelly on top of him as he did. His hands cupping her butt, her fingers still wrapped around his erection, he held her there poised, his gaze dark with passion roaming her body. She wiggled again, rubbed the tip of his penis against the edge of her folds—close, so close.

He lowered her an inch. Back and forth, she moved against his erection, the moisture beading at the tip of his penis mixing with her own. Another inch. He was hers now. She gloried in the feeling, held his gaze with hers, then plunged down, taking his full length inside her in one swift, almost orgasmic move.

Panting, she waited for her body to adjust, to calm enough she could continue. Kol's eyes closed; his hands moved from her buttocks to her breasts, squeezing and caressing until she knew she couldn't wait any longer.

Pulling in a breath, she raised up to move against him over and over until her body tightened around him and his body shook between her thighs. Then with one final plunge, when she could feel his orgasm taking over, she let go, and as the last waves of pleasure rode over her, she collapsed on top of him. Only her lips left with the energy to move, she pressed a kiss to his chest.

Heather sorted through the things in her desk, dumping into a box the few things she valued…a book of spells she'd bought online, the wooden dowel Kelly had made for her the second week she worked here, and finally a picture of her and Kelly standing in front of the one case they'd solved together—before Aesa approached Heather and her life had gone downhill.

She stared at the picture. A mom-and-pop grocery store had had a little produce problem. As in everything from apples to zucchini seemed to rot to mush right before their eyes. Kelly had suspected some kind of curse, maybe for revenge, but it had been Heather's suggestion they ask around a bit, question other grocers. Turned out the problem wasn't at the store at all—but at the delivery company. They'd been trying to make a few extra bucks by employing a simple charm that made produce look weeks fresher than it really was. Only problem was, the charm wore off within a day of delivery.

The success made Heather cocky and when Aesa approached her to help convince Kelly to take on Kol, she'd figured, why not? Kelly already had issues with Kol, and the thought of power to rival Kelly's was beyond tempting.

She hadn't bargained on being part of setting a veritable battalion of monsters loose on the city. Or on how much guilt she would feel for deceiving Kelly.

She picked the picture back up then threw it down into the box.

She'd traded her job with Kelly, a position that while

not exactly glamorous could have eventually really led to something, for a shot at quick and extreme power.

Like all get-rich-quick schemes, it had been too good to be true. Now she was stuck serving a fanatical garm, who at any wrong move might very likely choose to rip out her throat.

Heather shivered. No way. Enough was enough. She wasn't going to be responsible for anything else that escaped through that portal, and she wasn't lying to Kelly anymore, either. She might have been a little power-struck for a while, but she was over it. Time to pack up and move on.

She flipped off the lamp on her desk and hefted the box onto her hip. The sound of the front door's knob rattling halted her next step.

Oh, please, let it be a salesman of some sort. The edge of the box digging into her hip, she watched the door slowly glide open.

One classic low-heeled pump appeared. The box slid out from under Heather's arm to land with a thump back on the desk.

"Heather? Are you going somewhere?" Aesa, back in loving-mother mode, carefully wiped her shoes on the mat inside the door.

Heather smiled, a tight move that made her cheeks ache. "Just picking up a few things."

"Now? I thought you were going to find Kelly. We need her." Aesa brushed some tiny bit of lint off her sleeve, then smiled at Heather.

She appeared so normal, innocent even, but Heather had seen the look in her eyes when she was a wolf—hungry, desperate, like a cornered animal. It was still there now, hidden, but visible. A glitter that said she wouldn't let anyone or anything stop her from getting to Lyngvi—not now that she was so close.

"I just thought I'd come by here first. In case Kelly was working. It's where she would expect to meet me, if…"

"If everything were normal?" Aesa wandered to the door to Kelly's office. "But it isn't, is it? As you said, she's on to us. Now we just need to secure her help—one way or another." She spun, pinning Heather with her glittering gaze.

"I…I know. I'll go to her house next."

"Good. I'll meet you back at the bar." With a tilt of her head, Aesa shimmered.

Heather exhaled all the air she'd been holding, and pressed both palms down on the desk to keep from falling on top of it.

Aesa was having her watched. It was the only explanation. Damn garm. As noisy and intrusive as they were at the cavern, they could be still and silent as the night. If a team were watching her, she'd never know it.

They could shimmer in behind her and tear out her throat before she had a chance to even be alarmed.

She stared down at the photo, now upside down in the box. If she wanted to make it out of this agreement alive, she had no choice—she'd have to deliver Kelly back to the bar.

Chapter 16

"Don't touch her, Vilfir." Kol's voice was low and loaded with menace.

Spooned against the warm muscular length of Kol, Kelly was slow to come fully awake, and even slower to process the meaning of Kol's words.

"I'm not touching. Just looking," a voice smooth as an ice-covered hillside replied. "We heard the guardian took a mate. What is she, *exactly?*"

Warm breath slithered over Kelly's cheek.

"Mine." Kol's arm shot across her as he reached for someone or something.

Now fully awake, and becoming more and more aware that someone besides she and Kol were in her bedroom, Kelly's eyes flew open. Her hands gripping the comforter, she shot upright.

A dark-skinned man with a slim build, and a disturbing leer darted out of Kol's grasp. Kol shimmered and reappeared behind the man Kelly assumed was Vilfir, wrapped one hand around his throat and lifted him off the ground.

"What are you doing here?"

Somehow still managing to look superior, even while struggling to breathe, Vilfir only pointed to where Kol gripped his throat.

Kol gave him a shake. "Talk."

His face changing from cocoa-brown to something more in the burgundy family, Vilfir rolled bulging eyes at Kelly. Seeing she was still watching, he lowered one eyelid in a lascivious and somehow threatening wink.

Kol growled and tightened his grip.

Realizing her staff was on the floor near her clothes, Kelly gathered the comforter more closely around her nude body and edged to the side of the mattress.

Vilfir managed a sigh and Kol, his face grim, murmured something Kelly couldn't hear.

Keeping her gaze glued to the two men, she bent to retrieve the staff. As she did, the murmur of voices arguing from somewhere in her house jerked her attention to the closed bedroom door.

"Kol?"

Still caught up in the battle of wills with their intruder, he didn't respond.

With quiet deliberation, she leaned over the side of the bed and grabbed both the staff and her clothing.

After quickly tugging on her shirt and underwear, she crept to the door.

"What's…?" Kol glanced from Kelly to the door, his head tilting as if he heard something, too. Without warning, he released his grip on the intruder, letting him fall to the ground.

Vilfir let out one quiet gasp, then pressed his hand to his throat. "How rude. I just came to talk."

Kol took a menacing step toward him. "Who?"

The man glanced from Kol to Kelly to the door, then back at Kelly. His gaze flicked over her bare legs, but at another growl from Kol he sighed and addressed the garm.

"Everyone. As you well know, the bar is closed. There is nowhere for anyone to go. And things are escaping the portal. Things we don't want around. You—" he leaped to his feet with catlike agility "—need to do your job. Not be…" He waggled his eyebrows toward Kelly. "Enjoyable though that might be."

Kelly angled her staff toward him, but Kol had already pressed him back against the wall, his forearm shoved against Vilfir's throat. "No more comments. You just answer what I ask, or you won't have a throat for asking. Understand?"

Vilfir's dark eyes snapped, but he gave a short nod.

Kol moved back, but still kept the man within reach. "Everyone? Svartalfar?"

His eyes locked onto Kol, the man replied, "Svartalfar, dwarves, giants, even some trolls—those who can travel in light. Everyone. All the—"

"Desperates," Kol murmured.

"Regulars," Vilfir finished.

Kelly's hand tightened around her staff. "You mean—"

Kol grabbed Vilfir by the back of his shirt and shoved him forward. "We have company." Then, Vilfir still in his grip, Kol flung open the door and strode out into the hall.

Kelly grabbed up her pants and followed.

As Kol turned the corner into her living room, what had been a murmur changed to a roar of angry voices and sounds. Kelly paused long enough to jerk on her pants, took a deep breath, then stepped into the room.

Practically every nasty, despicable, dirty creature she had ever encountered at the Guardian's Keep was perched somewhere in the room, mouth open and fist raised.

Every drop of blood in Kelly's body drained to her feet.

It took half an hour, but Kol finally managed to get the motley group in Kelly's living room under control.

After designating the dwarf Bari as their spokesperson, the desperates settled around the room and listened with only a few outbursts.

Kelly stood in the back, her arms folded over her staff and her eyes darting from one member of the group to another.

Confident she was safe, Kol sat in the recliner two dwarves had shoved to the center where everyone could see him.

"I'm not the guardian anymore," he stated. "The Council suspended me and I'm cut off from my…the portal."

Bari blew air through his lips like an annoyed stallion. "Council don't know shit from sugar."

A rumble of agreement flowed through the rest of the group.

Kol crossed his arms over his chest. "Maybe, but they're in charge."

"You're the guardian." The dwarf stood, the axe hanging from his belt bouncing against his leg, and pointed one gnarled finger at Kol. "You don't just stop being 'cause some—" He glanced at Vilfir sitting cross-legged near him. "What humans call them?"

The dark elf made a writing motion in the air.

Bari nodded and continued, "Pencil pushers say so. They have no power over you. Not really."

Kol frowned. It was true, but without the Council then what? And even if he ignored Magnus's command to stay away from the portal, he couldn't take it back by himself. Not if what Magnus and Kelly had told him were true. "I can't fight off hundreds of rogues, not alone and not now that they have the benefit of the defensive position. It's one thing to stop them from taking the portal in the first place, but getting it back once it's lost…that's a lot more difficult."

Bari nodded toward Kelly. "You have her."

Kol glanced at Kelly. Her lips set in a thin line and her eyes huge, she nodded.

"And…" Bari drew himself up to his full height and jabbed a thumb into his chest. "You have us."

The room erupted with battle calls and stomping feet.

Kol glanced around. The outcasts and misfits of the nine worlds. How could he even consider going into a battle with them at his back?

Kol leaned his chair against the lavender wall of Magnus's waiting room. Lavender—who'd have thought it? Kol hadn't even been sure what the color was. He'd had to ask Magnus's receptionist.

It was calming, apparently.

Knowing the kind of beings Magnus called here, Kol doubted it had much effect.

The receptionist lifted a hand and gestured for Kol to enter. He gave her a nod of thanks as he stood, then shimmered through the opaque glass wall into Magnus's office.

"Kol. What are you doing here?" Magnus turned to face him. A map of the human world hung on the wall behind him. Flashing colored pins dotted the region around the Guardian's Keep.

"I heard Holi made it through." Magnus turned and twisted a pin until the flash slowed and turned dark. "We haven't located him yet, but we did get the last of the draugrs. Praise be."

He gestured for Kol to sit.

Choosing to remain standing, Kol approached the older garm. "I want to take back my portal."

Magnus lifted a brow. "I thought we settled that. It isn't yours at the moment. And the Council will decide if and when we will recover it."

Kol tensed. "If?"

Magnus hesitated, then strode to his desk and sat down. "I suppose you deserve to know. There's been discussion of sneaking someone inside and shutting it down—permanently."

"Why? We haven't even tried to take it back yet."

Magnus opened a small cardboard box and poured a pile of the colored pins onto his desktop. "Even if we defeat them, there are too many of them. Humans are going to notice the battle."

"You don't think humans have noticed the undead walking the streets?" Kol asked.

Magnus counted three orange pins onto his palm. "Not yet. We were quick."

Kol shook his head in disbelief. According to Kelly, plenty of humans saw plenty of things they wouldn't be forgetting anytime soon. Another example of the twisted reality the Garm Council created for itself.

He strode to the desk. "I won't let my portal be shut down."

Magnus stared up, his eyes hard. "You don't have any say in the matter."

Kelly picked up an overturned plant and dropped it in the trash. The last of the desperates had left two hours earlier, and she was still cleaning up after her uninvited guests. She'd never bothered taking any magical steps to guard her house, hadn't seen a need, but now…she stumbled over a forgotten battle axe. She picked up the weapon and measured its weight in her hand. Shaking her head at how a dwarf could heft such an item, she returned to her thoughts. Not a single desperate had had an issue with getting inside her home. Definitely time to consider designing a few well-thought-out wards.

As she was contemplating exactly what she would need to set a protection ward, the doorbell rang.

She glanced at the axe in her hand. She couldn't believe the dwarf who had left it found some manners. The weapon held up in had front of her, she strode to the door and whipped it open.

Heather blinked then hopped back a step. "Kelly. You're home."

Kelly gazed at her assistant through narrowed eyes. "You came by expecting me to be out?"

Heather emitted a rather high-pitched laugh and gave the neighbor's shrubs a glance. "Can I come in?"

Kelly ran her hand over the flat edge of the axe's metal head. Should she let her in? Kelly knew or at least majorly suspected her assistant couldn't be trusted—but if she didn't talk to her, how would she know for sure? Decision made, she stepped back and gestured with the hand holding the axe for Heather to enter.

Her gaze darting to the shrubs again, Heather quickly slid inside.

"So." Kelly gestured for her assistant to have a seat in one of the wooden kitchen chairs some of the desperates had dragged into the living room.

Heather glanced around, her brow lowered. "Did you have a party or something?"

"And not invite you? Never." Kelly drove the axe head into the coffee table.

Heather's gaze locked onto the weapon now protruding from the furniture's wooden top. Eyes rounded, she looked up at Kelly. "Listen, I know things might have looked strange—"

"Strange? You mean that little scene at the bar—you pounding away on the computer trying to hack your way into the portal while monsters and their minions flooded the city?"

Heather flinched.

Kelly relaxed against the sofa cushions, her arms folded over her chest. "No, not strange at all."

A noise sounded from outside. The neighbor's dog chasing a squirrel or something. Kelly ignored it.

Heather shifted in her seat, her head turning to glance over her shoulder toward the window behind her. She stood. One hand twisting the ring on her index finger, she wandered to the fireplace. "I need your help."

"Really?" Kelly tapped her fingers against her upper arm.

"Really." Heather's eyes were wide, her face drawn and pale.

Huffing out an angry sigh, Kelly replied, "With what?"

Apparently sensing a crack in Kelly's angry facade, Heather licked her lips then inhaled deeply. "Aesa. She wants you to come back to the bar. To open the portal to Lyngvi."

"What makes Aesa think I *can* open the portal?"

"Well…" Heather glanced around. "She thinks Kol will tell you. That he…you know…loves you."

Kelly pulled back. *Love?* No mention had been made of love—did Kol love her, was that why he'd done so much for her? She shook her head, struggling to keep the thoughts from leaking into her conversation with Heather.

"And if he does? She thinks I'd betray him?"

"Well, you have—"

Kelly shifted, her foot knocking against the coffee table with an angry thump.

Heather took a step back. Her butt hit the rough bricks of the fireplace and she jumped.

Kelly raised a brow. "What's going on, Heather? Why do you care what Aesa wants?"

Heather glanced down at her brown leather boots. "If you don't help, she'll kill me."

Kelly stared at Heather for what felt like hours. Heather hadn't meant to blurt things out quite that bluntly, but she was on edge—sure every sound outside was one of Aesa's garm showing up to rip her into bite-size morsels.

Her hands began to shake. She fisted them at her sides.

When she could stand it no longer, she looked up.

Kelly glanced away, but Heather caught a glimpse of her expression. Concern. Concern was good—gave Heather hope.

"Does Terje exist?" Kelly asked.

"Terje?" Heather repeated.

Kelly turned her face back to Heather. "The son. Aesa and Fenrir's son. The one she asked me to rescue. Does he even exist?"

Not sure what this had to do with saving Heather from becoming kibble for an angry Aesa, Heather chewed on the inside of her lip. "I think so, but he's an adult. Fenrir's been on Lyngvi a long time."

Kelly shook her head and mumbled something under her breath. She seemed angry, but the emotion didn't appear to be directed at Heather—thankfully. "But she's obsessed with freeing Fenrir. That's why she wants through to Lyngvi."

"And the rogues? Why are they helping her?"

Heather uncurled her fingers and wiped her sweaty palms down the front of her pants. "It's hard to explain. It's all garm politics."

Kelly edged sideways, until her body faced Heather, then leaned forward as if expecting Heather to continue.

Heather swallowed and complied. "I don't really understand it all, but they think if Fenrir is freed, they'll all get a portal or something to guard. Some kind of greater purpose." She emphasized the last two words by making air quotes with her fingers.

"Not a horrible goal," Kelly murmured.

Heather shrugged. "I guess not." She was so sick of the garm and their cause, nothing they said or did seemed worthwhile to her anymore—not to mention the fact that with a twitch of Aesa's nose any one of them would willingly snap through Heather's windpipe.

She shook off a sudden chill.

"But Fenrir's being held for a reason," Kelly added.

Realizing dissing the garm's cause wouldn't help her own, Heather imitated the passion she'd heard so often in the rogue's voices. "But not necessarily a good one."

"No…" Kelly frowned, then pinned Heather with suspicious gaze. "Why'd you get involved?"

Heather ran her fingers through her hair. Could she out-and-out lie to Kelly again?

Kelly waited.

Jerking her hands free from her hair, Heather blurted out the truth. "I wanted a shortcut. I wanted power, and I didn't want to have to work for it. I know that's sounds bad—is bad, but it's the truth, and I can't do anything to change it now." Suddenly drained, she walked to a recliner sitting in the middle of the room and collapsed into it.

"Well, at least you're being honest," Kelly replied.

Slumped in the chair, Heather ran her finger over the silver ring that once was her mother's. Yeah, she was finally being honest—question was, would it save or doom her?

When Kol returned to Kelly's, she was sitting on the couch staring at a battle axe that protruded from the top of her coffee table.

"Did one of the desperates…?" he asked.

She shook her head. "No. All me." Then she grabbed the axe by the handle and tugged it free. After dropping it onto the table top, she looked up. "So. How's the Garm Council?"

Kol picked up the axe and ran his thumb over the sharpened edge, then held it out to Kelly. "Might not be a bad idea to learn how to use this. Look's like we're going to war."

Chapter 17

Two in the morning and the troops were assembled outside the Guardian's Keep. Kol glanced around the small circle of leaders, one chosen by each group of beings: Bari, the dwarf; Vilfir, the dark elf; Gusir, a giant; and Morn, a troll.

"What's the plan?" Morn asked, her tail snapping against her leg.

"Garm are hard killing," Bari said. "Best go for containing them somehow."

"That's the plan." Kelly stepped forward, a red backpack slung over one shoulder. She reached inside and pulled out a crystal the size of Kol's fist.

Bari plucked it from her palm. "What that going to do? It explode?"

"Watch." She stepped back and tossed, one by one, five stones to Kol. On her signal he placed them just as she had instructed him the night before.

Morn grunted. "Pretty, but I don't see how—" She took a step toward Kelly and collided with an invisible wall. "What the—"

"This won't hold." Bari jerked up his axe and swung. The earth beneath them tremored, but the barrier held.

Vilfir smiled, his gaze roaming Kelly's body. "Talented, isn't she?"

Brows lowered, Kol slapped his silver bat against his palm. "One less elf won't hurt our cause any, Vilfir."

The Svartalfar grinned and slipped behind Gusir, out of Kol's view.

With a quick glance at Kol, Kelly murmured under her breath and retrieved the crystal closest to her—breaking the barrier.

Morn stepped away from the stones, her silver eyes narrowed. "There are a lot more of them. Can she build a trap big enough?"

Kelly bent down to pick up the crystals and began dropping them back into her bag.

Kol faced the troll. "Not a problem. The trap is already built. Your job is just to herd the rogues where we tell you."

Four pairs of eyes slid from side to side, each being assessing the other's thoughts.

Finally, Bari stepped forward. He held an open palm out to Kelly. "Worthy plan. We agree."

She stared down at his outstretched hand as if not sure how to react, then slowly swiped her own across the top.

Bari grinned, white teeth almost glowing in the dark. "We will wait for the signal."

With one final nod, all four blended into the darkness.

Beside him, Kelly hefted the bag onto her back, then stood perfectly still, her gaze on the currently quiet bar across the street.

"What's going to happen?" she asked.

His gaze also on the bar, Kol replied, "I don't know." He pulled her hand into his. Her hand was cold and stiff. He rubbed his thumb over the bones on the back and felt, as much as heard, her sigh. He tugged her closer, until her thigh pressed against his. With another, even softer sigh, she wove her fingers between his.

Her hand curled in his, he had to fight his natural inclination to keep her safe, to order her home, away from the impending battle. The rogues wouldn't give up their position easily. Both sides would suffer—there was no doubt of that, and Kol couldn't bear the thought of anything harming Kelly. But he knew she wouldn't go. He also knew she had to prove something to herself. Had to fight this battle to defeat whatever guilt she still harbored—for what had happened to her friend, for releasing what she saw as monsters on this world, and for not trusting him.

He wouldn't take that chance away from her.

Kelly glanced around the dark street outside the Guardian's Keep. How she'd wound up teamed with such a ragtag group she couldn't say—beings she hadn't been sure existed a few months ago. Now her life was pinned to them.

From behind the Dumpster, Bari waved—a battle axe with one hand, a short dagger with the other. The giants had taken a station farther away, to better keep out of sight. The dark elves and the trolls managed to blend so well with the background even Kelly wasn't sure where they were.

"Ready?" Kol's voice boomed in her head.

He'd changed so he could communicate with everyone without alerting those in the bar.

"Bari, you're on."

The dwarf flipped over the Dumpster, landing squarely

on his feet. Behind him a dozen more dwarves did the same. Then en masse they trooped to the Guardian's Keep's door.

Everyone had agreed the best idea was to first try drawing the occupants of the bar out, maybe even lead them to the trap without any bloodshed. At least Kelly had thought the no bloodshed part was a good idea; the dwarves and giants had been pretty much dead set against that part of the plan.

Bari in the lead, the group reached the bar. With the flat side of his axe, the dwarf leader pounded on the door. A minute passed with no answer. Then just as Kelly could hear something murmuring in the shadows—the Svartalfar or trolls—something clanged and the door swung open.

Aesa stood on the other side. "What do you want?"

"Passage," Bari declared. "We have business to work through this portal. You have no right to cut us off."

The door started to slam shut. With a forward thrust, Bari shoved his axe in the last few inches of opening. "Let us in, garm, or we attack."

The door edged open a bit more, and Aesa's voice floated across the street. "Really? Okay."

The dwarves exchanged surprised looks and began to shoulder their way forward. As the last one reached the stairs to the small stoop, the space around them began to shimmer and twenty-five rogues all with silver bats materialized.

They were on the dwarves before the smaller beings had a chance to turn.

"Now!" Kol leaped from the shadows into the middle of the fray. A troop of dark elves followed, their short thrusting swords slashing the air as they ran.

The garm spun, forming a circle, their backs to each

other. The rogues closest to Kol followed his lead, changing into wolf form. Those remaining swung their bats—the ring of silver hitting steel echoed down the alleyway.

"Kelly, behind you," Kol's voice again. Kelly spun and found five new garm creeping toward her. She held out her hand; within seconds, a glowing ball of power crackled on top of her palm.

The rogue in front held up his silver bat. Kelly recognized him as the man who had held her and almost killed Kol at the Guardian's Keep.

"Why are you fighting us?" he asked.

She frowned, a bit confused by the question. "You stole the portal." Taking a step to the side, she kept her gaze moving from one rogue to the other and back again.

His face earnest, he replied, "For a just cause. We don't want to hurt you. Come with us. Don't let your mind be clouded by…" He glanced toward Kol.

Kelly kept her gaze on the threat. "My mind finally isn't clouded."

"No?" He took a step forward. "You don't even know what you're fighting for—what we're fighting for."

"I know you've unleashed every monster in the nine worlds on this one."

He shrugged. "Spilled milk. We have bigger concerns."

"Freeing Fenrir? How would that be a good thing?"

His chest expanded and his chin tilted upward. "Respect? The chance to be treated as an equal? You don't value those things?"

"Of course I—"

Something screamed behind them. Unwilling to turn her back on the rogues facing her, Kelly had no choice but to ignore the spine-chilling noise.

The rogue addressing her didn't bother to glance

away, either. "They won't beat us. We have the portal on our side now."

"What's that supposed to mean? Portals don't take side." *Did they?*

"You'll see." With a sad smile he and the others shimmered.

Where did they go? Kelly searched the mass of bodies. Weapons and teeth flashed. Curses and blood flowed. But she couldn't find the garm who'd been speaking with her anywhere.

The main group had moved. Kol, the dwarves, and dark elves had managed to shift the battle closer to the corner where she had set up her trap.

"Almost time," Kol whispered in her head.

Forgetting about the rogues, she picked up her backpack and sprinted to her station.

The giants and trolls appeared at the flank of the battle, increasing the push toward her and the crystals. More rogues shimmered into the battle—some as wolves, some as men.

Four in wolf form jumped on the lead giant, Gusir, pulling him to his knees. Bari leapt on top of the fallen giant, his battle axe singing a deep bass as it plowed through the air, knocking a rogue off the giant and onto the asphalt.

Kelly's palms itched, her heart pounding with the need to jump into the fight—but her job was very specific. She was the only one who could spring the trap.

A rogue grabbed Bari by the neck, his teeth piercing the dwarf's skin. Blood streamed down Bari's neck, but he didn't waver. Just pulled his dagger free and shoved the blade deep into the rogue's stomach.

The responding howl made Kelly's own stomach twist and turn. Eyes flashing, the rogue's companions—those remaining on Gusir—turned to join in the attack on the dwarf. Kelly took a step forward. She couldn't let the dwarf die, but Kol's voice boomed in her head. "Hold. We're almost there."

Kelly glanced around. Kol was right. In her concentration on the scene playing out between Bari, Gusir, and the rogues surrounding them, she'd missed the shift of the overall battle. Only around twenty feet now separated her from the edge of the struggle.

But Bari…

A whistling sound turned her attention back to that small section of the fight. Vilfir spun through the air like a Chinese acrobat. He landed, feet wide, sword ready, beside the fallen Gusir and pale Bari. The high pitched sound of his blade slicing through air and garm told Kelly he was moving before her eyes could register what was happening. Within seconds, he'd forced the garm back and jerked Bari to his feet. The less agile Gusir waved them away as he lumbered to a stand.

"Almost there," Kol yelled.

Kelly jerked the final crystal from her bag and stepped back into the shadows. The garm moved closer. First one then five moved in between the crystals. Not enough. She needed most if not all of them contained, and the desperates out of range, before she laid the trap. The beings with the fastest reflexes, trolls and dark elves, would follow the garm into the enclosure. When Kol gave the signal they would have only seconds to escape the trap before Kelly laid the last crystal and murmured the words of entrapment.

As Kelly crouched in the darkness, the crystal cold and ready in her hand, an eerie screech escaped from the bar. Her gaze flew to Kol. He stood facing the Guardian's Keep, his back and tail rigid. His ears slowly pulled back until they were tucked against his head.

Then perhaps forgetting he was connected telepathically to Kelly, he growled—a low menacing sound that sent Kelly stumbling backward until she remembered it wasn't directed at her. She clutched the crystal tighter and shifted her gaze to where Kol's was—the bar door.

The knob rattled. Someone inside screamed. Then the door burst open, Heather, her eyes huge, her mouth open in a silent shriek, bounded out the opening. In her hurry she tumbled down the steps and onto the pavement.

Kelly's breath caught in her chest. She started to scream at her assistant to get up, to run, but before she could Kol shimmered, grabbed Heather by the collar and shimmered again, this time next to Kelly. He paused a second, then shimmered back to where the desperates still fought, unaware of what was happening.

Beside Kelly, Heather, still on her knees, heaved, losing whatever meal she had last eaten on the pavement near Kelly's feet. Kelly pulled Heather's hair back from her face and looked back at the bar.

Tendrils of blue-black smoke twisted their way through the doorway. At first Kelly thought the bar was on fire, but immediately realized it wasn't smoke she smelled but the cold dampness of earth and decaying flesh. She gagged, struggling not to join Heather still kneeling on the asphalt.

"What is it?" she murmured.

"Draugrs," Heather choked out.

"What—?"

"Undead. *Revenge of the Zombies* meets *Dracula*." Heather wiped the back of her hand across her mouth and hazarded a small smile, but despite her attempt at humor, fear shone from her eyes.

In front of the bar, the first column of smoke began to morph. Within seconds a towering blue-white giant with only gaping holes where its mouth, eyes and nose should have been reached out and plucked a dwarf from the ground. The small man spun to see what held him, his axe swinging as he turned, but as the first waves of horror registered on his face, the draugr opened its mouth and swallowed him whole.

The sound of bones crunching battered against Kelly like physical blows.

Another draugr formed. Another dwarf, then a dark elf disappeared.

Kelly reached down and grabbed Heather by the hair. Yanking her face up to look at Kelly, she asked, "How do you kill them?"

"You don't. Only a hero can."

Kelly shook her head, by her count the parking lot was filled with heroes.

"A certain hero. It's like genetic or something, only a very few can kill a draugr and no one knows who they are until…"

Until they fought one and didn't get devoured.

Kelly's gaze shot to Kol. She couldn't let her mind go there.

She glanced back at Heather. "What else? There has to be something else."

Heather swallowed. "Their graves. They need to be returned. It's the only place they're under control. I heard the Garm Council managed to get one back earlier. I don't know how."

Cursing, Kelly dropped her grip on the other woman's hair.

"Kelly." Kol's voice again. "Are you ready?"

Kelly stared blindly into the battle. Was he serious? With these things free, he still wanted to trap the rogues?

"Keep with the plan. We'll trap the draugrs, too."

Trap the draugrs? Kelly clamped onto the thought. She could do that.

Trying not to think about anything except her part in the battle, Kelly readied herself for Kol's signal.

Tail rigid behind him and eyes alert, Kol mentally barked orders to the desperates. Their task had been complicated with the arrival of the draugr, but it hadn't changed. They just had to squeeze a few more bodies into the cage now.

A draugr grabbed for Bari, but the dwarf folded into himself and rolled across the pavement out of the undead's reach. Vilfir danced in front of the creature, his thrusting sword catching the light from a nearby lamppost. The draugr stumbled forward, his mouth gaping open as he stalked the Svartalfar. The undead's companions followed.

Kol waited, counting in his head to keep from signaling too soon. As the last draugr lurched into the cage, he yelled telepathically to the desperates, "Leave."

Almost as one, dark elves flipped backward and wind trolls whirled into miniature cyclones, squeezing between the bodies of rogues and draugrs.

Two seconds that was all they could afford. Then without looking to see if all had escaped, he called to Kelly. "Now. The trap. Spring the trap."

She glanced up, her violet gaze meeting his, the final crystal in her hands. She bent to drop it into place and froze, her gaze locked on the rogues and draugrs about to be trapped together in her cage of magic and will.

* * *

Time slowed. The weight of the crystal pulled at Kelly's arm. She only had to drop it, utter a few words and the rogues would be trapped…but…

A draugr slashed a huge pawlike limb through the air as the last Svartalfar flipped hands over feet and landed outside the line of crystals.

"Now," Kol yelled in her head. Her lower lip between her teeth, she plunked the crystal between the others, and glanced up. The rogue who had approached her earlier stood only a few feet away, his gaze locked on hers. The first words fell from her lips.

She paused. *Just one more and the circle would close.*

The rogue frowned, the first flickers of understanding that something was wrong—for him and his companions at least—showing behind his eyes.

Kelly's heart sped. She knew they didn't stand a chance. There was no way the rogues could shimmer before Kelly could say that last word—no way for them to keep from being trapped inside the crystal cage with the undead draugrs.

She licked her lips, started to form the word, then stopped.

She couldn't. God help her. She couldn't trap the rogues in that cage with the draugrs to be eaten alive—even knowing the rogue staring at her was almost surely responsible for the monsters' release. That's what he had meant when he said the portal was on their side. The thought made Kelly sick, deep in her gut, but she still couldn't bring herself to utter the last three syllables.

A furrow formed between the rogue's eyes. His gaze flicked to the crystals and back at Kelly. Silently, she willed him to understand. His eyes rounded, she could almost see realization clicking in his brain. She shut her own, unable to witness what might happen next.

Kol yelled again, but she didn't move, didn't say the final word. Her heart pounding, she waited, until she felt power wash over her, then opened her eyes and watched as the rogues in one uniform wave shimmered out of the trap.

Her chin dropping to her chest, Kelly murmured the last word, then somersaulted away from the circle.

Rolling to her feet a few yards away, she waited. The draugrs, just like the desperates earlier, didn't realize they were trapped, not at first. They lumbered forward, arms waving, mouths opening in hungry roars.

Praying the circle would hold, Kelly took another step back. The air beside her shimmered and Kol appeared beside her. He grabbed her hand and gave it a squeeze.

Her gaze still on the group of screaming, lumbering monsters, she whispered, "I couldn't do it. They set those things free on us, but I couldn't trap them inside with them. I just couldn't."

Kol gave her hand another squeeze, a silent sign of support that almost sent Kelly to her knees.

The front draugr hit the barrier, then exploded into a dark cloud of smoke. She held her breath, her mouth silently counting, praying the creature wouldn't reform. *Five, six, seven...*

Mouth gaping, the draugr pulled itself back into a solid human form and screamed—harsh and chilling like metal on metal.

Kelly shivered.

Kol squeezed her hand again, then tugged her closer and pressed a kiss to her temple. "Everything will be okay."

Unable to take her eyes off the raging monsters caught inside her trap, Kelly nodded and blinked back the hot tears threatening to form.

He was lying.

This was his one chance to save his bar, and she had ruined it.

Chapter 18

Kol held onto Kelly's hand as the four leaders of the desperates approached. Vilfir, looking somehow amused, arrived first.

"Not quite as we planned it." The dark elf plucked a rock off the ground and began tossing it up and down. Head cocked, he watched as the frenzied draugrs threw themselves against the invisible walls of the cage, disintegrated into smoke, and then reshaped themselves only to repeat the process again and again. The rock landing squarely in his palm, he smiled.

The draugrs were in their third round of reincarnation when Bari, Morn, and Gusir arrived.

"What happened?" Ignoring Kol, Morn stepped in front of Kelly, and glared down at the petite witch.

Her jaw jutting to the side, Kelly stared straight ahead as if memorizing the bright paisley design on the female troll's shirt.

Bari flung his axe at the ground, the heavy blade slicing into the asphalt. "We had them."

"We did," Gusir seconded, his voice reverberating in his chest.

"She…" Morn twirled one finger in a circle before letting it slow to a stop inches from Kelly's nose. "Let them escape."

Arms folded over his chest, Bari rolled back on his heels and studied the two females. "That true, witch?"

Still smiling, Vilfir turned his attention from the draugrs to the scene beside him.

Kelly pulled her hand from Kol's. He took a step forward, attempting to place himself between her and the others, but she placed a hand on his arm, and looked directly at her interrogators. "Yes, I did."

Curses erupted from Morn and Bari. Vilfir took a step back and continued to watch, and Gusir just frowned as if not fully comprehending what was happening.

Her gaze level, and her chin firm, Kelly seemed to let their venom wash over her.

Tail snapping, Morn spun toward Kol. "This is what you chose as a mate? What you trust?"

Very aware Kelly stood beside him, weighing each of his words, Kol lowered a warning gaze at the troll. "She isn't like you." He glanced at the others. "Like any of us."

Bari strut forward. "She scared? She freeze?"

Before Kol could respond, Vilfir turned on the troll. Kol stepped forward, between the two females. "Fear wasn't the issue. If fear ruled Kelly, I wouldn't be standing here facing you. She's battled beside me—saved me."

Vilfir grinned. "Must be true, Morn. Not much scarier than you right before dawn."

"Then what?" Morn shot spear-sharp glances at both Vilfir and Kelly. "What kept her from following our plan?"

Her back rigid, Kelly stared back at the troll.

Barely able to restrain himself from reaching out and brushing the hair away from her neck, from pressing a kiss to the tense muscles he knew he'd find there, Kol blew out a breath. "Compassion. She showed compassion."

At the disbelieving looks on the other three's faces, Vilfir laughed. "Can't blame her for that, now can we?"

Kelly ground her jaws together. "No, you can. I cost everyone what they worked for."

"Not to mention the lives lost." Bari's fingers danced over the handle of his sheathed dagger.

"In my world, traitors die." Morn leaned forward.

Kol stiffened. His silver bat was out of reach, but Kelly was only inches away. He could grab her and shimmer long before either Morn or Bari could harm her. He started to move, to attack Morn or save Kelly he wasn't sure, but before he could decide, Vilfir began to laugh.

"Well, isn't this grand? Place a new seat at the hanging— the Garm Council has arrived."

His hand brushing against Kelly's arm, Kol turned.

Magnus, Birgit, and five goons strode across the parking lot, stepping over fallen desperates without even a glance downward.

Kelly pulled back, putting distance between her and Kol. He didn't need to be associated with her right now. She glanced at the leader of the Garm Council, Magnus, striding toward them. His brow lowered and his gait steady, it didn't appear this was going to be a friendly visit.

Frowning at the draugrs still struggling to escape Kelly's cage, Magnus ground to a halt. "What happened here?"

The desperates all seemed to melt into the background,

still physically near, but less obvious. Her heart fluttering, Kelly wished she shared the talent.

Kol stepped forward. "We captured some draugrs."

Birgit flicked her gaze around the parking lot, her gaze stopping pointedly at the fallen desperates she and the other members of the Garm Council had stepped over. "How convenient you were nearby when they escaped. Having a reunion of sorts?"

With a grin, Vilfir slid out of obscure mode. "We Svartalfar try to be of service." His gaze ran down the length of Birgit's body, then back up.

She pinned him with a glare.

Ignoring, or perhaps not even noticing, the exchange between Birgit and the dark elf, Magnus addressed Kol. "You were told to stay away from the Guardian's Keep."

Kol turned slightly, blocking Magnus's view of her, Kelly realized. "Did you prefer the draugrs weren't caught?"

"I prefer the draugrs weren't set free."

The two men stared at each other with steady gazes, neither giving ground.

Kelly gripped the nylon backpack fighting the urge to step forward and draw attention off Kol. However, such an act would only make matters worse, she knew that.

Birgit huffed out a breath. "Give it up. We heard about the battle. I can't believe you teamed up with these—" she glanced around "—broken toys, and expected to win."

Jerking his axe out of the asphalt, Bari broke cover. "What you been doing? Chasing your tail?" He swaggered forward, his nose hitting Birgit mid-abdomen, he glared up at her.

She curled her lip in a snarl.

Rolling the rock he'd picked up earlier around in his palm, Vilfir added, "You have to admit, it didn't appear the Council was doing anything to rectify the problem."

"The Council doesn't work for you," Birgit replied.

"Really?" Morn slid forward, too. "I was under the impression the Council worked for everyone involved in portal transport…" she glanced around the group at Bari, Vilfir and Gusir "…which we are."

"But you're not—" Birgit shook her head and turned to face Kol. "The point is, you went out on your own. That's rogue behavior."

Something uncurled in Kelly's stomach—a long twisting ribbon of dread.

Magnus took a step forward away from Kol, Birgit and the desperates, his arms folded over his chest, he studied the trapped draugrs. "Birgit, call the others; we have draugrs to transport."

"But what about—?"

"Call them," he repeated, his voice firm.

With a muttered curse, Birgit spun on her heel and shimmered.

Magnus turned and jerked his head at Kol, signaling for Kol to join him.

Still trying to stay unobtrusive, Kelly studied the pair, but was unable to make out anything they were discussing or to even decipher their body language. Both were tense, but neither seemed ready to strike.

Morn slithered next to her. "Want to know what they're saying?"

Kelly narrowed her eyes. She wasn't fond of the troll. Of all the desperates, Morn was the one she might have been tempted to leave in with the draugrs. Annoyed she needed her help, Kelly gave a short nod.

Morn swirled into a wind and spun away. A few seconds later as Magnus and Kol seemed to be ending their conversation, she reformed next to Kelly.

"Magnus knows you're the problem. That you're the reason the rogues got control of the portal in the first place, and that this plan failed. But he doesn't want to lose Kol, and Kol won't give you up." The troll shook her head.

Kelly frowned. "Give me up?"

Morn shrugged. "Not sure what that means. I think there's been talk of trying you. Whatever it means, you're going to be the downfall of the guardian. If he sticks with you, he's going to have to go rogue. The Council won't even talk to him with you in the picture."

"It's me or his portal?" Kelly murmured.

"Best case for the guardian. Could be neither. They might decide not to give him back his portal—assuming they ever get it back—and they might try you and kill you." The troll said the words with a complete lack of emotion, like she was discussing a lunch order.

"What if Kol got his portal back himself, and I…" Kelly licked dry lips "…disappeared?"

Morn tilted her head, interest popping into her eyes. "That might change things, but you'd have to get the Council to forgive Kol for going against their mandate to keep away from the bar *and* you'd have to get Kol to forget you. We've all seen how he watches you, touches you whenever he can. The guardian wouldn't let you just disappear."

"But they blame me, right? For everything? Think I corrupted Kol somehow? So, if they saw him choose the portal over me and there was no doubt I was never coming back…they'd have to let him keep his portal."

Morn slapped her tail against her open palm. "The Council doesn't *have* to do anything. They're hard to understand, but, yeah. I think that might work."

Might work. Might not. No promises. No definites. But it was all Kelly had. She just hoped she had the guts to go through with what she had to do.

Kol reached into Kelly's kitchen cabinet and pulled out a bottle of whiskey. He wasn't much of a drinker—bad habit for a bartender—but tonight he really needed one. Magnus had been as direct as he could be—Kelly or the portal, maybe neither. But no Kelly, not unless Kol went rogue and took them both into hiding.

The Council was giving him twenty-four hours to turn her over, then they were coming for her. Magnus assured Kol she'd get a fair trial, that Kol would even be allowed to testify at the hearings, but that would be it. Based on everything that had happened they didn't feel they could trust a guardian under the influence of someone like Kelly. She was untrustworthy and therefore if Kol stood by her side, he was untrustworthy.

Kol had asked what would happen if Kelly was found innocent, but Magnus had just stared at him. They both knew there was no hope of that. Kelly had admitted to working with Aesa. Birgit would testify against her; the desperates would very likely tell how she had released the rogues today. And any testimony Kol gave would be considered suspect.

It was a hangman's court—no winning.

He was staring into the glass of amber liquid when Kelly sauntered into the room, her hips swaying side to side.

"Kelly." He slid the glass onto the table beside him. "We need to talk."

She dipped her finger into the whiskey and ran it over his lower lip. "I don't think we do—not now."

He licked it off and tried to focus on what he had to say.

Kelly paused in front of him, lifted one leg and slid onto his lap, her breasts pressing against his chest. She exhaled lightly, in a soft moan that sent a shiver dancing across his skin.

His fingers dug into his thighs. "Kelly," he managed to grind out between clenched jaws. "We have to leave here. Magnus gave us twenty-four hours. Where's your sister? You'll be safe with her."

Kelly leaned forward, her lips brushing his. "Don't know."

Kol growled in frustration. Kelly and her sister together were damn near unstoppable. If he could just get Kelly to her twin, he wouldn't have to worry about keeping her safe. She'd be fine while he came back and dealt with the Council.

Kelly's tongue darted between his parted lips. "She never answers my calls."

Kol closed his eyes, his mind scrambling to focus on the problem of keeping Kelly safe.

Her fingers tiptoed down his chest. She grabbed the tail of his shirt and tugged. Then before he could form another question, her hands slipped under the material and began stroking; her lips moved from his mouth to his ear. She pulled his lobe between her teeth and nibbled.

He growled again, but this time from a different type of frustration. Using the last few strands of control, he whispered, "Kelly?"

With a low laugh, she ignored his plea, slid her hands higher and returned her mouth to his.

All hope of resisting melted away, and Kol ran his hands up her back, into her hair and pulled her mouth back to his.

"Bedroom," she murmured.

Kol hesitated. His body had no desire to move from where it was—Kelly pressed against him, nothing separating them but a few layers of cloth.

"Here," he replied, and shoved her shirt up off her body and onto the floor.

She pulled back, placed a hand on each side of his head and slowly shook her own. "No." Then she reached for the glass of whiskey, dipped another finger into the amber liquid and trailed it over the curve of her breasts in one long tantalizing movement.

Kol leaned forward to lick the liquor off, but Kelly laughed and danced backward, off of his lap and through the doorway that led to the bedroom.

When Kol arrived in the bedroom, Kelly was already draped across the bed, the whiskey glass dangling from two fingers—the other hand busy toying with the front close hook of her bra.

Nostrils flaring, he placed his palms at the bottom of the mattress and crawled up its length until he was poised over Kelly.

She took a tiny sip of the liquor. Whiskey glistened from her lips. Kol lowered his body and slowly pulled her lower lip into his mouth. The taste of honey and apricots sweetened the kiss, the warm smell of alcohol adding to his need. He released her lip, nuzzled her mouth one last time; then with cool deliberation took the glass from her hand and placed it on the bedside table.

"Wait." She held up one hand, a suddenly unsure smile tilting her mouth. He cocked a brow and with his gaze on her eyes, lowered his lips to the mound of flesh peeking from her bra—where she'd trailed whiskey earlier.

With a playful shove, she flipped, pushing him over until he lay beneath her.

"Wait," she said again. This time pressing a finger to his lips. Then with a shy smile she pushed herself off of him to stand next to the bed.

Her hands reached for the front of her bra. "People have told you a lot of things about me," she said. She undid the hook with a tiny snap, her foot kicking something under the bed as she did. "And I know you didn't believe them," she continued.

He lay back, his arm behind his head, his calm posture belying the passion raging in his body.

She mumbled something under her breath, something he couldn't understand. He tilted his head, confused, then she sighed, resnapped her bra and stepped away from the bed. "But you should have." Without a look back, she turned and left the room.

Kelly clicked the bedroom door shut behind her. Her heart hammering and her knees bending, she leaned against the wood just to stay upright.

She'd done it. She'd tricked Kol, not only into the trap she'd laid out with crystals hidden beneath the bed skirt, but hopefully into believing that she didn't care—that she'd been using him all along.

From inside the room, she heard a thump and the squeak of the box spring—Kol's body repelled by the walls of the trap falling back onto the mattress—then a disbelieving curse.

Tears streaked her cheeks.

She had to do this. It was the only way to keep him from following her, from trying to save her yet again.

He had to hate her.

"Kelly," he yelled.

She squeezed her eyes shut and pressed her palms to her ears.

"Why are you doing this?" he yelled again.

Swallowing a new bout of tears, she heaved in a breath, and pushed herself away from the door.

In the kitchen, she felt him change. The power from his transformation filled her tiny house—rage, he was filled with it. A round of squeaking springs this time, then a roar.

Desperate to get out of the house and on with what she had to do, Kelly jerked on her shirt and grabbed her cell phone from its charger. On her way to the bar, she'd call Kara—leave a message. Say goodbye. Maybe ask her to explain things to Kol…after.

No. Kelly scrubbed the back of one hand over her face. Better for him if he just hated her.

"Kelly?" his voice in her head now, soft, questioning.

She had to escape, before he ate away her resolve. Choking back another sob, she tugged open the door.

"Kelly, why?" he asked.

Both feet outside, her hand resting on the knob, ready to push it shut, she closed her eyes, and murmured, "Because I love you."

Chapter 19

Kelly stared at the Guardian's Keep; despite the bright sunshine that illuminated the parking lot, the ugly squat building looked even darker today than normal.

She hated this place—and loved it at the same time. The worst and the best moments of her life were all tied in some way to this bar. How fitting that this was the setting for her final act.

She'd retrieved her coat and hat from her car for the visit. It felt right walking back in clothed in the same outfit she'd worn the night she met Aesa, the night Kol dumped her out in the rain.

Squaring her shoulders, she flipped up the collar of her coat and placed one booted foot off the curb.

Heather jumped as the door to the Guardian's Keep banged open. Bright sunlight cast the intruder in silhouette.

Heather blinked, her eyes permanently dilated from living in this dark hovel for the past week. The coat…the hat…Kelly.

She'd come back.

Hope curling inside Heather's chest, she edged toward the door, but before she got more than a foot, Leifi and a dozen of the other rogues shimmered into the bar, cutting off any access to Kelly.

"What are you doing here?" he asked, his question directed at Kelly.

She stepped across the threshold and let the door shut behind her of its own accord. "I thought about what you said. About what Heather said. I've come to join you."

He glanced toward Heather, one eyebrow raised in disbelief, then back at Kelly. "Did you? Why do I find that hard to believe?"

One of the other rogues mumbled something, and Leifi laughed. "Oh, yeah, now I remember. Maybe it's because you almost trapped us inside your crystal cage with the draugrs."

Kelly pulled off her hat and dropped it on a table. Her gaze was cool, controlled, but there was a slight shake in her hand.

Heather swallowed and prayed Leifi didn't notice. Weakness to a garm was like blood to a shark. She'd learned that the hard way.

"But I didn't, did I? Do you honestly think you could have escaped if I hadn't let you?"

Leifi pulled back, his head tilting.

"She had time," Heather piped in. "I was there. All she had to do was say one word and you would have been caught."

"You were there, weren't you?" Aesa appeared in the doorway that doubled as the portal. "We still need to discuss that little fact."

"The draugr—" Heather began.

Aesa cut her off with an impatient wave of her hand. "Not now. Maybe…" she studied Kelly "…not ever."

Kelly reached into her coat pocket and removed the wooden dowel she used to store power with two fingers. Carefully, she laid it on the table. "Good faith gesture. Now I'm unarmed."

Aesa smiled. "We do know you better than that, but still the gesture's a good one." She nodded at Leifi.

With a grunt, he placed the silver bat he seemed to constantly carry with him onto the table next to Kelly's dowel. The other garm all followed suit.

"So." Aesa gestured for Kelly to pull out a chair. "Why should we trust you?"

After a quick glance at the rogues, Kelly sat, her hands folded neatly on the table in front of her. "Haven't you heard? I'm a marked woman."

"Really?" Aesa glanced at Leifi.

He shrugged.

"The Garm Council thinks I'm responsible for losing this portal. Thinks I'm probably behind everything."

Leifi exhaled loudly out his nose. "They won't even give us *that* much credit."

Aesa flicked him a look. He crossed his arms over his chest, and fell silent.

"They've put me on the short list for trial and possibly…execution."

Heather inhaled, a sharp sound that cause Aesa to pin her with a gaze. She followed Leifi's example, snapping her mouth shut.

"I have nothing to lose by joining you, and I assume…" She glanced at Heather. "You have something to offer me if I do."

* * *

Kol spun on four legs, his head lowered, his hackles raised. Kelly had tricked him—trapped him inside a cage. His anger grew so dark he could barely see past his rage.

No one trapped a garm. He had thought there was nothing worse than losing a portal, but this… He reared up onto his back legs and flung himself against the invisible barrier. For the hundredth time, he collided with a roadblock as solid as a cement wall.

Bruised and exhausted, he lay on Kelly's comforter, his tongue hanging from him mouth, his breaths coming in short pants—his ears laid back against his head.

There had to be a way out of here. There had to be.

Kelly waited for Aesa's reply. She didn't care what Fenrir's lover offered her. She was going through that portal no matter what, but she needed the woman to believe Kelly was on her side, to trust her. The way Kelly saw it, the best way to accomplish that was to pretend she expected a payoff—a big one.

"What about the guardian?" Aesa asked, her lips twisting in thought.

"He told me what I needed to know," Kelly responded.

"He did?" Aesa leaned back. "And you're willing to betray him?" Her eyes narrowed.

Kelly stared at the other female. "I don't have any choice. If I stay out there—with him—the Garm Council will put us both on their list. We'll both be tried and—" she flattened her hands onto the table top "—killed."

"So, you're doing it to save him?" Something fluttered behind Aesa's eyes.

Not sure if she was playing Fenrir's lover correctly, Kelly pulled her fingers back in to her palms. "Neither of us will survive—or if we do, it will only be by being on the run. I—" her voice cracked, her response coming too close to the truth "—can't do that to him." She snapped her head to one side, refocusing. "But if I help you, you can give me what you promised Heather—power, right? With that, anything is possible."

Aesa tapped a finger against her lower lip. "And the portal? You want that?"

Kelly blinked. It hadn't occurred to her that she could get the portal in trade for helping Aesa. "But the Garm Council—"

Leifi leaned down to place one palm on the table. "Won't exist after Fenrir is freed."

Aesa smiled. "That's right. You bring him back to me, and you'll get your power and the portal."

Leifi placed a second palm on the table and growled, "What about us?"

Aesa lifted her eyes in a cool stare. "There are plenty of portals. Enough for every garm who's been loyal— don't worry. You will get yours." She looked at Kelly. "So?"

Wishing it were as simple as Aesa seemed to think it would be, Kelly nodded.

"Hello, anyone home?"

Still in wolf form, Kol's body tensed. Recognizing the voice, but not able to place it, he waited.

The door to the bedroom swung open. Morn, arms folded over her chest and a grin on her face, stepped into the room. "What have we here?"

Kol raised one lip.

Morn strolled closer, her tail dancing behind her. "Been here long?"

"Look under the bed—the crystals, just move one," Kol ordered in Morn's head.

Morn didn't even glance down. "You shouldn't have trusted her." She moved no closer to the stones.

"Move—"

She held up one hand. "I will, but you need to tell me what you're going to do first."

Kol frowned. Do? Look for Kelly, of course.

"You still trust her, don't you?" Morn shook her head. "You garm are just way too loyal. Pick a side and you won't let go."

"What do you know, Morn?" Kol sat back on his haunches.

"Your witch betrayed you. She was seen going into the Guardian's Keep earlier. You didn't tell her anything you shouldn't have, did you?"

Kol's tail twitched. There was nothing to tell Kelly, except what happened between Kol and Magnus. She already knew everything else.

"Like how to operate the portal. Did you tell her that?"

Kol tilted his head, studying the troll. Something wasn't right. Morn knew, or thought she knew, too much…and why… "What brought you here, Morn?" he asked.

"I was looking for you." She walked over and leaned against the bedroom wall, her toe just inches from the closest crystal. "When I heard your lover defected to the other side—or maybe I should say gave up pretending she wasn't on their side—I started wondering where you were. Thought you might be in a bit of a pickle." Her eyes flashed. "And look, you are."

"And that's it? You were concerned. I'm touched."

She snorted. "Like all wolves, you're an ass, but lucky for you, I'm not." She pulled back her foot and sent the crystal spinning across the floor. "There. You're free. Go do something stupid." Then, tail snapping, she dissipated into wind and blew out the door.

Kol leaped from the bed. He flexed his feet, letting his toes dig into the carpet as he thought. Kelly had tricked and trapped him. He'd had hours to work out that fact, but Morn's appearance had put a new light on things.

She hadn't wandered by worried about him. A troll? The idea was ludicrous. No, someone had sent her. Someone who knew he'd be trapped—Kelly.

Kelly trapped him, but didn't want him to stay that way. And Kelly loved him—he believed that as strongly as he believed in the power of the portal, the need for order, or even his own heartbeat. Kelly might still be denying it to herself, but she couldn't hide the truth from him.

Confident in that, he lowered his head and tried to sense her.

Nothing. It was like she had disappeared all together. A fist tightened around his heart—dead? No. He shook off the thought. He'd have sensed that, too. So outside of his reach, but alive?

He growled. He knew where she had gone.

Kelly waited until the rogues were lined up ready to pass through the portal. Aesa and Heather were staying behind to reopen the doorway for their escape—except Kelly knew it wouldn't happen. Kol and the Council would arrive and shut down the portal. She and the rogues would be trapped on Lyngvi.

A shiver traveled down her spine.

"You okay?" Heather whispered.

"Just cold," Kelly replied.

"I…I wanted to say thank you and I'm sorry."

Kelly raised an eyebrow.

"Sorry for lying to you, getting you into this mess. And thanks for coming back. If you hadn't…I don't know what would have happened."

"Don't thank me yet," Kelly replied, her gaze on the rogues. If things went as Kelly planned, Heather would be answering to the Garm Council soon. Somehow she doubted Heather would be singing her praises then.

"They're ready." Aesa raised her arms. The garm crowded in front of the doorway parted to let her pass.

Kelly quickly typed the password into the computer and clicked on the portal program. Everything worked just like it had before.

She took a deep breath.

"That's it?"

Heather's question caused her to jump. "Yeah, then you just click here." She pointed the mouse at "Lyngvi". "Say yes a few dozen times and you're through." She glanced at her old assistant. "Can you take it from here?"

Heather nodded. "Sure."

Kelly started to squeeze past the two women, but Aesa stopped her. "So Heather can operate it now? Did you give her the password?"

A nervous laugh bubbled out of Kelly. "No, sorry. I forgot. Here." She grabbed a pen out of a cup and scribbled a word onto a napkin. "Now you're set." She turned to join the rogues.

"Kelly." Aesa placed a hand on Kelly's arm. "Thank you. And don't take too long. It's been years since I've seen him. If I have to go much longer…" Her voice cracked, and Kelly actually felt sympathy for the woman again.

Another sign she was doing the right thing. She couldn't

be trusted—she couldn't even trust herself not to fall for Aesa's tricks.

Brushing the woman's hand off her arm, Kelly moved to her place in front of the portal. "Okay, Heather. Let's go."

The doorway shimmered, and silence fell over the group. The sound of the energy streaming through the portal and the breath of the rogues crowded around her were the only noises Kelly heard—that and the pounding of her heart.

She swallowed, then huffed out a breath and glanced up at Leifi. "Let's go."

Back in human form and with the silver bat in his hands, Kol stood in the shadows and stared at his bar. *His* bar. *His* portal. And *his* mate. He was tired of playing by other being's rules. Tired of losing what he loved.

He'd had enough. He was going in that bar and he wasn't leaving until he had everything he valued back.

He shimmered, reforming behind his bar. Kelly's assistant, Heather, glanced up from the computer. A gasp escaping her lips, she lunged for the bar top.

With a growl, Kol grabbed her by the back of her shirt and jerked her off her feet.

"Where's Kelly?" he asked.

Eyes round, she looked over her shoulder at him. Kol waited, expecting some kind of plea, but her gaze darted behind him and all color dropped from her face.

"You're too late, Guardian." The words formed in his head seconds before a wolf slammed him from behind, teeth sinking into his upper back.

He fell forward, dropping the witch, but maintaining his hold on his bat.

"They've already left. Any minute now and they'll be back with Fenrir." The wolf, a female—Aesa, Kol guessed—sunk her teeth deeper into his muscle and growled.

"You ever been to Lyngvi?" he asked through teeth gritted against pain.

She loosened her hold slightly. "No, why?"

"Because—" He took advantage of her shift in attention to push himself up and flip over, swinging the bat with as much force as his awkward position allowed as he did so.

She leaped backward, her wolf form giving her much more flexibility and speed than his human one. Head lowered, she growled. "Why, Guardian?"

Leaning forward, his weight balanced on the balls of his feet ready to fight, he replied, "Lyngvi isn't a summer camp. You can't just pull up the bus and wait for Fenrir to find his way on."

She laughed. "I'm not that simple. I sent reinforcements—plenty of them. If Fenrir can be freed, he will be."

She turned her body, circling back toward him, but Kol could sense her desperation—see it in the flicker of panic that passed behind her eyes.

He let the bat fall to his side. "I'm sorry. He can't be."

"He can." Rage pouring from her eyes, Aesa leaped, her open mouth aimed at Kol's throat. Knowing he didn't have time to shimmer before she would strike him, Kol raised his arm and waited for the impact.

A streak of silver flashed overhead. Aesa paused seemingly frozen for one second in midair, then began to twist, lunging for her attacker. Something metal and heavy clanked onto the cement floor and power replaced the streak of silver, two orange beams that hit Aesa in the chest, holding her off the ground. Kol placed his hand on the bar, bracing himself against the sudden wave of energy. Aesa's back stiffened, her eyes widening then dulling and with a hollow thump she landed in a limp heap beside him.

Breath heaving out of her, Heather fell to the ground. "They haven't been gone long, maybe you can still get her back."

Kol stepped forward, his hand held out to thank the witch.

"Get who back?" a voice called from the front doorway. Birgit waited, hands on her hips, the official Garm Council emblem shining at her neck.

The smell, the dampness in the air, the almost complete lack of light. All of it familiar and terrifying to Kelly. Pressed from behind by the eager rogues, she stumbled forward, her hands waving in front of her, as if that would help her avoid invisible dangers.

Leifi moved next to her, his hand wrapping around her arm. "Is this it? Are we here?"

Kelly jerked free of his hold. "Yeah. We're here."

"Fenrir. Where is he?"

Kelly waved into the darkness.

"Is it night?" he asked. The other garm murmured similar questions as they shuffled forward. The area outside Lyngvi's portal seemed to be expanding with each additional body, but there was still barely room to breath.

Trying to keep some amount of space between her and the rogues, Kelly shrugged. Day. Night. She suspected both were the same in this dismal place.

"We can't fight like this. We can barely see," one of the garm complained.

"We change," Leifi announced.

"I wouldn't," Kelly replied. She didn't know what

would become of her here on this island, but she did know she didn't want to be trapped with a hundred rogues on the crowded shelf of rock. "To get to the main isle, we have to climb. Once we're up there—then you can change."

Discussion rippled through the group.

Leifi placed a hand on her back.

She fought the urge to shove her elbow into his gut— not because she particularly disliked the rogue or even wasn't sympathetic to his cause—but because she knew what he didn't, that anything they did here was for nothing.

They could get to the top of this cliff. But they wouldn't free Fenrir and she wouldn't escape this place—not again.

Chapter 20

Barely giving Birgit a glance, Kol reached into a cabinet and pulled out the binding ties he used when extra control was needed for a creature being transported through the portal. He tossed one to Heather and nodded his head toward Aesa. "Do her hind feet. I'll do her front. These will keep her hobbled and keep her from changing."

Her eyes darting to Birgit, Heather nodded, then bent down to tighten the plastic tie around Aesa's legs.

"What's going on Kol? Where are the rogues?" Birgit glanced around the bar, her gaze wary.

"They're gone." Kol looked down at Heather. She held up a hand. He frowned then slipped another tie into her fingers. Her eyes focused on Aesa, she wrapped the plastic strip around the female garm's muzzle and yanked it tight.

"You got the portal back?" Birgit took a step forward, but hesitantly, like she suspected a trap.

Kol looked down at the trussed up Aesa. "Looks like it."

"Great. I'll call the Council." Birgit reached into her coat and pulled out a phone. "The troll told me you wised up. I didn't believe her, but…" Birgit shrugged and flipped open her phone.

Kol looked at Heather. "Can you operate this?" He nodded to the computer.

She nodded. "Kelly showed me."

"Once I'm through—shut it down. We don't want the rogues coming back, and we can't let Fenrir escape."

At his feet, Aesa's eyes flew open. "No," she murmured in his head.

Heather placed a hand on the mouse, her mouth a thin line. "But you and Kelly will be trapped, too."

Kol inhaled and glanced around his bar—his bar, a business he'd built up from nothing, a portal that served all nine worlds and more. A sliver of sorrow cut into him. He would miss it, maybe even more now, knowing he'd had it back even for just a few minutes. Looking at Heather, he leveled his gaze. "I know."

"Kol." Birgit held the phone away from her face. "What are you doing?"

With a nod at Heather, Kol picked up his bat, stepped over the fallen Aesa and stood in front of the portal. Energy shimmered and power pulsed. The portal was active.

He took a step forward. A stream of curses flowing from Birgit was the last thing he heard before his feet hit the hard rock ledge of Lyngvi.

Kelly dug her fingers into the dirt at the top of the cliff and pulled herself up. The rogues quickly followed.

"Now what?" Leifi asked.

Kelly glanced around. It was quiet, just the sound of the

waves beating against the rocks—no nightmarish screams or ground-shaking roars. She could almost convince herself she was on any dark rocky coast.

She glanced around, the hair on her arms beginning to raise. Almost, but not quite. The feil were near, watching. Why weren't they doing more?

"Do you feel them?" she asked.

"Who?" Leifi turned, scanning the darkness. "This is impossible. We have to change. Is there more climbing?"

Wrapping her arms around herself, Kelly whispered, "No."

As one, the rogues changed. Kelly reached out, soaking up as much of the powered emitted by their mass transformation as she and the wooden dowel in her closed fist could hold. In the human world the amount would have been massive. Here, Kelly just hoped it would be enough to…her brain stumbled. To what? What did she hope for?

Tears welled up in her eyes and she blinked them away. This was her choice. She'd make the best of it—she might be stuck on this isle, but whatever life she had left, she was going to live it. She certainly wasn't going to spend it tucked in a ball sobbing.

And despite the fact that her gut told her freeing Fenrir was not a good idea, she wanted to be there to see what happened, and extra power could only be a good thing.

The rogues, now all in wolf form, pressed against her from all sides.

She inhaled, taking in the now stronger scent of garm, the sea air, and the wet dog smell she'd noticed her first trip. They were close now. She might not believe freeing Fenrir was the right move, but she didn't know that it wasn't, either. And the rogues certainly thought it was—they'd come this far, they deserved a shot at their dream.

Trying to focus on only the next few moments, she dropped her arms to her side and stared at the gleaming wolf eyes around her. "Fenrir's cave is this way. Let's go."

Hand wrapped around the dowel in her pocket, she stepped onto the path. A hundred wolves flowed onto the rocks behind her.

"There." Kelly knelt next to Leifi and pointed to the lone lantern illuminating the entrance to Fenrir's cave. The lantern moved as if struck by a breeze, but all else was still—deathly still.

Where were the feil?

"No guards?" Leifi projected into her head.

Another wolf bumped into her, forcing her forward on her hands. A rock bit into her palm. Leifi twisted his head to growl a warning at the others as she bit back a cry of pain.

After she had righted herself, she replied, "There should be. I don't know where they are. I can feel them, but I don't see them anywhere."

"A trap?" Leifi asked.

"Probably," Kelly whispered.

Leifi's eyes scanned the clearing. "So close," he murmured. "I could shimmer inside, see what's happening, then decide."

Cold fear washed over Kelly. Suddenly, she didn't want Leifi to leave. She might not share his cause, but some strange level of trust had built up between them.

"Send someone else," she urged. "If something happens to you, the rest won't know what to do."

Leifi tilted his head as if considering her words. Then without explanation, the wolf who had bumped her shimmered. A new edge of unease knifed through Kelly. Kol had said he couldn't shimmer. Why could the rogues?

Before she could dwell on the thought too long the garm had returned.

He stood next to Leifi, obviously communicating telepathically with the rogues' leader.

"What?" Kelly asked when the conversation seemed complete.

Leifi's gray eyes met hers. "He says Fenrir is alone, bound by a thick rope—dwarf-made he thinks. It's wrapped around his legs and muzzle."

Kelly stared into the darkness—too easy. It was all too easy.

As if reading her thoughts, Leifi continued, "It smells like a trap, but what are our choices?"

Kelly didn't bother replying. They all knew the answer. There were no choices, not on Lyngvi. "You picked a path…" she began.

"Time to trod on it," he finished, then flashed her a canine grin.

Kelly's lips moved into a sad smile in return. She might not believe in Leifi's cause, but she couldn't help but respect his dedication to it.

"You stay here. This is our fight." And with that, the wolves shimmered.

Kol felt the shimmer. How could he miss it; the wave of power rippled over the island. He clung to the side of the cliff, his fingers clamped around stones that barely protruded from the hard rock and dirt wall, his feet balanced on other stones that felt as though they would give way at any second.

As the ripple faded away, he reached over the edge of the cliff, flung his leg onto the flat surface of the cliff's top, and immediately rolled to a stand, ready to fight.

Nothing but the beating of the waves greeted him.

Then he felt her—Kelly. His nostrils flaring, he bent over and placed his hands on his thighs. Just feeling her, knowing she was alive, almost knocked him to his knees.

He murmured a prayer of thanks, and centered his thoughts. Where was she? The rogues had shimmered? How? What was happening? He concentrated on Kelly, tried to pick up her emotions. Very little came back to him—like some kind of blanket was muffling the flow between them.

Something was different on the isle this time, something Kol didn't like. As the thought twisted inside him, a boom sounded from the center of Lyngvi, and the ground beneath his feet shook—so hard he stumbled, had to brace his feet to keep from falling. Then the crunch of falling stones, shrieks and howls.

His thoughts again centered on Kelly, Kol shimmered.

The ground heaved beneath Kelly's feet, knocking her onto the hard shale and packed earth. A crevice appeared beside her, she rolled, dirt caking her face, getting into her mouth and eyes. She spat and let her eyes tear, blinking, but not waiting for sight to return before crawling forward, away from where the ground cracked and moved.

Inside Fenrir's cave, the rogues shrieked. Rocks tumbled from above, rolling across the clearing, shale followed, glass-sharp shards sliding in sheets toward her.

Kelly's hand shot out, a shield spell on her lips. Before she could vocalize the words, an arm shot under her waist and jerked her upward. Her body tingled, prickled like thousands of icicles were piercing her skin. Then she was standing, her back pressed against Kol, her head hanging in front of her and tears of relief and failure running down her cheeks.

Damn him. He came for her. She bit her lip until blood mingled with the tears.

And damn her for being glad he did.

Kol turned Kelly in his arms until the front of her body was flush against his. He pulled her tighter, wanting to feel the beat of her heart, to stand there forever knowing she was safe.

The earth shook again. A boulder tumbled from above Fenrir's cave and landed with a crash in the clearing, smashing a small wooden cart to splinters. Kelly jumped and pushed her face more firmly against his chest. He pulled them back farther from the chaos. Even with everything going on he couldn't resist pressing a kiss to the top of her head and murmuring, "It's okay."

She looked up, her eyes wet with tears. "Is it? What now? You weren't supposed to follow me."

He dropped his forehead to hers. "I know."

From inside the cave, something roared—a strange sound like rock breaking against rock.

"What's happening in there?" Kelly asked.

Kol shook his head. "We should leave."

Kelly glanced back at the cave, uncertainty creasing her face. "The rogues…" Then she squared her jaw and looked back at him. "Where do we have to go? Birgit won't let us back through."

"How did you…?" He let the question fade. Kelly. He'd guessed she'd sent Morn to free him, had she also sent her to Birgit?

Another roar sounded from inside the cave.

He shoved the questions forming in his brain to the

side. Hopefully there'd be time for answers later, and if not…it didn't matter. Nothing would change how he felt about Kelly. He knew that for certain.

"I know they stole the portal, unleashed all kinds of foul things, but they don't deserve—" she waved a hand toward the cave "—whatever is happening in there."

"Fenrir," Kol began, then stopped himself. The mighty garm had helped Kol escape with Kelly before. Did Kol owe him something for the act?

Kelly watched him, her eyes filled with determination. She wasn't going to just walk away, and there was no way Kol was leaving her.

Shaking his head at his own stupidity, he nodded, then his arms wrapped around Kelly, they shimmered into the cave.

Inside the cave, the rogues were broken into groups— snapping and snarling at humanoid figures that seemed constructed from bits of Lyngvi—mud made up their main bodies, with dirt and pebbles forming their faces, and shale jutting from their shoulders and chests like armor.

"The feil?" Kelly whispered.

"The feil," Kol replied.

"But…"

"The feil are Lyngvi—the dirt, the rocks, even the sea. They can use every part of the isle to take a solid form. Looks like today they got a bit more creative."

A feil raised up like a wave then crashed down toward a rogue. The garm danced to the side. The feil collided with the earth, setting off a new set of tremors under their feet.

Kelly braced her hands against the cave's wall to keep from falling. As she swayed, something glimmered, catching her eye. She crept forward, clinging to the walls and shadows.

Hidden behind a group of swaying feil stood Fenrir, what appeared to be some type of cable wrapped around his feet, body, and snout. He stared at Kelly, his eyes snapping with rage.

Behind her Kol cursed under his breath.

They'd bound him. Kol bit back another curse, unable to believe what he was seeing. The cable, it had to be dwarf-made. It was cutting off all of Fenrir's powers—the gods had stopped his ability to shift long ago, but now…they'd cut off his ability to communicate, even telepathically. The great wolf was truly trapped—not just on this isle, or in this cave, but within his own body.

Kol couldn't even imagine the hell Fenrir was enduring.

The great wolf swung his head to the side, the expression in his eyes turning to a question.

Kelly took a step forward, but Kol reached out stopping her. They couldn't free him, but…

"Guardian." One of the rogues leaped, darting side to side as a feil ripped pieces of shale off its chest and flung them like deadly frisbees. "Join us."

Kol tightened his grip on Kelly's arm. The wolf in him wanted to jump in the fray, be part of a fight. But the part of him that respected order, understood the importance of balance screamed that it would be a huge mistake.

"Kol?" Kelly asked. Her fingers tugged at his shirt.

He stared down at her, sensing she was just as confused as he. His gaze went back to Fenrir. The wolf stumbled to a stand, lowered his head and met Kol's gaze.

Kol couldn't do it. He couldn't leave the garm, not like this.

"How much power do you have?" he asked Kelly.

She smiled. "Enough."

"Enough to break that?" he nodded to the cable.

She shook her head. "I don't know."

"That makes two of us," Kol replied, then slipping an arm around her waist, he shimmered them into place next to the great wolf.

They materialized behind the line of feil. The closest shifted sideways, the mud slurping against the hard earth telegraphing its next move. Kol shoved Kelly out of the way and ducked. The air above him whistled as razor-sharp shale sliced through the air, missing him by inches.

Kelly, her stomach pressed against the rock floor, squirmed forward until she grasped the silver cable that held Fenrir in both hands.

Another feil swiped an arm toward Kol. He kicked out with one foot, hitting the mud creature in the leg. The feil flung its arm downward, bits of rock that had formed its fingers flying off to pierce the ground around Kol. He shimmered, then shimmered again, as more and more pieces of the rock shrapnel flew toward him.

To his side, a feil grabbed a rogue by the tail and swung the wolf overhead like a lasso. Without warning it released the garm, sending it flying toward the cave wall. Seconds before colliding, the garm shimmered, reappearing in a heap not far from Kol's feet. Kol squatted next to the prone garm, pressed his palm to his nose, checking for breath. A slit appeared between the rogue's eyelids.

"Change," Kol ordered. "The feil were created to control Fenrir—a wolf. Here on Lyngvi, it gives them the advantage."

"Why should I trust you?" the rogue murmured in Kol's head. He recognized the voice as belonging to the rogue he'd battled before, the one who had drawn Kelly's blood. His hand fisted into the garm's fur, instinct telling him to kill.

"Kol," Kelly called from her place next to the cable.

Power poured from both her hands as she gripped the silver line. "I don't think I can break it."

Kol glanced back at the garm.

"Kol, help me."

One of the feil, slid closer, stopping only a few feet from where Kelly worked.

With a curse, Kol pulled his hand away from the rogue and shimmered directly in front of the creature that threatened Kelly.

Damn it. The cable writhed in Kelly's hands as if fighting against the power she poured into it.

Behind her, Kol fell to the ground, dodging as one of the feil swung an arm toward him. Another lifted its foot and stomped down, missing Kol as he rolled away, but shaking the cave and causing rocks to drop from overhead, smashing into both feil and garm. Even this onslaught didn't slow the battle.

Kelly turned back to the cable, if she could just hold it still, concentrate the power she had left in one place. She shot a desperate look around. Fenrir's brilliant green eyes stared back at her. She felt the same gut punch of fear she had the first time she'd visited Lyngvi and gained Fenrir's notice.

Fenrir shuffled his bound feet, inching closer to her. Kelly pulled back, her heart hammering, but she had nowhere to go—pinned into place between the mighty garm, the rock wall of the cave and the battling feil. Seeing her movement, Fenrir's eyes changed, darkened—as if he was straining to communicate.

Licking her lips, Kelly forced herself to stay where she was, to wait. A loud huff of air escaped Fenrir's nostrils and he shuffled again, this time making it to her side. He gave her one more piercing stare, then shifted his gaze down to the cable.

Kelly's gaze followed. Fenrir's foot hovered inches from the fetter. Suddenly understanding his intent, she shoved the cable forward, under his foot. With a nod, he held the line in place while she continued to pour power onto it.

Sweat dripped from her brow. The cable grew hotter and hotter until it burned into her skin. She squeezed her eyes shut and shoved the pain to some small part of her brain where it wouldn't interfere with continuing the torture.

"Kelly?" Kol stood beside her, but she didn't look up, just keep letting white-hot energy pour out of her blistered hands. "Kelly, you have to stop. What are you doing to yourself?" Just as she felt the cable bend, weaken, he tugged at her shoulder.

"It's coming," she replied.

"We have to go." She could hear that he'd turned, as if addressing someone other than her. Then he was back, squatting next to her, his hands reaching out to pull hers from the cable. "Now the feil are increasing, and they've done something. I can't shimmer. We have to run."

Fenrir's foot moved, pushing Kelly's hands away from the cable. She looked up and saw understanding. His eyes shifted from her to Kol.

She placed a hand on the garm's leg, ignoring the dirt and debris that marred the silver fur. "I'll tell Aesa that you're well," she whispered. "I wish we could have done more."

His gaze darted to the door of the cave—telling her to leave.

With one last glance at the cable, Kelly let Kol grab her by the arm and, dodging feil and fallen stones, they raced out of the cave and down the path that led to the portal.

Chapter 21

Kol dashed down the path, Kelly keeping pace beside him. While Kelly had been working on the cable, something had changed. He'd felt a shift in the energy of Lyngvi. He'd tried to shimmer to Kelly's side and been stopped cold, just like before, his body not even managing the tingle that normally preceded the act.

His stomach churning, he'd glanced past swarming bodies in the cave and seen feil after feil shooting up from the ground outside. Someone or something had shifted Lyngvi's defense up a notch.

To their right, mud bubbled upward and took shape—another pack of feil flowed over the ground toward them.

Moving at a jog, Kol stepped to the right side of the path, placing himself between the feil and Kelly. They had just reached the cliff and the climb down, when the ground shook and a thunderous roar split through the darkness.

Thrown off balance by the movement of the earth and the unexpected noise, they staggered forward. Then as Kol watched, Kelly tripped and fell over the side of the cliff.

Kelly fell forward, her hands in front of her, expecting to hit the hard stone ground. Instead air swept back her hair, and her body began to twist. Bile rushed to her throat as she realized what had happened, that she had tumbled off the cliffside. Hours seemed to pass, her mind going so fast time almost stopped, then a hand grabbed onto her shirt and Kol pulled her body to his. A tiny breath of relief passed through her lips, but then she realized they were still falling, just hugged together as one.

He'd caught her. Kol gripped Kelly tight against his chest. Unable to shimmer, his only hope was he could twist, cushioning her fall with his body. Would it be enough to save her? He had no idea.

"Guardian," Fenrir's voice bellowed in his head.

One of Kol's feet knocked against the cliff wall, dirt and pebbles flew loose, spattering the pair as they continued their descent.

"Shimmer," Fenrir continued.

Blood rushing to his head, Kol could barely make out the mighty garm's words, much less their meaning.

"Shimmer." This time the order was so loud, Kol couldn't ignore it or miss the meaning. Praying Fenrir knew something he didn't, Kol squeezed his eyes shut and concentrated on relocating to the bottom—safe with Kelly in his arms.

Kelly felt the tingle, but it didn't register. Nothing did except that her last moments were whizzing past her, too quick for her brain to even formulate a plan out of this disaster.

The tingle intensified and just as suddenly as it started, it quit. She wobbled, her feet sinking in loose dirt. Her burned fingers curled against Kol, her hand, even in its blistered state, able to feel the too-fast thump of his heart.

She stared up at him. Safe. They were both safe.

Then the air around them began to bend, turning into waves, that shifted and morphed until the rogues, still in wolf form, surrounded them.

"All right, Fenrir. What say you now?" The giant Kelly had seen on her first visit, the one who had seemed somehow in charge of Fenrir's care, appeared a few feet away, light haloing out around him. He stared up at the top of the cliff, raised one arm and shot an illuminating beam to the top. Kelly's gaze followed.

Staring down at them were the phosphorescent eyes of Fenrir. His silver hair blew forward in the breeze, making him appear even larger.

He was free. A gasp caught in Kelly's throat.

"I can't guarantee what will happen once they're through," the giant yelled again, his face still turned upward.

He paused, then ran a hand over his face. "Agreed—but you first. I won't open the portal otherwise."

Fenrir lifted his nose to the air, his face pointed to the sea, then lowered his head to scan the group of beaten, in cases half-dead, garm beneath him. When his eyes lit on Kelly, he paused.

"Don't forget your promise," she heard in her head. She lifted her chin and gave a slight nod. Kol's arm tightened around her waist.

Fenrir shook; debris flew from his fur. He lifted his nose one last time, the wind playing along his snout, then stepped back almost out of view. Kelly raised on her tiptoes, straining to see what was happening.

A line of feil appeared, the chain that had held Fenrir during Kelly's last visit slung over their shoulders. Slowly, they approached the garm and wrapped the chain around his neck, each clink of the metal knocking into Kelly like a physical blow.

He'd had a shot at his freedom and given it up. Why?

Kol watched as Fenrir let the feil wrap the heavy chain around his neck.

Tyr, the god in charge of keeping Fenrir under control, waved a hand and the front pair of feil began moving back toward the cave. Fenrir swept the group at the bottom of the cliff with one last gaze, then, nose held high, followed.

Kelly dropped her head.

Kol ran his fingers against her scalp. "It's for the best," he whispered. A truth he knew, but he couldn't help feeling the same disappointment and sorrow that he saw tugging at her face or the loss he saw echoed in the eyes of the garm around them.

For the first time in his life, Kol questioned if things were as cut-and-dry as he'd always believed—as simple as he'd tried to make them. Maybe Kelly had been right from the beginning, maybe being a guardian should involve more than just following the rules.

"Guardian." Tyr's voice knocked Kol out of his mental wanderings. "I've opened the portal. If you would use it to get these—" he waved his hand over the garm "—wolves out of here, I would appreciate it. Then follow with your woman." He turned as if to leave.

"What about Fenrir?" Kelly took a slight step toward the god.

Tyr paused midstep and raised a brow. "Fenrir? He stays, of course."

"Will you rebind him with…?" Kelly folded her hands closed, a grimace of pain crossing her face.

"Hapta?" Tyr's gaze wandered to Kelly's curled fingers, then back to her face, interest in his eyes. "Hapta is broken. It took the dwarves many years to forge the fetter, and it proved faulty. It will take them many more to replace it with something truly unbreakable."

He turned back to Kol. "It should go without saying, but somehow…" He glanced at Kelly. "I feel I need to make sure you understand…you, your woman, and these rogues are never to set foot on Lyngvi again. If you do, I won't be so generous."

"What about—" Kelly began.

Tyr leaned forward, his brow lowered. Kol took a step toward him. Tyr waved him aside. "Let her speak, but last question, little one." He pulled back, his fingers tapping against his forearm.

"Visitors. Can Fenrir have visitors?"

A huge laugh rolled out of Tyr's throat. "Visitors? Like the group of you? Why would I allow that?"

Seeing where Kelly was going, Kol moved forward. "This…" He nodded to the other garm. "Was all caused by one female, desperate to see her mate, Fenrir."

"And you think if we allowed this visitation, we might save a repeat of today?" Tyr lifted his chin. "Interesting." He leaned forward again. "I'll give it consideration." Then he turned and took a step, disappearing as his second foot left the ground. "And don't forget…" his voice drifted back on the wind "…my warning."

As Tyr's voice faded, Kelly turned in Kol's arms. "You think?"

Kol shrugged. "Who knows? Tyr prides himself on being evenhanded."

The garm Kol had identified as the rogue who had attacked Kelly previously padded forward. He tilted his head from side to side, then with a shake, changed. Within seconds he stood in front of them, human and naked.

Kol snarled and started to reach for the other garm. Kelly reached out, her burnt hand scratching the skin of Kol's forearm where she touched him. Kol flinched at the feel, guilt for letting her damage herself in such a way, causing him to drop his hold on the rogue. "We need to get you back," he said, ignoring the other male.

She brushed him aside. "You heard Tyr. Them first." She gestured to the rogues.

A growl formed in the back of Kol's throat as he switched his gaze back to the rogue in front of them. "Forget them."

Kelly shook her head. "You just fought beside them."

"That was—" Kol huffed out a breath. "Fine. We get them out of here." Not looking at anyone, he strode to the portal and crouched down beside it. "Not to the Guardian's Keep though. I don't want them near there any more than Tyr wants them here."

The rogue crossed his arms over his bare chest. "Send us anywhere. We're used to surviving."

Kol mumbled a curse under his breath. He didn't want to feel sympathy for the rogues. He wanted things to be simple. He glanced to where Kelly stood, her burned hands hanging at her sides. Unfortunately, he knew things would never be as black-and-white as they had once been. Kelly brushed a hair away from her forehead with the back of her hand and shot him a small smile.

Of course, a little variation in his outlook on life probably wasn't a bad thing.

* * *

Kol's arm wrapped protectively around her waist, Kelly walked through the portal. She wasn't sure where Kol had sent the rogues, but he had consulted with Leifi before opening the doorway and the rogue had seemed to agree with Kol's choice. It had taken only a few moments for the rogues, all in wolf form, to file through.

Her sister's voice was the first thing to register after her feet hit the solid floor of the Guardian's Keep. "Thank goodness."

The second was the row of eyes staring at them. Everyone seemed to be gathered around the portal—Birgit, Magnus, Morn, Bari, Gusir, and Vilfir formed the first circle. Behind them stood her sister, Kara; her new husband, the hellhound, Risk; and the troll king, Holi. Heather sat on the floor next to wolf Aesa, also bound by plastic ties.

And everyone seemed to be talking.

"Where are the rogues?" Magnus stepped forward.

"Well, you did it, wolf." Morn shared a glance with the other desperates.

"How did you get back through?" Birgit's gaze shot from the portal to Kol.

"Enough," a voice roared, and Kara was shoved through the crowd by her hellhound husband.

Kara didn't wait for another opening, she flew at Kelly, knocking her back against Kol. "What was that message you left me? It sounded suicidal. I was scared." Tears darkened her eyes.

A stab of guilt shot through Kelly. She opened her mouth to reply, but Kara just pulled her into a hug. "If I'd lost you...don't ever do that again. This was my fault. I should have checked my messages. I should have—"

"No." Kelly shook her head. "It's not your fault. Don't even say that. We make our own choices, right? I just made some bad ones."

Kara gave Kelly's hand a squeeze. A hiss of pain flew from Kelly's lips.

"What—" Kara jumped back, her gaze dropping to Kelly's blistered palms, but Kol had already grabbed Kelly and started ushering her through the group to the space behind the bar.

"Kol, we need answers." Magnus followed them, Birgit close behind.

Busy pulling a first aid kit out from under the bar, Kol didn't even bother with a reply.

"What answers? The portal is back—that's enough." Bari shoved his way past the two Garm Council members. "You—" he pointed his axe at Magnus then Birgit "—can leave."

Birgit snarled, her arm moving to grab the dwarf, but Vilfir slid between them, his brow raised in question. "I'd look around. You are not in the majority here."

Birgit continued her forward movement, but Magnus placed his arm in front of her. "Enough."

With Birgit and the desperates watching each other through narrowed eyes, Magnus turned his attention back to Kol. "We need to talk, privately."

Kol picked up a tube of ointment and squeezed some onto Kelly's palm, with a featherlike stroke he rubbed the medication onto her palms. Kelly wanted nothing more than to just sit still and let Kol minister to her wounds, but she knew at some point they had to deal with the group around them.

"Talk to them," she said, pulling her hand free. "They won't go away until you do and we have talking of our own to do."

Kol reached for a bandage.

"Kol. Talk to them. I'm fine. Really."

A frown creased his forehead. "I don't have to talk to them."

Kelly sighed. "Yes. You do. I'll wait."

Kol picked up her hand and studied the damage on her palm. Then so gently she could barely feel it, pressed a kiss to the scarred flesh. "You better," he whispered.

Kol crossed his arms over his chest and stared Magnus in the eye. "What did you want to talk about?"

Magnus blinked. "The portal. What happened to the rogues. Where you stand with the Council."

Kol angled a brow. "The rogues are gone. The portal is safe. And I don't particularly care where I stand with the Council. Anything else?"

Magnus's jaw hardened. "You'd better care, unless you're going rogue yourself."

Kol ran his hand down Kelly's arm. "There are worse things than going rogue."

Birgit shook her head. "You have completely lost it."

"No, I think I'm just starting to get it." He glanced from Magnus to Heather and Aesa who still lay bound on the floor. "What are you doing with them?"

Surprise flitted through Magnus's eyes. "Trial, then…" He shrugged.

Kelly gasped and pressed Kol in the back.

Birgit held up her hands. "They stole the portal and unleashed every degenerate beast in the nine worlds on this one."

Kol stared down at Aesa. Her blue eyes flicked from Kol to the Council members. "But why? Don't you think the reason matters?" Kol asked.

"No, I don't."

"Well, I do." Kol carefully pulled Kelly's arm through his. Then staring down at her, said, "I assume you want to spend some time with your sister?"

Confusion washing over Kelly's face, she nodded.

He shifted his gaze to her brother-in-law, the hellhound. "I thought I told you to stay out of my bar."

Risk shrugged.

His hand on Kelly's back, Kol continued, "Since apparently this place isn't mine any longer, I'll let it pass." Glancing down at Kelly, he asked, "You ready?"

Before she could answer, Bari scrambled to the top of the bar, and shoved his axe in Magnus's face. Morn, Vilfir and Gusir pushed forward until they ringed the Garm Council leader from behind.

"The guardian keeps his bar," Bari announced, the sharp edge of his axe pressed against Magnus's neck.

Kol raised a hand to object, but Holi, the troll king, dropped a meaty hand on his shoulder. "It's decided. I don't like this world I got tricked into. Morn say, only you keep others from wandering here by mistake. This Council agrees." He leaned forward, his breath blowing Magnus's hair back from his face. "Right?"

With a grin, Morn stepped closer, her tail running up the inside of Holi's leg. Vilfir leaned back against the bar, his dark gaze on Birgit and Magnus, while Gusir bent at the waist, towering over all of them but Holi. "The guardian stays," he announced. "Or the desperates revolt."

His brow lowered, Magnus studied the group for a second before turning back to Kol. "This is how you show I can trust you?"

Kol shook his head. "I'm not showing you anything. Do what you like."

"As long—" Holi tightened the hand perched on Magnus's shoulder "—as this guardian in charge."

His mouth a grim line, Magnus glanced from the troll king's hand to Birgit. "You did say Kol recovered the portal."

"Yes, but—"

Holi opened his mouth, revealing jagged teeth.

Suppressing a shudder, Birgit snapped her lips together.

"That said…" Magnus turned back to Kol. "It makes sense we give you another chance."

Kelly's blistered hand tightened on his arm. He slid his on top of hers, silently telling her to wait—they hadn't quite got everything yet.

"What about them?" He nodded to the two bound females.

"I already said—" Magnus stopped himself. "What is it you want?"

"Let them go. Trying them, killing them, will only increase the legend and strengthen the rogues' cause."

"I don't think—" Birgit began.

"Release them," Magnus ordered. Two of his thugs stepped forward and quickly snapped through Heather's bonds, then pulled her to a stand. Aesa scrambled to her feet on her own. Magnus gave them a cursory glance then began to shimmer. "I'll leave them in your care. Just don't lose the portal again. I might not be so understanding next time."

Birgit and the two thugs followed.

"So…" Kelly smiled up at him. "I guess you got what you wanted."

"Did you get what you want?" he asked, his voice low.

"Hmm." She cut her gaze from him to the portal. "Not quite."

"Really?" His heart heavy in his chest, he waited for her to continue.

"There's still them." Kelly pointed to Aesa and Heather who both stood waiting, their gazes wary.

Kol stared at the two females for a second, then glanced back at Kelly. Her eyes, blue, trusting and filled with hope gazed back at him. With a resolved huff, he grabbed a knife and reached for Aesa's bound paws. "No tricks," he said, but waited for Aesa to nod before continuing. Kelly stepped beside him, Aesa's clothing in her hands.

Within seconds, Aesa was back in human form and dressed. Her expression grim, she rubbed her wrists. "We were so close," she mumured, almost as if she couldn't keep the words inside. Then, a determined glint in her eye, she stepped forward. "I didn't lie to you. They did take Terje. They used him to trap Fenrir."

Her brows lowered, Kelly glanced from the female garm to Kol and back. "But Fenrir's been at Lyngvi for years."

"Almost two hundred," Aesa replied.

"So, the picture?"

Aesa shook her head. "Not Terje. I don't even have that to remember him by."

"You mean…" Kelly placed her bandaged hand on Kol's forearm. "He never came back?"

Aesa shook her head, then dropped her gaze. "I've been alone—no husband, no son, no one." She lifted her chin. "I won't apologize for tricking you. I'd do it all and more for just one more look at my family."

"Maybe…" Kelly glanced at Kol.

His gaze snapped her direction. "No. I can't go that far."

Aesa turned, her shoulders falling.

Heather spoke. "Tell the rest Aesa. Tell them who took your son." She looked at Kelly. "I didn't know about Terje when you asked me, I swear, but later when everything was going to hell, I asked."

Something twisted in Kol's stomach. Before Aesa turned and said the words, he already knew what she was going to say.

"The Council, or the beginnings of the Council, anyway. They took Terje and forced my mate to give himself to the gods to save him. Then, they wouldn't even return my son—said he could be as big of a threat as Fenrir. They wanted to make sure he was raised *right*." She almost spat out the last word.

Kelly turned, every inch of her posture saying she wanted Kol to do something, but he'd already moved— toward the computer. He snapped the machine to life and tapped on a location.

"I can only get you there. I can't control what happens after that."

An hour later Kol glanced around the empty bar then pulled Kelly's body flush against his. "I've never shut down the portal before," he murmured.

"You've never gone against Council rules before, either."

"Or sent someone to Lyngvi," he added.

"Or another to…where did you send Heather?"

Kol smiled. "I thought a bit more time with the rogues might do her some good."

Kelly snuggled a little closer. "She wasn't bad, just naive. I hope she keeps out of trouble, and finds what she's looking for."

With one finger under her chin, Kol tipped her face up to his. "I know I have," he whispered.

Her lips brushed his. "About closing the portal—we should make good use of the time, don't you think?"

Kol bent and scooped her into his arms. "I most certainly do." With a growl, he shimmered them upstairs.

Epilogue

Aesa stepped into the darkness. Everything was as Kelly had described—the pounding waves, the impenetrable dark, and the cold damp. Her hands in front of her, she shuffled forward until she hit the rock wall. Also as Kelly had described.

What now? Was Fenrir really here? Too many past disappointments kept her from believing he truly was.

Should she climb? Kelly and Kol had told her to stay in her human form, that is was her best shot at getting past the feil…at least long enough to get a glimpse of Fenrir.

Fenrir. If Kelly and Kol spoke the truth, he was close…so close. Her hands shook at the thought.

"Aesa?" The question formed in her head, the voice familiar even after two centuries apart.

Trapped on the tiny ledge with no room to change and thus no ability to reply telepathically, all she could do was bow her head and listen, try to keep the sob of joy that threatened to drown out his voice from escaping her throat.

"You came?" A whisper this time.

She nodded, even though her lover couldn't see the gesture, and moved her hands over the wall in front of her. Kol had told her not to shimmer unless she had to, that any such move might attract the feil. He'd told her to climb then to follow the path to the cave. She would find Fenrir there.

Her fingers found the first indentation in the stone, then another. Blinking back tears she'd been holding since her son and husband had been stolen from her, she shoved her fingers into a niche and began to pull herself up.

"I'm coming," she murmured. And this time no one— not the Council, the gods, nor the feil were going to stop her.

Glossary

Alfheim—Land of light elves.

Asgard—Land of the Aesir.

Draugr—Corporeal undead. Can take a rough human form and a bluish skin or travel as smoke forming dark clouds. Not very intelligent, but deadly. Can grow in size and smell of rotting flesh. Crushes or eats their victims alive. Only a few "heroes" can kill them.

Feil—Guardians of Fenrir. Make from the earth of Lyngvi, they can only exist on the isle.

Fenrir—Most powerful garm of all time. Son of Loki, brother of Jormun.

Garm—Human/wolf shape-shifters. Garm are guardians by nature. Garm serve as guardians to portals, other paranormal beings and worlds. Being a guardian is an essential part of what garm are. Losing their charge, whether a being or a portal, is like losing their purpose for existence. Without such a duty, they become rogue.

Garm Council—A small group of garm who oversaw the guardians of the most important portals, landmarks and beings.

Helheim—Land of the dead and Hel which lies within Niflheim.

Hellhounds—Human/massive dog shape-shifter. Hellhounds are hunters by nature. In the past they were used by the gods to run the Wild Hunt—dragging back souls of the evil (or those deemed evil by the gods). Today, with the hunt a thing of the past, they survive as they can—working for whoever has a need of their deadly skills.

Hraesveig—Giant corpse-eating eagle who sits at the edge of Helheim. The flapping of his wings creates a terrible wind.

Jotunheim—Land of giants and trolls.

Kara Shane—Heroine of Unbound. A witch, half of a set of identical twins. Twin witches are believed to be the most powerful witches to ever exist.

Kelly Shane—Heroine of Guardian's Keep. A witch, Kara's twin sister.

Kol Hildr—Hero of Guardian's Keep. *A garm and owner of The Guardian's Keep bar, which hides a portal to other worlds.*

Lusse—*Immortal witch who keeps a kennel of hellhounds, and uses them to hunt down other witches whose powers she drains to build her own.*

Lyngvi—*Mist-covered, rocky isle. Prison of Fenrir.*

Midgard—*Land of humans.*

Midgard Sea—*Sea that encircles Midgard, world of humans. Also home of Jormun.*

Muspelheim—*Land devoured by fire, impassable to anyone not native. Guarded by Surt and his fiery sword.*

Nidavellir—*Land of dwarves.*

Niflheim—*Land of freezing mists.*

Ragnarok—*The legendary final battle, which will destroy all nine worlds.*

Risk Leidolf—*The hero of* Unbound. *A hellhound owned by Lusse.*

Svartalfar—*Dark elf.*

Svartalfaheim—*Land of Svartalfar/dark elves.*

Tyr—Lesser god in charge of watching over Fenrir on Lyngvi.

Vanaheim—Land of the Vanir.

Wild Hunt—Hunt for souls led by various gods and other powerful beings using hellhounds.

Yggdrasill—The world tree which holds the nine worlds of Norse mythology.

* * * * *

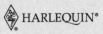

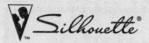

REQUEST YOUR FREE BOOKS!

2 FREE NOVELS PLUS 2 FREE GIFTS!

Silhouette®

n o c t u r n e™

Dramatic and Sensual Tales of Paranormal Romance.

YES! Please send me 2 FREE Silhouette® Nocturne™ novels and my 2 FREE gifts. After receiving them, if I don't wish to receive any more books, I can return the shipping statement marked "cancel." If I don't cancel, I will receive 4 brand-new novels every other month and be billed just $4.47 per book in the U.S. or $4.99 per book in Canada, plus 25¢ shipping and handling per book plus applicable taxes, if any*. That's a savings of about 15% off the cover price! I understand that accepting the 2 free books and gifts places me under no obligation to buy anything. I can always return a shipment and cancel at any time. Even if I never buy another book from Silhouette, the two free books and gifts are mine to keep forever.

238 SDN ELS4   338 SDN ELXG

Name   (PLEASE PRINT)

Address   Apt. #

City   State/Prov.   Zip/Postal Code

Signature (if under 18, a parent or guardian must sign)

Mail to the **Silhouette Reader Service™**:

IN U.S.A.: P.O. Box 1867, Buffalo, NY 14240-1867

IN CANADA: P.O. Box 609, Fort Erie, Ontario L2A 5X3

Not valid to current Silhouette Nocturne subscribers.

Want to try two free books from another line?
Call 1-800-873-8635 or visit www.morefreebooks.com.

* Terms and prices subject to change without notice. NY residents add applicable sales tax. Canadian residents will be charged applicable provincial taxes and GST. This offer is limited to one order per household. All orders subject to approval. Credit or debit balances in a customer's account(s) may be offset by any other outstanding balance owed by or to the customer. Please allow 4 to 6 weeks for delivery.

Your Privacy: Silhouette is committed to protecting your privacy. Our Privacy Policy is available online at www.eHarlequin.com or upon request from the Reader Service. From time to time we make our lists of customers available to reputable firms who may have a product or service of interest to you. If you would prefer we not share your name and address, please check here. ☐

SN07

Silhouette® Desire

You can lead a horse to water…

When Alyssa Barkley and Clint Westmoreland
found out that their "fake" marriage was never
rendered void, they are forced to live together
for thirty days. However, Clint loves the single
life and has no intention of being tamed, but
when Alyssa moves in, the sizzling attraction
between them is ignited and neither wants the
thirty days to end.

Look for
TAMING CLINT WESTMORELAND
by
BRENDA JACKSON

Available February wherever you buy books